ARCANE WONDERLAND

BITTER SPIRITS

JAMI GRAY

Cover Art: Deranged Doctor Design, www.derangeddoctordesign.com
Publisher: Celtic Moon Press First edition, 2026
ISBN: 978-1-948884-78-5 (ebook) ISBN: 978-1-948884-79-2 (print)

sign up for free reads from jami!

Join Jami's newsletter to be the first to hear about new releases, free books, special prices and other nifty events.

Sign up at: https://www.subscribepage.com/jami-gray-books

what readers say...

About Arcane Transporter:

"Taking a refreshing approach to fantasy magic, this fast-paced, economical thriller is told from a highly likable perspective." —Red Adept Editing

About PSY-IV Teams:

"This story is an emotional roller coaster, from betrayal, anger, fear, love..." —InD'tale Magazine

About the Kyn Kronicles:

"...a fantastic paranormal action novel is quite possibly the best book I've read this year. I could not put it down, and had to exercise serious self-control to keep from staying up all night to finish it." —The Romance Reviews

About Fate's Vultures:

"...if you like your characters with a bit more bite, with secrets, with hidden agendas, and all those sorts of things, and your worlds are a far more deadlier place, then this is for you." —Archaeolibrarian

also by jami gray

ARCANE WONDERLAND

Last Call

Bitter Spirits

Rune & Tonic

ARCANE TRANSPORTER

Ignition Point (*Prequel Novella*)

Grave Cargo

Risky Goods

Lethal Contents

Collision Course

Blind Spot

Terminal Drift

THE KYN KRONICLES

Shadow's Edge

Shadow's Soul

Shadow's Moon

Shadow's Curse

Shadow's Dream

Shadow's Fall

Tangled in Shadows (*Short Story Collection*)

FATE'S VULTURES

Lying in Ruins

Beg for Mercy

Caught in the Aftermath

Fear the Reaper

PSY-IV TEAMS

Hunted by the Past

Touched by Fate

Marked by Obsession

Fractured by Deceit

Linked by Deception

BOX SETS

PSY-IV Teams Box Set I (Books 1-3)

The Collapse: Fate's Vultures (Books 1-4)

The Kyn Kronicles Box Set (Books 1-6)

Arcane Transporter Box Set I (Books 1-3)

Arcane Transporter Box Set II (Books 4-6)

"Death is a bitch who sometimes wears my face."

- Isa Serrano

acknowledgments

My stories center around found family and survivors - not the kind that go to tribal and vote, but those individuals targeted by life in various ways, who managed to stay on their feet and hit back. The stubbornness involved to hold that belligerent position speaks to an inner core of steel that can hide a multitude of cracks, and sometimes life lands a sucker punch that can weaken that core. Sometimes life lands a flurry of them. When it does, it's those we hold as our "family", the trusted beloved few who we don't have to pretend perfection or try and excuse our faults with, who reach out, grab our hand and drag us back up. They don't stop there, they stick, to our sides or our backs, they won't leave us to face things alone.

Those connections are what my stories celebrate, and Arcane Wonderland is my love letter to those of my "family" who've been with me during this whole wild ride. A trio who found their place in a family of their choosing. I believe that's what keeps us sane, being able to cultivate our own family, however that looks.

Luckily for me, I have many to thank for keeping me sane in this wild ride of life. As always at the top of my list are my boys: Ben, Ian, and Brendan. Then there are these wonder peeps that I'm eternally grateful can't get rid of me: Robin, Shirl, Kristin, Derrick, and Lisa. Even better, I found a treasure trove of love and acceptance from these chosen family members: Kim, Diane, Camille, Dave, and Erin. And, as a writer, there are the precious gifts of my reader family: Maria, Joanna, Sandy, and Cat.

Even better, you, readers, who keep picking up my stories and sharing your lives with me. I can't thank you enough, you keep me going when I can't see beyond my screen.

Much love,

Jami

contents

chapter 1

Isa

"I'M HITTING THE LOT NOW." Isa's headlights swept over the gray cement-block wall and the dumpster in front of it. The low-slung building crouched in the shadows of its taller siblings in downtown Phoenix.

"I'm right behind you. Wait for me," Desmond ordered.

Only the fact that Des was one of her best friends kept her from snapping a sharp rebuke. "Whoever is inside knows the alarm code," she said with patience and a hint of sarcasm as she put her car in park. "That generally takes murder out of the equation."

"Not funny, Isa."

"Lighten up, Des," she shot back.

It was freaking three thirty in the morning, and instead of being curled up in her extremely comfortable bed after ten hours on her feet, she was back at Wonderland, the bar she co-owned with Des and Cass—her bestie—wondering which employee was holed up inside. Normally, Cass would be the first in line to handle shit like this, but she was in Vegas, dealing with her toxic family. That had left Isa and Des on speed dial when things hit the fan.

Sometimes being a bar owner sucked balls.

She activated the charm in her earring, switching the phone's audio from her car to her ear. "If we were being robbed, they wouldn't have bothered with the code."

"That doesn't make it safe." His voice was rough with irritation.

"I've got my Taser." She grabbed it from her cupholder then shoved open the door. "If I solemnly swear to use it, will you chill out?" Isa hip checked her door closed and crossed the cracked-pavement-and-packed-dirt parking lot as Des's curses filled her ear. "Look, I'll stay on the phone until you get here."

He continued to grumble in her ear, but she let the sound wash over her as she kept an eye on her surroundings and crossed to the front entrance lit by an overhead security light.

"Putting you in my pocket," she warned him before tucking her phone away.

Then, holding the Taser at the ready, she set her other hand against the security ward embedded in the metal door. Magic washed under her palm, flashing from bright orange to pale green. There were no further indications that someone had messed with the security ward, just the snick of the lock releasing.

"Yep." She kept her voice low. "Definitely had the code."

She pulled the door open, and the hinges released with a muted squeak. Shadows filled the narrow staircase leading down to the bar, the soft glow of the security lights barely holding them in check. Isa slipped inside and froze just over the threshold as the weight of the door hit her back. She eyed the stairs disappearing into the darkness and regretted her agreement to keep the dim, atmospheric lighting.

Built in the late 1940s, the building had initially been an art gallery that sat below street level as a concession to the desert temperatures. Even though logic promised nothing lurked in the inky depths pooling at the bottom, tension clawed its way up Isa's spine and sank deep as her pulse ticked up. She drew in a breath, held her Taser at the ready, and inched forward, easing the door closed.

She stopped on the bottom step and strained her ears, trying to catch any noise that didn't belong. The only thing she heard was the hum of the air conditioner. Cool drafts danced over the exposed pipes curling out of brick walls and wound through the hollow areas surrounding the thick wooden beams before spilling to the shadow-strewn floor. The windowless space was filled with nebulous shapes, but the graffiti-style tags and sigils covering the double metal doors on the back wall glowed softly, offering glimpses of upturned stools on top of scattered pub tables. The arcade side of the open floor was quiet and dark, as the electric machines had been powered down at closing time. Security lights, installed under the booths lining the wall, offered some relief to the gloom, their illumination reflected in the long mirror behind the bar.

"Talk to me!" Des barked in her ear, startling her.

She'd forgotten he was on the other end. "Doesn't look like anyone's here."

"I'm turning in now."

"Cool." Reassured, she started across the floor, her goal the door behind the bar that led to the office and compact kitchen. "I'm going to check out the back."

Isa rounded the end of the bar and flipped the pass-through, while in her ear, Des muttered to himself as he parked. She moved into the back as the clunk of his car door closing was followed by the rapid crunch of footsteps. A light burned bright over the stove in the kitchen, but the space was empty of life. She got to the office and had her hand on the knob when she heard movement.

"Shit."

"What?" Des demanded as a familiar squeak indicated he'd hit the entrance door.

"Someone is in the office."

"Do not go in, Isa."

Ignoring him, she tightened her grip on the doorknob, held a finger over the Taser's trigger, and threw open the door. A sharp scream greeted her, along with the clatter of something bouncing off the desk, the dull thud of a chair hitting the floor, and a rush of movement. In that fraction of time, recognition flashed, and somehow, she managed not to launch the Taser.

"Don't shoot! It's me!" someone sobbed.

In Isa's ear, Des thundered down the stairs.

"What the hell, Kelly?" Relief, irritation, and the weird letdown that chased an adrenaline rush left Isa both pissed and shaky. She hit the switch, and the office filled with light.

Behind the battered desk stood Kelly, one of Wonderland's servers. She was dressed in a gorgeous goth clubbing outfit, her hands held high, her pale face blotched and covered in smears of tear-smudged mascara as well as more ominous shadings that indicated the rise of fresh bruises. There was a small, raw cut on her lower lip, and the hands near her tangled, sweat-matted hair carried streaks of what Isa thought might be dried blood.

"I'm sorry, I'm sorry," Kelly babbled, her tone sliding along the edge of hysteria. "I didn't know where else to go." She started to lower her hands and motioned toward the floor. "I was calling you beca—"

The slam of the door to the back area reverberated down the hall. Kelly flinched as a half-strangled screech escaped her. The fast-approaching heavy tread that followed belonged to Des.

Isa kept her voice soothing. "It's okay, Kelly. Shh, it's okay."

Kelly scrambled back, almost tripping on the overturned chair behind her, and gave a panicked sob. Her eyes widened, and her hands flew forward as if to ward off an imminent attack. “No, he’s here! He’s goin—”

“Kelly! It’s just Des!” Isa said in the stern tone that never failed to lower the drama level when shit went south with the serving staff. “Look at me!”

Kelley’s gaze jumped to Isa as Des pulled up short in the doorway.

“It’s just Des,” she said, softer now, trying not to lose her mind at the sight of long, deep scratches marring Kelly’s arms. “Take a breath with me. Come on.” She drew in a lungful of air and waited until Kelly did the same before letting it out.

When Kelly pulled in another broken inhalation, her eyes darted to Des, but they came back to Isa on her shaky exhalation. Isa inhaled again, silently encouraging Kelly to keep it up, as she slowly set her Taser on the arm of the sofa. Then she exhaled as she cautiously moved toward the shaken young woman. When she got close, she saw that Kelly’s pupils were so big they almost erased the whites, and there was a concerning reddened knot coming up on her forehead.

Worry about a possible concussion was drowned under a simmering protective fury as Isa took in the other signs of violence—tears near the neck of the black lace shirt. Singe marks on the short red skirt that wrapped around black hot pants. A scattered collection of what looked like small cuts in the exposed skin of her thighs and the deep red coloring her knees above thick-soled lace-up boots. Isa looped a careful arm around Kelly’s waist and guided her to the sofa, biting back a slew of curses as she spotted a ring of red that looked scarily like finger marks high on Kelly’s scratched arms.

“Come, let’s sit over here.” With effort, Isa kept her temper out of her voice.

Kelly gingerly sat on the sofa and wrapped her arms around her middle. When her shoulders curled inward, Isa grabbed a nearby throw and settled it around the shaking girl. A hint of smoke and alcohol rose from Kelly's clothes.

A low growl from the doorway had Isa turning to Des. Based on his thunderous expression, he had come to the same conclusion as Isa. The shadows behind him deepened with a weighty sense of a menace.

This could be bad. Very bad.

Hoping to head off the explosion, she said, "Des, why don't you get Kelly some water?"

The storm building around Des retreated as he shot her a quizzical look, complete with raised brows. She canted her head and looked pointedly at his hands, which were fisted at his sides. Those hands flexed open, causing the intricate ink on his skin to shift as he shook out his arms. The oppressive air around him lightened as he blew out a silent breath and then turned on his heel and left.

Isa crouched in front of Kelly and fought the urge to growl when she caught sight of the marks on the girl's neck. "First things first—how hurt are you? Do we need to go to emergency?"

Kelly shook her head. "No, no, I'm okay."

She wasn't, not by a long shot, but this was not the time to argue. "Okay," Isa said calmly. "Can you tell me what happened?"

Kelly started to nod then winced, her hand going to the knot on her forehead. "It was a farewell thing, you know? Leo wanted to go out one last time before I left town, so we met up with some friends at the Obsidian Club."

That explained the Goth-inspired outfit.

"It was absolutely bussin'. Everyone was having a blast. Then just before the club closed, Leo crashed out."

"He freaked?" Isa asked, and Kelly nodded. "How so?"

"He was getting paranoid—thought someone was watching him."

"Did you pick up on that vibe too?" Isa asked. Kelly wasn't the flighty type—she couldn't be if she wanted to work at Wonderland—and wouldn't detect a vibe unless it was really there.

Kelly bit her torn lip, flinched, then stopped. "No, but he was off, way off, being cringe to Em and Olie. Saying how they treat him like shit because he's a muni."

Isa tried not to wince. The derogatory term referred to those who held little to no magical ability in a world that was all about Arcane power. "So he's a Traditionalist?"

She shrugged. "Yeah. His magic is, like, small, you know? He can try to turn lights on and off, juice up a minor charm, but it's always a crapshoot. I didn't think it bothered him much. I mean, we laugh about it all the time, but tonight, he... he... just..." She closed her eyes and pressed her lips together as a single tear rolled down her face.

Isa got up to grab a box of tissues. On her way, she picked up the old portable handset from where Kelly had dropped it and set it on its base on the desk. She sat back down next to Kelly and handed her the box. The younger woman murmured a quiet thanks then pulled out a handful of tissues and blew her nose.

"Sorry," she whispered.

"Nothing to apologize for." Isa heard Des moving back their way. "So, you were at the club, and this Leo guy was getting upset?"

"Who's Leo?" Des asked, stalking back in with a highball glass full of water and handing it to Isa.

"A friend." Whatever she saw on his face had her quickly adding, "Just a friend, I swear."

Considering the state Kelly was in, Isa wondered if the girl was in denial. She offered the glass of water to Kelly, who managed a couple of sips before handing it back. Isa set it on the floor to the side of the sofa.

Des headed to the desk and the toppled chair. He made quick work of righting it before taking a seat, giving Kelly space. "And where is Leo now?" He opened one of the desk drawers and pulled out a healing kit.

The tissues Kelly was twisting between her fingers tore, and what little color her face had held disappeared. A curious blankness hit her gaze as her breathing became erratic. "I… I don't… He's…"

Alarmed, Isa caught Kelly's hands in hers and squeezed. "Kelly, look at me. Come on. Look at me and breathe. Yeah, just like that, again. Good. You're good."

As Kelly breathed in and out, the strange blank look slowly faded from her eyes. When Isa was sure the younger woman wouldn't pass out, she got to her feet, took a seat next to her, and tried again. "Okay, so you're at Obsidian, Leo's getting weird, and then…?"

She dipped her chin in a slow nod. "We were at the club, and it was closing, so there was a discussion about where to go next. The others were getting pissed at him being so weird and wanted to ditch him for the Alchemist in Tempe, but I figured he was just hammered. I started walking him home, since we were close, hoping he'd sober up, but instead, he got worse, which made me wonder if he had taken something at the club."

Isa caught movement from behind the desk and risked a glance. Des raised a small ice pack in silent question. She nodded and lifted her hand as she kept on topic with Kelly.

"Is he the kind that would do that?"

"I didn't think so," Kelly said as Des tossed over the ice pack and Isa caught it. "You know I don't like that scene, but when he went to pay for his drinks earlier, something fell out of his pocket, and I went to pick it up, but he got there first. Snatched it up quick and stuffed it away while he was acting kind of squirrelly. So maybe?" She said the last as a question.

"Do you know what it was that he dropped?" Des asked.

Kelly's brow furrowed. "It was one of those tiny baggies" —she lifted her hand, with her forefinger and thumb about an inch apart—"with a couple of red pills." She dropped her hand and looked worriedly between Isa and Des. "I got upset and asked him about it. He said he was holding it for someone, that it wasn't his, and we kind of argued about it, you know?"

Isa did know because Kelly had lost an older sibling to an addiction. "Okay, so you're taking him home—"

"Which is where?" Des interrupted.

Kelly's attention went to Des. "Evermore."

Isa recognized the name. The popular high-rise condo, about five blocks north of Wonderland, catered to the downtown university crowd. "So you walked from the bar to his place, right?" Isa asked. The younger woman nodded, her attention on Isa's hands as they unwrapped the charmed ice pack. "Then what?"

"I got him up the stairs and inside his condo. He told me earlier that his roommate was out of town until next week, so I knew no one was home, but I didn't want to just leave him alone and whacked-out, you know?"

"You were worried." Isa activated the ice pack's rune and handed it to Kelly.

"Yeah." Kelly pressed the pack to the knot on her forehead. "He kept muttering and pacing in the living room, so I went to the kitchen to get him some water and aspirin. I was at the fridge when..."

Her gaze went dark as she tightened her hold on the throw, huddling. Misery radiated off of her. Isa rubbed a comforting hand along her stiff spine but stayed quiet, letting Kelly tell the story at her own pace and fight her way clear of the memories.

In a few moments, Kelly spoke again. This time, there was a distance in her tone. "He slammed me into the fridge so hard I dropped the glass. Heard it shatter, but I couldn't move. He had me pinned..." Her voice cracked, and a violent shudder tore through her. The hand clutching the throw rose as if to touch one of the bruises by her eye but stopped. "He said how he'd make me pay attention. How he wasn't a useless muni, how things were going to be different now, then..." Her shock-glazed eyes met Isa's. "I tried to talk him down, but it wasn't working, and it should have, Isa."

She wasn't wrong. Her skill as a Charmer was part of the reason they'd taken her on as a server. A mage who could calm a rowdy crowd with a few magically backed words was invaluable.

"It was like every time I spoke, it just made him angrier, so I fought back, doing that thing you taught us, where you just drop. That's where I got these." She shifted her weight and loosened her grip on the throw, exposing the cuts and scratches on her thighs. "There was glass on the floor." She touched one of the shallow cuts with a shaky hand. "But then he grabbed my hair and started to drag me across the floor. I needed something, anything, to stop him, and there were knives on the counter, you know, in one of those block thingies. I tried to grab one but knocked it over just before he hit me again. I couldn't really see, just picked up one of the knives, and... and..." She turned her hand over, revealing deep, ragged tears along her palm and small cuts on her fingers.

Isa hissed at the blood-smeared mess, wondering if stitches were going to be needed. She took Kelly's wrist carefully to keep her from using it. "Des, can you get me some wet paper towels?"

While Des headed out, Kelly kept talking. "I used it to make him let me go." Her fingers curled up as if holding something, and Isa's heart ached as she realized the cuts had been made when Kelly's grip had slipped on the knife. Kelly kept staring at her blood-streaked hand. "Everything kind of blurs after that."

Des came back in, handed over the damp paper towels, then stepped to the desk as Isa gently wiped away the blood. He came back and handed Isa a healing charm. As soon as Kelly's palm was somewhat clean, Isa activated the charm and was relieved to see the worst of the cuts start to close under its soft glow.

"I was trying to get out of the kitchen," Kelly said, her attention on what Isa was doing, "when this flash hit me." She touched the singe mark in her shirt. "It hurt so bad. I think I screamed." She turned to Isa with a dazed look. "I don't get it. He's not an electro mage or a pyro, but he was standing there, wielding magic he shouldn't have, eyes wild. And that magic — like some weird cross between electricity and fire—" She shook her head. "All I could think was he was going to kill me. He tried for another strike but missed. The magic he was using, it was scary wild, and I just wanted to get out of there. He came after me again, and I knew I wasn't going to make it out. He got an arm around my throat, and I stabbed him over and over again until he let me go. Then I ran." She lifted her head, her gaze going from Isa to Des as she swallowed hard. "I think, maybe, I might have killed him."

chapter 2

Locke

"GOT a possible lead that might intersect with your case." Locke didn't bother with a turn signal as he nudged his Charger around a sedan with out-of-state plates, doing the speed limit on the westbound 202. He zipped forward, knowing by the time they clocked him and started to move over, he'd be long gone.

"I thought you were tracking down Isaiah Holmes." The voice emanating from his speakers belonged to Zev Aslanov, the intimidating Cordova Family Arbitrator but, more importantly, Locke's friend.

"I am." As soon as Locke cleared the sedan, he glided back into the left lane. "Does the name Leo Starini hit any bells?"

"Nothing's ringing," Zev said. "How does he tie into the Forge Foundation?"

"Other than being a Traditionalist, I haven't a clue, but according to Jigz, he's not only a friend of Isaiah's but is flashing around a new product as well."

"You think it's the stuff I'm looking into?"

"I'll find out tonight." As Locke passed the sign for Twenty-Fourth Street, he angled the wheel to the empty right lane to catch the exit for east I-10.

"Are you hitting another club?" Zev asked.

Locke's lips twitched as he steered into the highway's connecting arc. "Check the time, old man. Clubs are closed."

"Fuck you, bro." Zev's refrain carried a familiar affectionate dryness.

"Lovely offer, but I'm going have to pass. You don't have enough curves for me," Locke shot back, but his amusement was short-lived. "I had Roxy dig up Leo's address. I figure if he's not already home, he should be soon."

"And you'll be waiting," Zev said grimly.

"And I'll be waiting," Locke agreed, his foot pressing down as the road ahead straightened out.

"Tag me if you run into trouble."

Locke stifled an amused snort. "Please. This will probably be the easiest thing I do tonight."

"Fine. Then how about you tag me if you get anything useful?"

"That I can do."

Zev's grunt was followed by a moment of silence before the familiar heavy beat and down-tuned guitars of Chevelle resumed. Locke let the music wash over him and rolled his tight shoulders. It didn't loosen shit.

That night had featured an annoying trek through a series of hot spots filled with the university students. It was not his scene. At the age of twenty-nine, Locke had long since left behind the overpriced clubs crammed with a glittery, hectic throng wanting to be seen. He preferred higher-end venues that understood the true meaning of ambience and served quality drinks to a less frenetic crowd intent on enjoying the moment and getting their money's worth.

As if it had just been waiting for a chance, the familiar image of a dark-haired siren hit his brain. With a low oath, he forced her back into the box she refused to stay in and turned his attention to the job at hand—a byzantine one guaranteed to keep him from dwelling on one frustratingly tempting bar owner.

Close to two years back, the sister-in-law of Locke's boss, Emilio—head of the Cordova Family—had been killed in retaliation for stealing highly classified biotech research that she'd hoped to leverage into a paycheck. She'd made the mistake of locking the information behind a blood ward keyed to her young son. After she and her husband were killed, the interested parties decided kidnapping the kid was worth the risk of angering one of the most powerful Arcane families in Arizona.

This proved to be a mistake on their part. Emilio, determined to retrieve his beloved nephew and the information in question, set Zev out to hunt. As the Family Arbitrator, Zev was judge, jury, and executioner for anyone stupid enough to cross the Family. It didn't take Zev long to track down the boy and the Guild Transporter who had accepted an off-the-books job involving an unknown package. That initial meeting of the Hunter and the Transporter had led to a shit ton more drama, which had uncovered a secret project that twisted inherent magic and a complicated conspiracy that stretched its sticky fingers to the highest corners of the Arcane society.

Locke's tracking skills had earned him a seat on the wild ride late in the game. As a Hound for the Cordova Family, he was privy to certain sensitive details the majority of the Arcane society would never hear. Like the very real possibility that the Delphi serum—a drug created from the stolen research—had not been contained by the Arcane Council and was now making its insidious way through the Arcane population.

The situation had come to light a couple of weeks earlier when, through a series of strange coincidences, two incidents were brought to Emilio's attention, and he, in turn, had called in Locke and Zev. The first involved Lilly Wright, a seventeen-year-old water mage whose father was a midlevel manager at one of the Cordovas' research facilities, and the second was twenty-two-year-old Micah Holmes, an earth mage and intern in the law offices of Cortez, Hamlin, & Blythe.

While Lilly's family had already reached out to the Western Arcane Guild to hire a curse breaker, Micah's friends had tried to keep things low-key by hiring a freelance Key at discounted rates, which only made things worse. When it was clear Micah wouldn't be able to make it in to work, they called his supervising clerk and explained that he was dealing with a nasty stomach flu. That excuse only stretched so far, and on day three, the supervisor got the full story out of Micah's friends and then took the situation to his boss, Maribel Ortiz, the Cordova Family lawyer. Mari, who knew all about the conspiracy and mad-science project, called Emilio. Wanting the best curse breaker available, Emilio had contacted the Western Arcane Guild. They, in turn, had assigned top-tier Key Lena Davis, who just happened to already be working with Lilly's father. At Emilio's request, Lena had taken on Micah's case as well.

Long story short, Lilly had been the target of a straight-up curse set by a jealous rival who coveted a spot on the swim team. Lena removed that hex and then tried to help Micah. It didn't take her long to discover that whatever was messing with his magic wasn't a standard active-level hex but something else, which eluded her. She suggested tagging a Dual-Key —Grayson Beck, out of Las Vegas—as he specialized in both active and latent curses. And just a few days ago, Grayson had confirmed Emilio's dark suspicions about what lay behind Micah's rapid deterioration and erratic magical behavior. The earth mage hadn't been hexed—he'd been poisoned with an unknown substance. Once tests were run, the results confirmed that whatever he'd taken was based on the Delphi serum. Not only did it screw with his magical ability, but it was killing him slowly as well. Currently, he was being monitored in a private medical facility under the name Patient Zero.

Emilio had initially wanted Zev and Locke to hunt down Micah's supplier and find irrefutable proof of the drug's origins before he took his next step, which included bringing the Arcane Council in on the investigation. Unfortunately, while retracing Micah's last known movements, the Hunter and the Hound had discovered that prior to his overdose, Micah had been trying to locate his missing younger brother, Isaiah. According to Micah's circle of friends, for the last five years, he'd been Isaiah's sole caregiver, taking on the role when he was seventeen and Isaiah was eleven. While Micah was focused on becoming a lawyer, his younger brother was pissed at the world in general and ran with a much wilder crowd, leaving Micah to habitually drag his baby brother out of whatever trouble he found.

That was how Micah had ended up dosed. Micah's friends confirmed that the weekend Micah started acting strange had been the one he'd spent tracking Isaiah through a series of underground parties and a handful of clubs that accepted less-than-legit IDs. At some point, Micah's behavior started to shift from focused and determined to easily irritated and quick to anger. Initially, his friends put it down to his having to deal with Isaiah, but when the level-headed law student with a minor earth-magic ability went after a snarky, drunken frat brat and tore multiple massive cracks into the club's asphalt parking lot—setting off numerous car alarms and rupturing city water lines—the friends knew something was not right. After hustling Micah away from the scene before authorities arrived—a law student with an arrest never went over well—they hunkered down at one of the friend's homes in the suburbs. When the sun rose, Micah was sporting a massive headache and a serious personality change. When his magic became scarily erratic, they feared he had been cursed. Cue the panicked hiring of a budget Key.

But as with all things, they got what they paid for, and the inept Key had only made things worse. By the time Lena got to Micah, his friends had resorted to sedation spells and restraints. Remorse plagued them, so when Zev and Locke started asking questions, they were quick to spill everything. They had no idea when or where Micah would have been drugged, but they were able to pin down when his behavior had started to change. Locke retraced their steps, checking video surveillance and asking questions, finally hitting pay dirt at the second club, the Alchemist, where video footage showed a known small-time dealer placing a roofie in Micah's drink. The club's security tagged the dealer as a regular visitor named Jigz.

Locke waited at the Alchemist, and sure enough, the wiry fucker made an appearance back by the bathrooms. When Locke stalked down the narrow hallway, the nervy dealer scented a threat and started to run. He didn't get far before Locke had him pinned to the cement block wall that ran behind the club and proceeded to ask questions. After a few strategically applied "encouragements," the story tumbled out.

Isaiah was one of Jigz's customers, and Micah's questions had started to interfere with Jigz's nightly endeavors. It didn't help that Micah kept pushing the issue even though Jigz hadn't seen Isaiah in over a week. To get Micah off his ass, Jigz decided to spike his drink with a party gift shared by another customer, who happened to be one of Isaiah's buddies and went by the name Leo Starini. Jigz had no clue what the party gift did or where it came from, but Leo promised it would rock his world. He provided a sample and said if Jigz wanted more, for the right cut, he'd be happy to facilitate. Jigz had no interest in taking on another supplier, but he figured if Micah's world was rocked hard enough, it would make him stop asking about Isaiah, so when he spotted Micah's drink at the bar, he dropped the pill and walked away. Problem solved. Locke had left a battered Jigz slumped in the alleyway and decided to track down this Leo guy. That was how he'd ended up rolling down Washington in the dead of morning.

He hooked a right on Seventh, grateful that at ass o'clock, the one-way streets of downtown Phoenix were empty. It was wild to drive here now that high-rise residential spaces had popped up like rabbits. In recent years, what had once been a small cluster of multistory buildings had grown into a dense urban canyon.

He made a right on Monroe and cruised the narrow two-way road as it carved its way between parking garages and high-rises until he hit First. Rising thirty-four floors into the night sky, the Evermore condos sat on the southwest corner, where a bland beige box of an office building had once stood. Locke bypassed the underground parking garage and managed to snag a metered parking spot across the street from the entrance. He took the time to pay the meter, since the HQ for the Phoenix Police Department was just down the road. Then he jogged across the street.

Locke used the access code pulled from the ethernet by Tana—the Cordova e-geek—to open the glass door to the lobby. Along with the code, she'd shared that no one would be on duty, as the concierge desk was manned from seven in the morning to eleven at night. He pulled open the heavily tinted glass doors and found the space empty of life. He headed straight for the elevators, noting the strategically placed security cameras tracking his passage. He didn't worry about being recorded. If his conversation with Leo went sideways, Tana would take care of any digital evidence.

The ride to the fourth floor was short and quiet. He got

off and did a check of the two closest unit numbers, 4001 to the right and 4009 to the left. Since the hall appeared to loop around, he figured there were only nine units on this floor. He'd started down the right hall toward 4005 when a dark smear on the floor caused a hitch in his stride. When his magic quivered, he stopped and sank into a crouch to get a closer look, and a touch of iron hit his nose.

Blood.

The smudge held the edge of a tread. He looked at the hall and found a couple more drops staining the floor a little farther down, their shape and spacing indicating that someone had been moving erratically and fast while wounded. The power that lived inside him came on point, urging him forward. He pulled a thin blade out of the hidden sheath in his belt and stood up. Holding the blade down at his side, where it wasn't easily spotted, he prowled down the hall on silent feet. At the corner where the hall turned was another smear, almost as if someone had bounced off the wall. He continued walking and wasn't surprised to find that units 4004 and 4005 shared that side of the hall.

His pace slowed as he released his magic, letting it sniff over the doorways and draw in the lingering blend of emotions and magic. It slipped over 4004 and homed in on 4005. In the entryway, the muddied scents of an illusion mage mixed with the diluted blanks of a nonmagic user. There was a sharp bite to the fading trace of an illusion mage, a hint of fear or apprehension—it was hard to tell.

He angled his body, putting his back to the door, and let his hand hover over the knob. A flex of magical muscle determined there were no active runes at play, so Leo used either standard electronic security or nothing at all. His fingers closed around the cool metal, and he carefully twisted, the knob turning smoothly.

He eased the door open. A rush of cool air curled around

him, carrying the sharp sting of fear, the acrid bit of anger, the tangle of an illusion mage, and the burnt ash of a fire mage, but it was the alluring darker scent winding through it all that had him cursing.

"What the fuck, Isa?"

chapter 3

Isa

CROUCHED next to Leo's sprawled body, Isa pivoted so fast she almost landed on her ass while her heart tried to beat its way out of her chest. She barely caught herself with a shaky hand on the nearby coffee table as she faced down the one person she had no desire to see that night.

With sickening sweetness, she said, "Good morning to you, too, sunshine."

"Don't be cute, Isa." Locke glared at her as he walked inside and carefully closed then locked the door behind him.

Afraid I'm going to run, are you?

Instead of letting her mouth run free, she kept a wary eye on him as he stalked closer, the air around him nearly vibrating with that fascinating tension he carried like a shadow.

He stopped next to Leo's outstretched hand, his unusually light eyes shifting from the body to her. "What did you do?"

"Not a damn thing." She kept her voice cool and tried to ignore the sting of his accusation. Of course he thought she was at fault. She rose slowly, relieved when her legs didn't fold. "I found him like this."

A long moment passed as he stared at her, but she refused

to look away first, a reaction that hadn't changed since the first moment he'd walked into Wonderland and hit her radar. To stand unmoving under that intense, predatory stare was a personal challenge, but she managed another win when he finally shook his head, sank into a crouch, and turned his attention back to the body between them.

"I'm assuming this is Starini," he said.

"Who?" Still rattled by the scene she'd walked into and the fact that her magic was acting like an overeager puppy wanting to play, she had to take a second to make the connection. "Oh, you mean Leo?"

"Is Leo the body on the floor?" Locke asked, his strained patience laced with sarcasm.

The familiar tone would normally set her hackles on end, but tonight, they barely quivered, too exhausted by her earlier emotional roller coaster ride with Kelly. "Well, I didn't check his ID, but I'm feeling like it's a safe assumption."

"Smart-ass," he muttered.

"Better than a dumbass," she shot back so fast it earned her a serious side-eye. She turned away, hiding a wince. How he managed to always reduce her to a bratty teenager, she'd never understand. It seemed to be his superpower. "Why are you hunting him?"

"Who said I was?"

"Now who's the smart-ass?" She rubbed her arms, trying to get the hairs standing on end to chill out. It wasn't working.

"You okay?"

She looked over shoulder to find him watching her. "I'm fine," she lied as she put a little more space between her and the temptation residual death presented.

That was the thing about being a Reaper. The minute she got near a recent death event, the urge to play with the lingering essence became nearly impossible to ignore. At the moment, the dark whispers were easy to drown out—all she had to do was focus on how irritating it was to deal with Locke. But that wouldn't hold them back for long.

She played with the scythe charm on her necklace as she stepped around the bloodied knife and moved to the island that separated the living room and the kitchen. One of the barstools was tipped over, and a hefty butcher knife lay under its padded back, its blade clean. On the island's stone surface, the block knife holder lay on its side, a couple of blades still gamely holding on. She rounded the island's far end and spotted the shattered glass on the floor near the fridge. One of the stainless-steel doors sported a dent, confirming that Kelly had a hell of a throwing arm. In the area between the island and the stove, the glass pieces were mixed with smears of blood and water, marring the laminated wood floor. More blood marked the lower white cabinets, along with scorch marks. Letting go of her charm, Isa skirted the mess on the floor and got close enough to brush her finger carefully over one of the burns. The surface was smooth, but her finger came back coated with soot.

Those aren't from cooking.

If Kelly was right and Leo was a muni, that kind of non-damage to the cabinet's surface shouldn't exist. Only a skilled fire mage could manage that kind of control. Straightening, she wiped her finger on her jeans.

She nearly jumped when she turned around to find Locke standing at the end of the island, watching her. "What?"

He leaned his hip against the island and folded his arms. "You going to tell me what happened here?"

"Only if you tell me why you showed up." If Locke was after Leo, then Kelly's problems might be bigger than Isa had anticipated.

There was a long moment of quiet before Locke grudgingly admitted, "I'm tracking a missing person. Leo was the one of the last people seen with them."

A jumble of questions clamored for attention. She picked one. "Who's missing?"

He shook his head. "Nope, I answered yours. Time for you to answer mine." He glided closer, deliberately invading her space. "What are you doing here?"

Her pulse, which had finally leveled off, kicked up again, this time with something a lot more dangerous than nerves. She could shove him away, but in the deepest pit of her consciousness, she knew touching him would be a huge mistake. Instead, she fisted her hands, lifted her chin, and gathered her irritation into an impenetrable shield. "There was a situation earlier, and Leo was involved. I was coming to talk to him."

"Talk?" he asked in disbelief. "Talking doesn't lead to that." He motioned back to where Leo lay.

She kept her gaze on him. "I told you, I found him like that."

"And you didn't call the police?"

His question held just enough condescension to trigger her temper. "Not like I had a chance, considering you barged in just after I got here." She pulled her phone out of her pocket. "But hey, I can fix that, and we can both spend the next couple of hours answering uncomfortable questions."

"Wouldn't be uncomfortable for me."

Of course not, because he's part of the all-powerful Cordova Family. The urge to snarl in frustration was so strong it escaped her clenched teeth in a feral hiss as she pushed past him.

She didn't get far. He caught her arm in a gentle but firm grip. "Tell me about the situation."

She was already shaking her head. "No."

His eyes narrowed at her bitten-out refusal. "What are you hiding?"

"I'm not hiding anything."

"Okay, then who are you protecting?" he asked. When she didn't answer, a muscle jumped in his jaw. "Des?"

She snorted as she tested his hold. "Please. Des doesn't need my protection."

"Then who?"

Recognizing that he wasn't going to drop this, she reluctantly said, "One of my servers."

He finally let her go. "So your server killed him?"

Seriously? He's a damn dog with a bone. She shouldn't have been surprised, since she was dealing with a Hound.

"I don't think so," she said as she remembered Kelly's horrified shock.

Initially, when she first walked in, she thought it was highly likely that Kelly had killed him, but... unable to resist the pull any longer, she inched toward Leo's body. Her magic shivered in anticipation, like a carrion bird fluffing its feathers before a feast. She ruthlessly reined it in and focused on the physical evidence.

In the kitchen were scattered drops of blood, likely from where Kelly had cut herself on the broken glass. On the other side of the island and trailing into the living room were more crimson smears but nothing big enough to indicate a fatal wound. The bloodied knife she'd stepped over earlier lay between the kitchen and living room. The four-inch blade wouldn't have offered much protection if Leo was tossing fireballs at the panicked girl. If Kelly had killed him, as Isa feared, there should be a blood pool somewhere nearby, but there wasn't.

That left Isa with serious doubts that Kelly killed anyone, so she didn't want to share the girl's name with Locke. Especially since she had no idea why the Cordova Family was interested in Leo.

She turned back to the man watching her and told a partial

lie. "According to her, he was still breathing when she ran out of here."

There was a disconcerting glint in his ice-blue eyes, but whatever he was thinking was well hidden. He shook his head. "Is she okay—your server?"

Ignoring how his obvious concern made her heart twinge wistfully, Isa gave a slow nod. "She's going to need stitches and some serious time with an ice pack." *And probably a good therapist.*

He folded his arms over his broad chest. "And you still came alone to confront him?"

She frowned. "He's a drunk kid, Locke. I didn't need a bodyguard."

"Even a drunk kid can do serious damage, Isa."

She barely refrained from rolling her eyes. "It's not like I can't protect myself."

"Did you tell Des about this?"

"He knows."

"And he let you come over here? Alone?"

"Your sexism is showing, Locke," she snapped.

His head jerked back, and he dropped his arms. If she hadn't been so upset, she would have found his affronted expression hilarious.

"I'm not. I'm just..." Flustered, he ran a hand through his hair as he looked away. "Dammit, Isa, you could've walked into anything."

Knowing he had a point, she blew out a long breath. "Well, I definitely walked into something." Her magic grew impatient, and to feed the monster, she inched a little closer to Leo. "This missing person—who is it?"

Those sharp eyes didn't miss her movement, but he didn't comment. "His name is Isaiah. He just turned seventeen. His older brother has been trying to track him down, with no luck."

"What happened?" She could think of a hundred reasons why a teen would take off, but the fact that Locke was trying to track the kid indicated something deeper was at play.

"That's what I came over to ask Leo."

"It's going to be hard to get your answers now," she pointed out.

"Maybe not."

She looked over her shoulder to find Locke studying her with those glacial eyes that appeared to glow. Not wanting to admit how much that eerie gaze unsettled her, she asked, "What?"

"What if you—"

"Uh-uh, nope." She shook her head as she backed away. "Nope. Not doing it, Locke."

He tilted his head, his gaze shifting from considering to calculating. "Your magic wants to," he drawled.

"It doesn't always get what it wants." The reminder was as much for her as it was for him. She turned away, rubbing her arms where, once again, her hair was standing on end. "Dial it back, buddy."

"I'm not doing anything."

She shot him a narrow-eyed glare. "Aren't you?"

His gaze went from her arms and to her face. That unearthly pressure in the room took a step back, like a wolf sitting on its haunches. "It's not just my magic running wild, babe."

She let go of her arms and sank into a crouch next to Leo. The power that lived inside her pulled against her control, eager to play in the echoes of death. "I've got it in check."

He gave a disbelieving huff. "Come on, Isa. I've got a missing kid, and this guy was my best lead."

And that sucks, but... "Can't you do whatever it is you do and sniff him out?"

Instead of answering, he asked, "Why won't you help?"

It wasn't that she didn't want to, but helping would cost her. For a moment, she wished Des had been the one to come after Leo. As a Tracer, getting answers for Locke would be a lot less deleterious.

For once, she decided to give him the unvarnished truth. "Because it's not right."

"Like that's ever stopped you."

And that snapped comment answered a long-held question. Clearly, Locke had investigated her. *But how deep has he dug?* She curled her hands into fists but refused to look at him as he muttered a vile word.

Then he was dropping into a crouch next to her, remorse heavy in his voice. "I took that too far, Isa."

He had, but it was also an accurate statement she couldn't argue with. She could feel the weight of his gaze, but she resolutely kept her attention on Leo.

Locke blew out a breath and, in a less aggressive tone, said, "You're a Reaper. All you have to do is check to see if his soul, or whatever, is close enough to pin down for some answers."

His oversimplification was typical of mages who had not the first clue about how those who played in the other realm worked. She didn't have time to school him in the intricacies of the Spiritualist classification. Still, that didn't mean she couldn't share a CliffsNotes version.

With studied patience, she explained, "First, I'm not Des. Talking to the dead is not my thing. Second, violent death damages the soul, leaving it chaotic and sometimes incoherent. What you're asking of me is to take a traumatized soul, trap what's left of it in my body, and force it to answer your questions." She finally looked at him. "Ever heard of 'my body, my choice'?"

He met her gaze, and she was surprised to see both remorse and determination in his eyes.

"It is—it so is—but I need your help." He paused then added the killing blow. "Isaiah needs your help."

Shit damn fuck it. It was her turn to look away. Sensing her acquiescing, her magic leapt with excitement even as her gut twisted into painful knots.

"Fine." Without looking at him, she waved him away. "Go stand over there and stay out of my way."

She felt him move back, taking the feral hum of his magic with him. She pulled in a deep breath, her fingers closing over the warm gold of the pendant resting against her skin. With skillful ease, she brought her soul's reflection into focus as she let the air out in a slow and steady exhalation. A figure formed in her mind's eye, created from iridescent ebony and dotted with tiny pinpricks of starlight. It was feminine and her but also not her. A tattered cloak of deepest black curled around her. The figure's hair moved like inky ribbons, her features vague, her eyes two pits of deeper darkness. Isa loosened her grip on her magic, and the figure pulled up the hood of the cloak until her blurred features were nothing but shadows, and those unearthly eyes took on a ghostly glow.

As an invisible wind whipped the cloak about, icy fingers twined around Isa, strangling the warmth of compassion, mercy, love, and understanding until only a pitiless resolve remained, leaving behind a Reaper once known as Isa.

chapter 4

Locke

LOCKE FOLLOWED Isa's directions and moved back, giving her room to do her thing. He had to admit to being curious about how this would all go down. Reapers weren't keen on working their magic with an audience, which maybe explained Isa's initial reluctance, but something told him there was more to it. His magic agreed, and it watched her carefully, prepared for anything.

She took a breath, touched the gold medallion that rested just below her throat, and let it out on a slow exhalation. Then things got freaky.

Ebony tendrils dotted with tiny flickers of light curled from Leo's body, moved around Isa's feet, and crawled up her legs like an inky pet snake. The temperature in the room dropped, creating an unsettling chill that pierced skin and bone with unnatural ease as the phantom sensation of ants crawling over his skin left Locke twitchy. His magic lunged, gnashing its metaphorical teeth at the unseen threat seeping into the room.

Isa's head snapped up and turned toward him with an alien disjointedness, which was bad enough, but it was the tide of black swallowing her eyes that raised his hackles. She stared at him like he was prey as shadows drifted over her face, twisting her features into a grim skeletal mask. The nightmarish vision chilled his soul, and his muscles tightened with the urge to strike out.

Instead of giving in to the violent impulse, he blinked. The weird apparition disappeared.

What the fuck?

The unearthly tendrils moved faster, circling her hips then her waist. When they reached her chest, she turned back to Leo's body. The vaporous ribbons rising from Leo had coalesced into a vaguely humanoid shape that now hovered in the air in front of her. The hand resting at her neck dropped, and those tendrils slithered over her arms, curled around her shoulders, and went no farther. They thickened into a writhing cloak that covered Isa from shoulder to toe, undulating in an unseen wind.

Power, thick and heavy, filled the space and pressed against him. Whispers teased his ears, but no matter how much he strained, he couldn't make out the words, if there were any to understand. He shook his head to dislodge distracting noise and narrowed his attention to what was happening around Isa, but the strange murmuring persisted. He couldn't be sure, thanks to the constantly shifting shadows, but he swore her lips were moving.

Time passed as a motionless Isa stood in the center of a whirling dance of darkness, facing the misty shape of Leo while the rush of haunting voices continued. He was unable to tell if it minutes or hours had passed when he realized silence had fallen—not a lack of noise but the kind of quiet that came from the absence of, well, everything. An unnatural stillness, as if the very air held its breath. Locke couldn't help an instinctive jerk when Isa moved, lifting her arms and opening them wide. The hovering form of Leo drifted closer and closer, its shape stretching toward her as if drawn by a magnet until whatever was left of the man had merged with the writhing shadows around Isa. A visible shudder ran through her, and only then did her arms fall back to her sides. For a long moment, she simply stood there, a statue of darkness deeper than night and more intimidating than a nightmare.

Worried, Locke forced his stiff body to move, taking a couple of steps toward her. "Isa?"

She turned her head and pinned him with an unsettling stare.

He barely caught his flinch. "What in the—"

One of her brows rose into an arrogant arch.

He swallowed down his reaction and quickly changed course. "Everything good?"

Her normal hazel was nothing more than a thin line of color around swirling black pools interrupted by starbursts of white. "It's fine." Her voice was flat, empty.

Disconcerted because Isa was normally all fire and flash, not this ice queen from hell, he asked, "You sure?"

She canted her head, her lashes coming down as she turned back to Leo. "Ask your questions quick. Leo's not doing so good."

The hint of sardonic amusement in her voice set his teeth on edge, but he ignored it and moved to the other side of Leo's body so he could face her. It was disturbing how the woman watching him wore both Isa's face and the casually cruel one with equal ease.

"How does this work?" he asked.

Her lips curved as something vicious slid through her inhuman gaze. "Ask your question. Leo answers."

He couldn't shake the sense there was more to this. "Can he lie?"

Her smile deepened. "Anyone can lie, Locke."

"Can you tell when he's lying?"

She inclined her head. "Yes."

Instinct kept him from asking what would happen to Leo if he lied. He was damn sure he didn't want to know because this being was not Isa. This was something older, colder, and far more callous than the firebrand who fascinated him. His magic agreed, prowling forward as it watched the unknown threat in front of him.

He folded his arms and got down to business. "Does he know where Isaiah Holmes is?"

The swirling in her eyes picked up speed as more tiny white pinpricks exploded across her black irises. A trickle of white noise, like a breeze rushing in, returned, and that weird whispering was back, teasing the edge of comprehension. Isa's features shifted subtly, as if someone else was setting up shop under her skin. Her posture changed, shoulders rounding, hands opening and closing, her attention dropping to the body at her feet. Then a whimper escaped her. Isa's voice, when it came, was all wrong—masculine, rough, with a touch of panic and confusion.

"Oh gods, that's me! What's going on? I can't—" Isa made a lurch toward the body only to be jerked back by invisible bonds. "Oh gods—"

"Leo!" Locke barked, trying to stop the spiraling hysteria of whatever remained of Leo. He waited until those wide eyes flew to his. "Where is Isaiah Holmes?"

Isa's head jerked back up, and that weird dual layer of expressions was difficult to watch. Eventually, Leo's confusion rose to the fore. "Isaiah? Was he with me tonight? What happened? Why can't I remember? Did he do this? Is this why—"

"Leo, I need you to focus. When did you last see Isaiah?"

"I... I don't—" Isa's head shook as she spun in place as if looking for something or someone. "Kelly was here. Where did—" She let out a pained hiss as her hands went to her temples and pressed in. "Someone's screaming. Who's screaming? Why won't they stop?"

Locke skirted the body on the floor until he was within arm's length of Isa. He reached out but stopped short of actually touching her—him—whoever the hell it was using Isa. Instead, he snapped his fingers inches from her face. "Hey, hey, man. Focus for me."

Isa stumbled back, her head twisting this way and that as if searching for an escape route. Locke braced because he could tell she was about to bolt, but just as she started to move, she froze, the writhing shadows picking up speed, and somehow, the darkness gained depth.

Her head came up, and it was apparent the Reaper was back in control. "Go to the next question. He's fragmenting too fast to hold on to."

Locke gave her a grim nod. "Leo, the pill you gave Jigz. Where did you get it?"

Comprehension flashed through the inky orbs. "Pill?" This time, the question wasn't confused—it was cagey as fuck. "What pill?"

"Don't fuck with me," Locke bit out as he got up in Isa's face. She jerked back as Leo's spirit tried to retreat. "Where did you get it?"

Isa's throat bobbed as she swallowed. Terror seeped around the pools of black and spilled from her sputtering response. "I can't... I don't know..."

Isa's features shifted, her voice mercilessly cold. "Lie."

Her face contorted into an agonized mask as Leo struggled against the Reaper's hold. Her aborted head shake and small jerky motions looked painful, as if Leo was fighting her. "I can't tell you. He'll kill me. I can't..."

"You're already dead," Isa said, eerily calm.

"No... no! That's not right." Isa stumbled back a step, her hands coming halfway up before freezing in place. "That wasn't supposed to happen! He promised!"

Isa's eyes widened, and the masculine pitch of her voice escalated in panic. "What are you doing? Don't! No! I can't... stop!" Her body gave a massive jerk, her eyes screwed closed, and her grimace deepened as her mouth opened to release an unearthly wail. An invisible wind whipped through the room as something unsettling darkened the air.

Unnerved by a sense of being hunted, Locke braced, retrieved his blade—the hilt a familiar weight against his palm—and pivoted. He dropped into a defensive crouch, keeping the blade hidden as his magic searched the swirling shadows for the unseen threat. Behind him, the power surrounding Isa beat against his back like an incoming storm as the agonized pleas became a jumble of sound.

A heartbeat passed, then another, before the agonized wail cut off, leaving behind a fading echo. The shadows pulled back, and he watched their path as they returned to coil around the woman behind him. He was startled to see Isa holding a grisly staff. Taller than her, it appeared to be made of graying bone or stone and had a curved black blade at the top.

But that wasn't the only change. The shadowy tendrils had solidified into an actual cloak. The change was so real he swore he could feel the brush of heavy material against his legs. Tendrils of shadow poured out of Isa, reforming into the amorphous shape from before. But it was less solid now and more tattered. She raised her staff and brought it down in a slashing motion almost too quick to follow. A shocking flash of white left Locke blinking his vision clear. When the living room came back into view, Isa stood stiff and straight, her attention aimed at Leo's body at her feet, the writhing shadows nowhere in sight. The air was once again warm, but it did nothing to expel the stubborn chill gripping his bones.

"I warned you."

It took him a moment to understand she was talking to him. "What?"

She lifted her head, her expression closed, her eyes back to hazel, but there was no hint of warmth in them. "What good was any of that, Locke?"

Her question caused a sting of guilt that he didn't have the luxury of addressing. Clearly, whatever cost she'd paid to indulge him had caused her pain, but this situation had ramifications that outweighed his remorse. "You tell me."

Without breaking eye contact, she slowly shook her head. "Uh-uh. You were the one looking for answers."

He caught a glimpse of something else behind that blank mask, just a flash but enough to cut through the weirdness in his brain. Instinct or magic, or both, shuffled her reactions and came up with a curious picture. He took a wild guess. "You saw something."

She continued to study him with that strange intensity.

He dug in. "You did, didn't you?"

Silence stretched between them like a rubber band forced to its limits. Just before it snapped, she nodded.

"And...?" he asked.

"And much like Leo's reactions, the images were... chaotic." She carefully stepped around Leo's body and inched back toward the front door, but she never stopped watching him.

He straightened and followed her retreat, not sure he believed her. Since calling her a liar would ignite an argument, he tried another angle. "You knew he was lying about the pill."

She stilled. "I did."

He held her gaze, pinning her in place, as he waited for her to elaborate. When she didn't, he pushed. "Who gave it to him?"

"I don't know!" she shot back, voice sharp, a little bit of her normal obstinacy reappearing.

He didn't hide his skepticism, letting it free with raised eyebrows.

She let out a frustrated noise, dragged a hand through her hair, and spun away to pace in front of the door. "I don't, Locke, but whoever they were, Leo was petrified of them. There was no name, no face that flashed through his mind when you asked, just this drowning depth of fear with enough pressure to break him."

Something in her voice warned him not to push, so he let that go. For the moment. "Who's Kelly?"

She flashed him a disgruntled look. "My server." Her answer was short and final.

Okay, moving on. "And Isaiah? What did he know about him?"

Some of her agitation eased as she stopped moving to face him. "Leo met up with him sometime recently. I'd guess within the last week or so, though I can't be sure. I got the impression they're friendly but not best buds or anything."

"Any idea where they met?"

Her head moved to shake but then stopped.

"Isa?" he asked.

She turned to him. "There was something about this building he was in, but I need to talk to Des—make sure I'm remembering things correctly."

"Where's Des now?"

"Back at Wonderland." She rubbed her temples. "With Kelly."

He nodded. "Good. Then we'll head over, kill two birds one stone."

Her gaze went to Leo's body then back to him. "And we what—just leave him here?"

"We can't exactly walk out with him."

"What about calling the police?" she asked.

"You want to spend hours answering questions?"

She grimaced.

"Exactly." He herded her toward the door.

She worried her bottom lip and frowned. "Doesn't seem right to just walk away."

"We aren't." He opened the front door and waved her through before following her into the hall. "I'll make a call on our way to Wonderland." He pulled the door closed and heard the lock engage.

"For what? A cleanup team?" Although she kept her voice low, there was no missing the edge to her question.

He put a hand at the base of her spine as they walked to the elevators. "No, to a detective."

She gave him a sidelong look. "One on the Cordovas' payroll?"

"We've offered him a private position, and he's turned us down." They reached the elevator, and he pressed the down arrow before looking at her. "Repeatedly."

She gave a soft snort of disbelief. A soft ding sounded, and the silver doors slid open. Isa stepped inside and waited until he followed before hitting the button for the ground floor. Then she studiously ignored him as the doors closed.

Amused, he invaded her space, watching as color rose under her cheeks, her breathing sped up, and her eyes widened just the slightest bit. She made an irritated hiss that sounded like an angry wet kitten.

Unable to resist teasing her, he asked, "Problem?"

She tilted her head back, chin lifted, so she could glare at him, the gold in her eyes fairly glowing with her temper. "There's plenty of room in here. You don't have to be right on top of me."

He bent his head just enough to breathe in the subtle

sweet scent of vanilla-laced cinnamon as he put his lips next to her ear. “Maybe I want to be.”

Her color deepened as she turned into him, her lips coming perilously close to his. “Fair warning—I bite.”

He let his grin free. “So do I.”

Those kissable lips parted in an aroused gasp, but before he could prove his point, the elevator dinged and the doors opened. His dark chuckle chased Isa out into the lobby.

chapter 5

Isa

Safely inside her car, Isa gripped the steering wheel as she watched Locke saunter down the sidewalk, his ass holding her attention. He jogged across the street, and when he reached a black muscle car with equally dark windows, he stopped and looked back. Caught staring, she swore and looked away, imagining his smug smirk.

"Ugh, what is wrong with you?" She started her car and continued to berate her bratty hormones. "He's nothing but trouble."

Ignoring the answering purr of contentment from her mind, she put the car in gear. A glance up showed Locke standing at his open car door, waiting for her. He motioned for her to go on ahead. Her teeth clenched, and instead of flooring it, she pulled out of her spot and drove sedately by. Her rearview mirror showed his driver's-side door closing and the bright glow of his headlights coming to life. She flexed her grip on the wheel and shuffled through the various boxes of her more problematic emotions in the hopes of finding one to safely stuff her current confusion into without breaking the lock. It should have been a simple exercise, but it was proving difficult.

Normally, dealing with the dead left her feeling disconnected from... well, everything, as if a layer of emptiness existed between her and the world. It was her coping tool, a way to keep a lock on her addiction to wallowing in those darker emotions and the chaos they created. Unfortunately, that wall could last anywhere from a handful of minutes to several hours, depending on the depth of her interaction with the tormented soul. And since Leo's violent death had shredded his soul to the point where stitching the remnants together had been challenging, even for her magic, she shouldn't be this riled up so soon. Leo had bounced all over the emotional spectrum, from shocked and scared to resentful and bitter and everything in between. He kept getting lost in his confrontation with Kelly. Although it was clear from the shit ton of guilt he held, he hadn't intended to hurt her, his attack had been sparked by an ugly layer of bitter envy that quickly spread into an inferno.

There were flashes of things that didn't make sense—like the strange split in personality, from guilt ridden to insanely furious, as if some switch had been thrown. His initial shock at wielding magic had bordered on horror, but when the magic came, he'd been manically elated. Isa had sensed scattered bursts of vicious satisfaction at proving "him" wrong, coupled with an arrogant need to gloat. The problem was, she'd had no clue who "he" was until Locke started asking questions. Under interrogation, Leo's wildly careening emotions kept disintegrating, shredding memories piece by piece, and she'd needed both elements to force him to tell the truth. In his confused state, his memories started to tangle, dragging Isa along for the ride, and her hold on the fragile pieces that made up Leo became even more draining. Only well-honed skill, and a depth of magic fueled by her battle-scarred will, allowed her to navigate the churning currents without going under. But among Leo's fractured flashes were familiar images that had left Isa not just worried but skating the edge of scared.

And Isa didn't do scared. Hell, she'd give anything to talk to Cass, her Oracle bestie. Cass was a great sounding board when Isa was dealing with Reaper shit, but since she was involved with her own drama up in Vegas, it was up to Isa and Des to handle things, and that required an urgent conversation with Des.

She pressed the accelerator a little more as she drove through the nearly empty downtown streets. Isa made the turn that would take her to Wonderland and cursed softly as she caught the glare of Locke's headlights behind her. She would have to make the most of her alone time because blindsiding Des with Locke would not be good. She sped up until she lost Locke's lights.

Then, since digging her phone out of her pocket while driving wasn't a good idea, she touched the charmed stud in her ear. "Call Des."

After a heartbeat, Des's voice filled her ear. "Are you okay?"

"I'm fine, but I ran into Locke at Leo's."

There was a pause. "Locke Turon?"

"You know any other Locke?" she asked.

That earned her a four-letter word that made her wince.

"Leo?" he bit out.

"Dead."

"Well, shit."

She couldn't agree more. "Locke's following me back to Wonderland." A charged silence filled her ear, so she asked, "How's Kelly doing?"

"She's holding, but I called River, asked him to represent her. He agreed and is heading over to her apartment to meet up with us."

Relief trickled through her. Kelly would be in good hands with River Ortiz, a friend of Des's who ran a private family law firm with a solid reputation. The two men had met in middle school, and although they'd taken different life paths, their friendship had stayed strong enough that when River had a client whom the justice system had failed, Des was happy to step in with a helping hand, and by extension, so were Isa and Cass.

"What time?" she asked.

"I was just waiting to hear from you before I took her home."

"Can't you hold off? I'm almost to Wonderland, and Locke's going to want to talk to her."

"You think that's wise?"

Probably not. "I don't know."

"I'm not feeling reassured, Isa."

"Yeah, neither am I." She took the last turn, seeing the parking lot in front of Wonderland, then pulled the proverbial pin. "Des, I think Angel's involved in this mess."

This time, the pause was heavier. "How?"

"I'm not sure, but I think Leo's been spending time at the Den."

"That's not good."

"No, it's not." She pulled into a spot and parked. "Look, I'm here and heading in."

Des's unhappy voice took on a warning note, holding her in place. "Isa, if Angel is mixed up in whatever this is, let Locke handle it."

She didn't want to acknowledge the painful hitch in her chest that idea caused. "It's not that simple."

"It is that simple." Des's tone was hard. "You confront Angel, and things are going to get messy."

Like they aren't already? "I know, Des." Isa didn't need him to spell it out—she'd lived the nightmare before. She threw open her door and got out, beeping the car's locks. "We need to see if Kelly knows anything."

"About the Den or Angel?"

"Either." She started for the bar's entrance.

After a beat of silence, he gave in. "You want to ask her outright?"

"You have a better idea?"

He muttered something she didn't catch then said, "If you put Locke and Angel in the same room—"

"I get it, Des." She yanked the door open and clattered down the stairs, too keyed up to be creeped out by the shadows enveloping the stairwell. "But you know Locke. He won't back off." And she couldn't live with herself if she let him walk into that vipers' pit alone.

"Fine." With that, Des's voice cut off.

She hit the main floor just as the door behind the bar swung open. Des held it as Kelly passed through, her face drawn and streaked with tears.

The girl spotted Isa and froze in place. "He's really dead?"

"He is," she confirmed, trying not to wince. Kelly paled further and started to wobble as panic and horror filled her face.

Des caught her, giving her something to lean against, but Kelly didn't look away from Isa. "It was an accident, I swear." Her voice teetered between hysteria and pleading.

"I know."

Kelly tore free from Des and rushed from behind the bar, leaving Des to follow at a slower pace. Isa met her halfway, capturing the younger woman in her arms.

"I can't... I don't know what to do." The words tumbled out as tremors ran through Kelly's slender body.

Isa tightened her hold, giving her a tether so she wouldn't fly apart. She wanted to console Kelly—reassure her that the paltry paring knife couldn't have possibly inflicted enough damage to be lethal, that something else killed Leo—but had no solid evidence, so she kept silent. She met Des's grim gaze, finding a reflection of the protective streak they each carried. It was what made Wonderland a strange family. Proof or no proof, there was no way they were hanging Kelly out to dry—that wasn't how they worked.

"We've got you." She loosened her hold and shifted so she could see Kelly's tear-ravaged face. "Locke's right behind me. He's going to ask you what happened." She held Kelly's reddened gaze. "You tell him exactly what you told me and Des. Don't elaborate. Don't try to charm. Just repeat what you told us, okay?"

Kelly swallowed hard then managed a jerky nod.

Isa forced her lips to curve up. "Good. Afterward, Des is going to take you home so you can talk to River. You remember him?"

Kelly nodded. "He's a lawyer, right?"

"Yep, and since he's on our side, you can answer any question he asks, but don't try to make things sound better than they were. You give it to him straight, then you do everything he tells you. Understand?"

Kelly's nod was smoother this time.

Isa looked behind Kelly to Des, who leaned a hip against a nearby table, and raised her brows in silent question. He gave a small head shake, so she turned back to the girl in front of her. "Kelly, did Leo ever mention the name Angel or a place called the Den?"

Kelly frowned. "No, why?"

The door at the top of the stairs creaked before Isa could answer. She lowered her voice. "Remember, keep your answers to Locke simple."

She turned so she could wrap an arm around Kelly's

shoulders as they both faced the man gliding down the stairs. He hit the floor in a fluid stalk, and Isa couldn't suppress the shiver that wound down her neck as he closed in. *Goddess help me if he ever decides I'm prey to his Hound.*

Locke's gaze darkened as it slid over Isa and the disheveled Kelly. His attention shifted to Des, whom he acknowledged with a slight chin lift. When his attention returned to the two women, Isa felt Kelly stiffen next to her. Locke's prowling intensity lessened as he gentled his features.

He came to a stop, careful to keep a few feet between them, and didn't offer his hand or try to touch her in any way. "Kelly, right?"

"Ye—" Kelly cleared her throat, and her voice strengthened. "Yes."

"I know you've had a long night, and I appreciate you hanging around. I just have a couple of questions about what happened." He half turned, motioning toward one of the booths. "Why don't we sit over here, okay?"

Kelly shot a look at Isa, who nodded and let her go so she could lead the younger woman to the booth. Isa scooted in first, leaving Kelly the seat on the open end. When Kelly stood there, stiff and tense, Locke took a seat on the other side. Kelly jerked and turned as Des dragged a nearby chair over, its legs scraping across the floor. She turned back and sat down, trapping Isa in the middle seat. Des set the chair at the table, between Locke and Kelly. Spine ramrod straight, Kelly kept her gaze on the tabletop as she worried her lower lip, her hands balled up in her lap. Isa wanted to reach out but knew she had to let the younger woman face Locke on her own.

Once everyone was situated, Locke spoke, his tone curiously gentle. "Can you tell me what happened?"

Kelly's nervous gaze came up and bounced from Isa to Locke to Des then back to Locke. Isa was close enough to catch the way her expression wavered between scared and calm. The girl's nerves were getting the better of her.

Isa kept her voice low, her warning subtle. "Kelly, Locke works with the Cordova Family, and it seems they have—had—some questions for Leo."

"The Cordovas?" At Isa's nod, Kelly's already pale face lost what little color remained, but the strange shimmer disappeared as she reined in her magic. No one wanted to tangle with an Arcane Family, especially one like the Cordovas. Her gaze darted to Locke. "But Leo's a muni." She winced. "Sorry, I know how that sounds. It's just..." She took a deep breath and started again. "Leo was a Traditionalist."

"We're aware," Locke said. "Leo is connected to someone else we're looking for. I was hoping to ask him some questions tonight, but..."

"But he's dead." Kelly's voice hitched.

"He is, so as the last person to see him, you might be able to share something that will help me out, but I won't know until you tell me."

"Right." Kelly's voice was shaky, her gaze skittering to Isa.

Isa gave her a tiny nod of encouragement.

Kelly sucked in a bracing breath, blew it out, and faced Locke. "Right," she said, her voice stronger this time. "Where do you want me to start?"

A charming smile curved Locke's mouth. "Was tonight special or just a regular thing?"

"It was a going-away thing because I'm leaving town soon. A way to get the squad together one last time."

"Who all is part of the squad?" Locke asked.

"Well, me, Em, Olie, and Leo." She stumbled over Leo's name but then continued gamely. "We met up at the Obsidian Club around ten."

Isa listened to Kelly retell the story she'd shared earlier, this time without jumping from scene to scene. The younger woman took Isa's suggestion to heart, keeping it simple. The friends had met up and had a good time, then Leo started acting out of character. Em and Olie took off for the Alchemist in Tempe, leaving Kelly with an obviously impaired Leo. Kelly had taken him to his apartment, and Leo had attacked her.

"Things happened so fast, and I..." She shook her head. "That's not normal for Leo. He's not like that." Tears welled but didn't fall. "Everything kind of blurs, but there was this moment when he had me pinned in the kitchen. I just wanted to get out, but he wouldn't let me go. He got weird. His eyes..." She shivered and huddled in her seat. "There was something really wrong in his eyes. I was so scared, and I needed something to make him move so I could get out. He kept backing me up between the sink and fridge. There wasn't much to use, but there were dishes in the sink and on the counter. I remember grabbing a bowl and throwing it at him, but it didn't do much other than piss him off. He just kept coming. So I was tossing whatever I could find, hoping something would get him to move. He had me pinned near the sink." Her hand brushed her throat, where fingermarks marred her skin, and her voice grew quieter. "I just wanted him to let me go. I... I must have grabbed a knife because he finally did." She dropped her hand to her lap, her shoulders straightening slowly as she lifted her head. "I was running for the door when something hit me. It felt like I was on fire, and I couldn't get my body to move. I was curled up on the floor, and he was standing there, magic pouring out of him." She swallowed and met Locke's gaze. "I know that makes zero sense because Leo doesn't have magic, but he must have gotten his hands on some kind of spell, because he was definitely flinging around serious magic."

Locke didn't appear surprised. A grim look lurked behind his composed expression. "How did you get away?"

Kelly's shoulders rose and fell in a jerky motion. "I tried to charm him into letting me go. For a moment, I thought it would work, but then he tried to zap me again, and whatever magic he had just kind of sputtered out. He was so pissed it was like he barely knew where he was, and while he was raging, I managed to get to my feet." Tremors erupted from her as she relived the moment. "It was like he was possessed or something. He was bleeding, but it was like he didn't feel it. The magic was, like, curling around him. I think it was starting to burn him, but he was pulling at his hair and screaming. I ran for the door and got out." Her breathing picked up.

"You're okay, Kelly." Isa reached out, covered her trembling hands, and gave them a careful squeeze. "You're good. Just take a breath." She waited until Kelly had sucked in air. "Now hold it... just like that. And let it out."

Once Kelly was calm, Locke returned to his questioning. "You said he started acting weird?"

"Yeah. I mean, I thought he was hammered, you know, because he'd been drinking pretty steadily." She scratched a nail across the table's surface.

"Is that normal for him?"

She thought about it. "No. I mean he drinks—we all do, you know—but he doesn't get lit on the regular, but..." She rolled her shoulders.

"But...?" Locke prompted.

Kelly's eyes darted to Isa in a silent question. Isa dipped her chin.

"But tonight hit different, and it made me wonder if he took one of those pills he said he was holding for someone."

The air around Locke came on point. "What kind of pills?"

Kelly shrugged uncomfortably. "I just know they were red

because I got a glimpse of them when he dropped them earlier."

Locke studied her with an alarming intensity. "And he didn't say who he was holding them for or where he got them?"

She shook her head. "I didn't ask. I was just pissed he had them at all."

"You said tonight he was different," Locke tried a different approach. "How so?"

The tension riding Kelly's shoulders eased back a fraction. "He hit the bar right off, ordering drinks, and he kept them coming. He was really keyed up. I asked what the deal was, but all he would say was that he was dealing with work stuff."

Locke frowned. "Work? You mean Tech Wizards?"

Kelly rolled her eyes. "Right? I mean, how much stress can there be helping oldies recover their deleted files?"

Isa suspected it wasn't just Leo's job stressing him out and, when Locke sat back with a considering look, figured he felt the same.

"Did Leo mention a client by name?" Locke's tone was so carefully casual Isa perked up. "Like one of the families or maybe a local business?"

Kelly shook her head. "I don't think so."

"Did he ever mention the Forge Foundation?"

Forge Foundation? Why does that sound familiar? She refused to look to Des, unwilling to give Locke any hint that she would be doing some digging on her own after this.

Kelly shook her head and rolled her shoulders. "No. He'd gritch about customers, but he had his own names for them, you know? Trophy Wife or Loser or Cracked—things like that."

Locked shifted in his chair, his fingers tapping absently against the table. "Was there anyone specific pissing him off tonight?"

"Other than Em, Olie, and me? No." Kelly tilted her head as something occurred to her. "When we got to his apartment and he started to go off about not being a useless muni, he said something about how Mr. Flex was delulu and he'd show him." She blinked and met Locke's gaze. "I don't know who Mr. Flex was, but I think he was the real reason Leo was all stressed."

Locke looked to Isa. "Mr. Flex?"

"Probably someone with deep pockets or flashy toys who likes to show off," Isa translated. "My guess, Leo was upset with someone who was bragging about their connection to someone they thought was important."

"Yeah, that," Kelly confirmed. "Leo kept saying how Mr. Flex had serious main-character syndrome. It really got under his skin because Leo's family has that same attitude. They put a lot of pressure on him to join their business, but he didn't want that."

Curious, Locke asked, "What business is that?"

"Oh, they own Polished Pros. Leo says they're always bragging on how they're the go-to cleaning service in the Valley." More of Kelly's nervous energy seeped away as she talked. "Leo was first-gen college, so his family really wanted him to take over and help expand their contracting services outside the Valley, but he wasn't as keen on that plan. He's tried a couple of start-ups, but they didn't get far. Hence, his current job. He kept saying it was temporary, but he's been there almost a year now."

"And you have no idea who this Mr. Flex is?" Locke pressed.

"No, sorry, not a clue."

"Do you know Isaiah Homes?"

There was zero recognition in Kelly's puzzled face. "Nope. Never heard of him."

Locke continued to ask more questions, but it soon

became clear that there wasn't much more Kelly could give him. By the time he brought the conversation to a close, Kelly looked like she was about to collapse.

Locke pulled out his phone. "Let me get your number and address, Kelly."

Panic flashed through Kelly's face. "Wait? Why? I answered your questions."

He looked up from the screen. "Because I'm not the only one who's going to want to ask you about what happened. Before I left Leo's, I called the incident in to Detective Thorn. He's going to want to talk to you. It'd be simpler if I passed your name and number on to him."

Des shot a frown at Locke, but he pulled out his phone and started typing.

Kelly's eyes rounded, the whites showing as she jerked back in her seat, and her gaze darted to Isa. "They'll never believe it was an accident. They'll throw me in jail. I'll lose my job offer."

Isa covered Kelly's fisted hand with hers and squeezed. "No, they won't, and you won't."

Kelly searched Isa's face and must have found what she was looking for, because she managed a tiny nod.

Isa looked beyond Kelly to Des, who raised his gaze from his phone and gave her a chin lift. She told Kelly, "Let River handle it, okay?"

"River?" Locke asked.

"Kelly's lawyer," Des smoothly answered.

Locke's lips thinned, but he didn't say anything else.

Kelly shot Locke a worried look. "Are we done?" When he nodded, she scooted out of the booth.

Des got to his feet and pocketed his phone. "I'll get her home and catch River up." He shot a dark look at Isa. "You going to be here when I get back?"

It wasn't really a question. She knew he wanted to talk

about Angel's potential involvement and the fact that they'd added Locke to the mix. Isa's body ached, and all she wanted to do was to go home and hide under the covers, but that wouldn't be happening.

"Yeah, I'll be here."

"Good." Des gave Locke a head tilt, nudged Kelly ahead of him, and followed the traumatized young woman out and up the stairs.

When the heavy door thumped shut, silence filled the space. Locke watched Isa steadily.

Uncomfortable under that unnerving stare, she snapped, "What?"

"You going to share?"

Damn the too-perceptive man. "Share what?"

Locke laid his arm along the back of the padded seat. "Whatever it is you and Des are hiding." She opened her mouth to deny his accusation, but before any words could escape, he dropped his arm, set his palm on the cushioned seat between them, and leaned in. "Don't, Isa," he growled. He gave it a moment then eased back. "There's something you're not sharing. At Leo's, you mentioned you saw something but wanted to run it by Des. I'm assuming you had a chance to do that on the ride over."

The urge to play with semantics was almost too much, but in the end, she caved, knowing it was useless to try to evade his questions. "I mentioned it, yes, but we haven't had a chance to talk."

"About...?"

She studied his face, taking in the steely glint that added an eerie shimmer to his light-blue eyes. She could try leading him on a merry chase, dodging questions and keeping things vague, but that would leave her with more than one predator on her ass and put a target on Locke as well. Better for her game to keep this particular predator on her side.

"I think Leo spent time at the Den."

He frowned. "What's that? Another club?"

If only. "Kind of. It's more like a vipers' pit."

A muscle jumped in his jaw as he caught a whiff of a scent. "Give me an address. I can check it out."

She was already shaking her head before he finished speaking. "That won't work. The Den is like Baba Yaga's house. It shifts locations on the regular. You have to know the right people to pin it down."

A hot flash of temper was quickly squashed as he drawled, "Let me guess—you know the right people."

Understatement of the year. She tried to ignore the ripple of discomfort whispering over her nerves. "I can reach out. If we're lucky, I might have something by tomorrow night and we can check it out after closing."

When his gaze sharpened, she knew she'd failed to keep her misgivings out of her voice. "And if we're unlucky?"

Isa would gain some seriously unwanted attention, but that would be her problem, not his. "We're back to figuring out who Mr. Flex is."

"There's no 'we' here."

She wished that were true, but something told her she wouldn't be lucky enough to shake him loose and pursue this on her own. Still, if he was determined to wander off alone, that was his choice. With deliberate casualness, she said, "Works for me." Then she shifted to get out of the booth, one hand on the table, one on the seat.

A warm weight pressed her hand against the cool wood of the table as Locke held her in place. His "Dammit" was closer to a growl than an actual word. "I'll be here at nine."

"Make it ten."

"Nine," he insisted. "And I'm driving."

An unwelcome bolt of relief struck deep, momentarily exposing old scars and leaving her decidedly unsettled. Then it was gone as old habits rose fast and hard. "Afraid I'm going to ditch you?" she asked, her tone cutting.

At her swipe of verbal claws, a slow, taunting smile curved his mouth and a knowing look darkened his eyes. "You can't run fast enough to lose me, Isa."

That was what she was afraid of.

chapter 6

Locke

THE NEXT NIGHT, Locke was in one of the booths lining the walls of Wonderland, watching Isa and Des work the floor. It was Sunday, and the scene was fairly quiet. As time ticked down to closing, patrons were settling up tabs and drifting away. Locke was beating back his lack of sleep with another cup of coffee. Detective Thorn had called him as he was pulling out of Wonderland's parking lot that morning, which meant Locke had made a return trip to Leo's apartment. When he got there, the Arcane Criminal Response Team was already on the scene, and Leo's body was on its way to the medical examiner's office.

Thorn wasted no time cornering him for a tense conversation, and Locke's vague responses meant the detective had ended up with more questions than answers. Although Locke could emphasize with Thorn's frustration, the detective had enough years in to know that for someone in Locke's position, Family came first, so Thorn could only push things so far. Thorn might not like the situation, but he understood it. For Locke, sharing information on a possible strain of the Delphi serum set loose in the wild was not an option. Hell, the existence of the serum wasn't even widely known in the Arcane world, much less among the local branches of authority. And if it got out, the delicate balance of trust between political and Family powers would be nothing but dust.

Locke manage to navigate the thin line between secrecy and transparency as the two men walked their respective sides. He did share with Thorn that he'd been tracking Isaiah when he stumbled across Leo. He omitted Isa's presence, but as he'd warned Kelly, he did give her contact information to Thorn along with a heads-up that her lawyer would likely be present when the detective went to visit her. That tiny peace offering eased some of the detective's ruffled feathers and earned Locke a resigned sigh.

At that point, Locke decided to press his luck and ask Thorn if he'd ever heard of a place called the Den. Thorn hadn't, but Locke clocked the minute stiffening of one of the ACRT evidence techs, who was clearly eavesdropping. The hyperawareness that was part and parcel of every Hound perked up. Not wanting to spook his prey, Locke spent a few more minutes finishing his conversation with Thorn, who offered to initiate a missing persons alert on Isaiah and then took his leave. Locke then made his way downstairs, where the emergency vehicles—including a clearly marked ACRT van—were parked. He picked a spot and waited.

Thorn left first and didn't seem to notice Locke standing off to the side. Shortly after, the ACRT crew came out, carrying evidence boxes. Locke's target trailed behind the other three crew members, a box tucked under one arm and a phone in his other hand. His head was bent toward the screen, on which he typed awkwardly with his thumb. He was so focused on what he was doing that he made it stupidly simple for Locke to fall into step next to him and cull him from the pack. For a moment, Locke thought he would have to chase the guy down, but the tech didn't bolt. Instead, he talked. At first, he was on the verge of panic, but one of his coworkers realized he'd been waylaid and came over to join the conversation, and Locke let them both stay. Only then did the tech calm a little. Locke read the remaining nerves as a reaction to being put on the spot rather than being guilty of anything.

It didn't take much prodding for the kid to admit that he'd been to the Den a few years prior but not recently. He backed Isa's claim that even then, it had moved around, and you had to know someone who knew someone to get access. He also reluctantly verified that it catered to an edgier crowd, but that was the extent of his usefulness. The short conversation wasn't much, but it did confirm Locke's concern that the place was way sketchier than Isa had indicated. And that worry dogged his heels all day as he and Zev chased down more empty leads on Isaiah. The unsuccessful hunt left Locke irritated and on edge. Either the kid was a damn ghost, or someone with skill was helping him hide. Locke was betting on the latter.

By the time he and Zev parted ways, Locke had only a couple of hours to kill. After changing into something more appropriate for trolling the Valley's nightlife, he hit Wonderland early and used food and coffee to erase the blur of fatigue. He wasn't one to ignore his instincts. He knew damn well that if he waited until nine to show up at Wonderland, he'd to find Isa long gone. To call her independent was like calling a porcupine prickly. Another man might be infuriated by such aggressive self-reliance, but not him. There was something intoxicating about tangling with a woman who knew who she was and what she was worth—the way she would watch him with a cool indifference he loved to shatter or how she would make him work for her attention. The thing was, once he had it—had her—his blood heated.

He knew himself well enough to understand that he got off on the chase and when he caught what he wanted, he tended to get bored. But he didn't think Isa would give him a chance to be bored. She was an enigma wrapped in secrets and guarded by lethal thorns, but all that protection lay over something exquisitely beautiful. When they'd first met months before, the sexual tension had been undeniably phenomenal, and while the intense reaction had initially thrown him for a loop, he was old enough to appreciate there was more to a woman than her physical attributes. And although Isa had that dark-haired, red-lipped, pin-up-curves thing going for her, a little digging revealed that her spirit and brain were even more alluring.

Being a Hound, he had a driving curiosity that led him to delve into the three bar owners' pasts, and he wasn't surprised to learn there wasn't much there, at least not publicly. What he did know was that Cassandra was an Oracle who was estranged from her highly influential family in Vegas. Interestingly, other than offering the occasional warning to Rory, she tended to keep her ability quiet. He wasn't sure why, and now that his buddy Grayson might be hooking up with her, he made a mental note to dig a little deeper.

As for Des, he'd popped up in Phoenix just before the group bought the bar, yet he somehow had a wealth of connections in the Valley. There wasn't much else out there on the guy, but Locke knew he was a Tracer because he recognized Des's tattoos as those worn by a couple of ghost whisperers Locke had worked with in the past. Why a Tracer and an Oracle, both with highly coveted skills, were working at a bar was anyone's guess.

Something to dig into later.

Then there was Isa, and unlike with the other two, there had been something to find. She'd grown up in the Valley, and based on the short list of her run-ins with the police as a teen, it was clear her home life had been far from happy. He hadn't bothered with the sealed juvenile records, preferring instead to hear the story from her, but he would have bet good money her thorns had emerged during that period of her life. They'd likely sharpened to lethal levels after she cut all contact with her family, some of whom still lived in the far-west part of Phoenix, and struck out on her own at sixteen. The next few years, her address bounced around from California to Vegas to Colorado then up to Oregon, with a brief stint in Washington, but she always came back to Phoenix. And all that moving ground to a halt once she tied herself to Des and Cass and Wonderland.

The trio bought the struggling bar years ago, and under their hands, it turned from a run-down pit into a jealously guarded jewel for the eclectic. The thing was, as he sniffed around, he caught faint hints that the bar was much more than a simple gathering place. It wasn't anything concrete, just a whisper here and a passing statement there, but put them all together, and they formed a ghostly trail that implied the three friends were acting as community guardians. Not like the stand-on-a-street-corner-and-keep-an-eye-out type—they were more like the ones to step in if someone was trapped in a situation with no way out.

As admirable as it was, it was also slightly reckless, but even Locke had to admit the role fit Isa to a T. The woman was highly protective once she let you in. Though he was still trying to figure out how to crack that code, he hadn't missed how she played the role of older sibling to her employees. Through the months he'd spent tangling with her, he'd been surprised at how a good sob story from someone she considered hers could sneak under her prickly armor and ignite the fiery defender. And when that happened, if you were her intended target, you'd best watch your ass before she burned it.

But with everyone outside her tight circle, she kept her distance. Except Locke. He might not have breached her inner circle, but he was steadily working his way in, no matter how much she hissed and raked him with her claws. Unfortunately, after what had gone down with Leo, he was worried he'd lose what ground he had earned as she slipped deeper behind her thorny wall. Locke was willing to spill blood to get to the heart of her—his or someone else's. He wasn't picky.

He shifted in his seat and took another sip of coffee as he watched Isa glide between customers and deliver drinks to three men at one of the high-top tables. She was dressed in black, from the heeled ankle boots to the wide-leg pants paired with a halter top designed to tease, the cowled neck dipping low in the front, leaving her back bare except for a single wide band. The gold medallion she never took off was joined by a flat gold necklace, a cluster of bracelets, and matching gold hoop earrings.

One of the men said something to her as she set their drinks in front of them. She gave him a flirty grin, the one she used on her male customers—a cute and edgy smile that ensured good tips but in no way revealed the real woman, who was an intriguing mix of fire and ice. And that woman was the one who kept his dick knotted up and had him fighting back an urge to stake his claim in a way no one could mistake. Of course, if he tried to make such a stupid move, she'd eviscerate him, but he still gave it serious consideration as a round of male chuckles came from the trio's table.

His hand tightened on his cup, but before he could do anything stupid, Isa was already sauntering back to the bar for her next order. He blew out a breath and forced his grip to relax. Being territorial was nothing new, but it when it came to her, the trait was growing worse. Maybe that fact should bother him.

"Need a refill?" The rumbled question came from Des, who had appeared at his table with a coffee urn in hand.

Locke nudged his cup toward him.

Des poured and, without looking up from what he was doing, said, “Need you to promise me something.”

Locke braced himself. “What?”

“Tonight, when you two hit the Den”—Des stopped pouring and met Locke’s eyes—“don’t leave her alone.”

Locke searched that intense gaze, trying to read between the lines, but darkness stared back. Tension set up shop in Locke’s shoulders and bled slowly down to the base of his spine. “Wasn’t planning on it.”

Relief filtered through Des’s shadowed eyes, and he dipped his chin. “She’s got one more table, then she’s clocking out.”

He didn’t wait for Locke’s response but turned and walked away, leaving Locke to wonder what exactly he and Isa were going to walk into.

chapter 7

Isa

In the back office, Isa set her phone on the desk, next to a tube of lipstick, and locked her purse in the bottom drawer. A text flashed across her screen.

Icehouse 11.

She dropped into the worn leather chair behind the battered desk that Des loved and rested her head in her hands. She needed just a minute, maybe two, to shake off the sense of impending doom.

What are you doing? She pressed her fingers against her temples, trying to ease the low-level ache that had settled in hours earlier, right about the time she'd sent the first text and slid back down a familiar rabbit hole, one she thought she'd finally left behind. The sound of knuckles against the doorframe had her raising her head and opening her eyes to find Des standing at the office door.

He wore a frown. "You okay?"

No. "Yes."

He looked at the phone sitting on the desk, his frown deepening. "Where are they setting up shop?"

"On the west side."

He wrapped a hand around the back of his neck, his head

doing a slow shake. With heavy resignation he asked, "The Cavern or the Icehouse?"

"Icehouse."

His hand went from his neck to his back pocket. "Here." He pulled something out and tossed it toward her.

Isa barely managed to catch the warm weight between her palms. She opened her hands to see what looked like a simple friendship bracelet made of braided string and a cluster of carved green and black beads. "What is it?"

"Protection." Des set a muscled shoulder against the doorframe and folded his arms. "The Zemi that came through last week made it—said she needed to give it to me for helping her out." The highly skilled warding mage who'd crafted it had been targeted because of her ability to create innocent-looking yet powerful objects like this. He angled his head toward the simple bracelet. "I'd feel better if you wore it tonight."

Since she could use all the help she could get, she slid the innocuous protection charm on. She tightened it until it sat snug on her wrist, a dark line almost lost among the various gold bangles. As the bracelet settled against her skin, Isa swore she could feel the invisible weight of the inevitable lighten. "Appreciate it, Des."

"You'll be careful." It wasn't a question.

"I will." She pushed back the chair and got to her feet. "Locke still out there?"

"What do you think?"

Sighing, Isa moved toward the wall safe. "I'm leaving my car. I'll pick it up when we're done."

She preferred to have her own wheels, but that wasn't happening without an argument, and while she normally got a kick out of pushing Locke's buttons, she couldn't find the will to do it tonight. Not when she was this keyed up about the impending meeting. She punched in the safe's code, opened the door, and moved the contents aside until she found what she was looking for—a small warded box. She pulled it out, disarmed the ward, and opened the container. Inside was a mismatched collection of objects.

"You sure you want to go through with this?" Des asked.

She picked out an innocuous-looking wooden disc and slipped it into her pocket. "Want to? No. Have to? Yes." She closed the box, reset the ward, put it back, then closed the safe. Turning back, she found Des watching her. "Anna said she'd be happy to help you and Leon with closing tonight." She collected her lipstick and phone from the desk before heading his way.

"We should be good," he said as she came up to him. "Did you reach out to Cass?"

Isa avoided his gaze. "I will, later."

"Isa..."

The warning note in his voice sliced across her nerves. She tilted her head back so she could glare at the man she considered a brother. "She's dealing with enough right now, Des. I'm a big girl. I'll be fine."

His lips tightened into thin disapproving lines. "I know you can handle your shit," he rumbled as he angled his body so she could step through the door. "It's Angel I don't trust."

"Me either, but letting Locke walk in there alone is not a good idea." They started down the short hall. "Something happens to him, and the Cordovas will be all over our asses." They couldn't afford to take on that problem, especially if Isa ended up on Angel's radar again.

She took his grunt as agreement and pushed through the door that led back into the bar. Des grabbed her arm in a gentle grip. Stopping, she turned her head and gave him a questioning look.

"Are you sure you want to do this?" he asked.

"No, but Locke's not giving me a choice."

"Maybe if you explained—"

She shook her head. "It wouldn't change anything. Locke is going in one way or another, and if I'm with him, Angel will focus on me, not him."

Des looked like he wanted to argue. Worry lined his face. "Promise you'll stick to Locke like glue tonight."

She tugged against his hold, and when he let her go, she leaned up on her toes to press her lips against his cheek before dropping back down. "I will. Promise."

He didn't look reassured, so she gave him one last smile before turning away. She went through the pass and headed toward Locke. He was already sliding out of his booth. The material of his short-sleeved, button-down shirt glimmered under the floor lights as he dropped a tip on the table and slid his wallet into a pocket of his tailored black slacks.

When she got close, he invaded her space, his hand going to the base of her spine. "Ready?"

The heat of his palm against her skin sent goose bumps cascading down her arms. "Yep." She tried to sound more confident than she felt, knowing that if Locke caught any hint of her unease, he'd go all alpha on her, which would make this whole thing even harder.

They walked across the floor, Isa returning a few utterances of "good night" from familiar patrons as Locke prowled at her back. He didn't say anything until they were in his car.

"You want to put in the address for me?" He started the engine, and it woke on a low rumble.

"Sure." She typed in the location, hit Enter, and sat back. In a sultry female tone, the GPS confirmed the forty-minute drive.

Locke shot Isa a look as she settled into the leather seat. "That seems a ways out."

"It's on the west side, out near the stadium." She dug into her pocket to retrieve the wooden disc and held it out. "And you're going to need this."

He took it from her. "What is it?"

"Our entry for tonight." She snapped her seat belt in place as he examined the token. "It's a marker that tells whoever is manning the door that you won't be bringing unnecessary attention to the event."

He curled his fingers around the token. "Yours?"

She shook her head, thinking of the young woman they'd managed to relocate a couple of years back without getting on Angel's radar. "No, someone else who won't be needing it."

Locke studied her for a long moment, but when she didn't elaborate, he shifted his weight, slipped the token into his pocket, and put the car in gear. He was quiet as he navigated the maze of one-way streets that made up downtown Phoenix. She watched the lights blur as he hit the highway and wasn't surprised when Locke finally broke the quiet.

"You want to tell me what we're walking into?"

No, she really didn't, but letting him walk in blind wasn't just unfair—it could be dangerous, as well, for both of them. "The Den started out as an underground rave for the college crowd, but over the years, it's morphed into an unconventional social club."

"You called it a vipers' pit."

"Vipers' pit, hunting ground—both would work."

"Hunting ground for what?"

"Whatever it is you're looking for. Whether you're a kid wanting an escape from a shitty home, a college student chasing a high, or a bored socialite looking for forbidden excitement, if you're there, it'll find you." She wrapped her fingers around the belt across her chest. "There's a high chance we're going to cross paths with some people from my past."

When she gave him nothing more, he prompted, "People or trouble?"

"Probably both," she said, torn between the knowledge that he needed to hear her story and her reluctance to share the painful details with someone who saw the world in black and white. After shifting uncomfortably in her seat until she was facing him, she fisted her hand in her lap and dove in. "Have you heard of the Idyl Devils?"

Light and shadows danced over his face as he frowned. "Sounds familiar, but I'm not making a connection."

"About fifteen years ago, they were just one of many neighborhood gangs in the West Valley. Over the years, they morphed from a group of rebellious teens with a bent for petty crimes to questionable businessmen managing sophisticated criminal enterprises."

"By 'sophisticated,' you mean…?"

"Extensive distribution channels for designer drugs." She watched the muscle in his jaw jump. "In the last few years, there have even been rumors of arms dealing and human trafficking."

"Any truth to those?"

"Not that I know of, but that doesn't mean much."

"So the Den is what? A front for one of these businesses?"

She rolled her shoulders. "My guess? At least one business, if not more."

"And the cops haven't come down on this group why?" he asked.

"I don't know." But she had some ideas. Knowing Angel and how far his sticky hands could reach, he had an in with the department. "What I do know is that the current head of Idyl Devils is using the Den to reel in new recruits to expand their business."

"And you think Leo was one of them?"

She couldn't shake the scattered snapshots dominating Leo's fear-soaked flashbacks. "Yes, and I think he met Isaiah at one of the Den's incarnations."

"But you're not sure."

"No," she admitted. "Because Leo's memories were pretty

ripped up, and I could be filling the blanks in with the wrong information."

He took a moment. "You said the location changes?"

"It does."

"But not always?"

"Certain sites are repeats."

"Like tonight?" he asked.

"Yes."

"But you didn't know that when we were talking to Leo, right?"

"What?"

"It wasn't until after you started questioning Leo that something tripped for you, right?" Locke didn't wait for her answer. "Which means it wasn't the location you recognized, was it?"

She swallowed. "No, it wasn't the location."

Quiet stretched between them. She kept her attention on the blur of lights as Locke continued down the highway. She tried not to feel or think, but the tension inside her coiled tighter and tighter with each passing moment.

Finally, he broke the silence. "You said this gang is known for dealing."

There was nothing in his voice to give away what he was thinking, so she responded in kind. "That's what I've heard."

"So it's likely Leo picked up the pills from someone there," he said, almost to himself.

"It's possible," she agreed reluctantly.

He gave her a quick look. "You said you didn't see who gave him the pills."

"I didn't," she shot back. "But drugs are kind of part and parcel of these things, so it would make logical sense if this was where he got them from."

He made a noncommittal hum then let a beat of silence

pass before switching gears. "Who are you and Des worried about?"

His question landed in her gut like a soft punch, leaving her off balance. She took a moment to shove her churning anxiety into a box and lock it. "His name is Angel Herrera." Proud of how steady her voice sounded, despite her pounding pulse, she finished coolly, "And he's the head of Idyl Devils."

"And who is he to you?"

My nightmare and the man who tore my family from me. Neither of those were answers she was willing to share, so she gave the one she could. "My stepbrother."

Instead of being shocked, Locke was surprisingly unfazed. "I take it you two aren't close."

Her laugh was bitter. "Not even a little bit."

Strangely, he didn't go through the opening she'd given him and instead asked, "Which parent goes to whom?"

Her brain stumbled over the question then found its footing. "My father met his mother, Pilar, when I was fourteen and he was nineteen. They married when I was sixteen."

"And your mom?"

The twinge was an old ache easily ignored. "Out of the picture—had been for years." Realizing her fingers were numb, she flexed her hands in her lap, feeling the blood rush back into them. "Pilar was good for Papá."

"And you?"

"For a little while," she said softly.

Just admitting that let the memories seep in. Papá dancing with Pilar in the small kitchen of the older, ranch-style home, their laughter filling the air. Pilar holding out a hand to Isa in an invitation to join them, her dark-brown eyes sparking with a warmth that Isa's teenage heart desperately soaked up. Sun-drenched afternoons when Pilar patiently taught her how to make albóndigas, a Mexican meatball soup with hearty vegetables and savory broth that was all about love. Pilar behind her, braiding her hair into a beautiful pattern she could never accomplish on her own. Then later, after Angel played his games, those same dark eyes had gone cold and cutting while Papá's disappointment sliced her heart to ribbons.

She waited for his inevitable question about what had happened, but it didn't come. Instead, he asked, "What do I need to know about Angel?"

She grabbed his offering with both metaphorical hands and held on tight. "He's a Harvester, so you need to lock your emotions down tight. Otherwise, he'll use them against you." Harvesters were masters at siphoning emotions, good or bad, to supercharge their personal power.

"How strong are we talking?"

"Strong." She thought of all the times Angel had bent the truth until even she wondered if she was the selfish, deceitful person he said she was. The twisted game had taken her years to escape. "He likes mind games. The more you let him under your skin, the deeper he gets, and once he has a hold on you, he doesn't like to let go."

"Sounds like a typical asshole," he said in a hard voice.

Oh, Angel is far from typical. At best, he's narcissistic. At worst? He's pathologically evil.

"If we're lucky, he won't be there," she said.

"And the chance of that...?"

With her luck, probably slim to none, but a girl could hope. "Depends on what's really happening there tonight. If it's just a party, I doubt he'd waste his time, but if it's cover for something else..." She shrugged.

"You got a picture you can share? That way, I know who I'm looking for."

She dug her phone out and pulled up a web browser. In seconds, she had his image on her screen. "Here." Ignoring the shudder quivering under her skin, she handed her phone to Locke.

He held it so he could see the screen and the road. "Streetwise Talent?"

"He heads up a commercial talent agency."

Locke handed back her phone. "When's the last time you saw him?"

"Three years ago." She put her phone back in her pocket. "Des and I were meeting up with some friends at this club, and he was there. He tried to approach us, but we left before he could make contact."

She remembered how she'd frozen when she spotted him. Des had picked up on her fear and stepped in, making himself a target as he blocked Angel from playing his games.

"And he didn't try to contact you afterward?"

"He tried a couple of times, but when I refused to give him the reaction he wanted, he finally got bored and stopped." Although the poltergeists Des had sent his way probably helped. Not to mention Cass's warnings, which had allowed Isa to avoid tripping over Angel's unexpected appearances.

"That's why Des doesn't want me to leave you alone tonight?"

Funny—she thought Des didn't want her to leave Locke, but whatever. She'd take whatever protection she could get when it came to Angel. "Yeah, that would be why."

Locke flexed his grip on the steering wheel and, with studied casualness, said, "You know, I can go in by myself."

"Nope, not happening." She couldn't, in good conscience, let him face Angel alone.

She played with the beads on the charm bracelet Des had given her. No matter what she told Locke, he'd believe he could keep Angel out of his head and away from his emotions, but Harvesters were subtle siphons. By the time you realized they were feeding on you, it was too late. If nothing else, her presence would distract Angel enough for him not to focus completely on Locke.

"Like I said, he may not be there."

Locke's disbelieving huff said it all. "If he is, you'll let me deal with him."

Since it wasn't a question, she didn't have to lie—she just kept her mouth shut because if Angel was there, she wouldn't be given much of a choice. She decided to change the subject. "So, what's your plan tonight?"

"Pardon?"

"What are you hoping to get out of this visit?"

"Ideally? Isaiah's location and the name of whoever is supplying those red pills."

"Getting a positive ID on your missing teen is going to be a long shot," she said. "Flashing a photo, asking questions—things like that will end with our asses getting kicked to the curb." *Or worse.*

"Not sure we can go in looking to score unless there's something you're not sharing."

Her shoulders snapped tight, and she gave him a sharp look, but the teasing curve to his lips had her biting back a stinging, defensive retort. "No, but it is an angle we can use. When something new hits the scene, word gets around."

It didn't take him long to put it together, and his humor evaporated. "You comfortable with that approach?"

She wasn't comfortable with any of this. Between shielding Locke and walking willingly back into hell, there wasn't much of a choice— at least, not one she could live with —but she knew enough about the man sitting next to her to be aware that he'd get his answers one way or another. If she took this on, there might be a slight chance of him walking away with what he needed.

"I think it's wiser than putting the Cordova name on everyone's lips," she said.

"I'm not an idiot, Isa. And I'm damn good at my job."

Realizing she'd stepped on his male toes, she softened her

tone. "No doubt, but in this crowd, you being all that's you, they're going to peg you as police or Family, and neither one is going to encourage a friendly exchange of information."

"Me being all that's me?" he repeated, focused on the wrong damn thing.

She waved a hand in his direction. "Stop fishing for compliments. You know what I mean."

"No, actually, I don't, but I'm dying to hear what it is you think makes me whatever it is you think I am." There was a dangerous purr to his voice.

She suppressed a shiver and tried to regain control of the conversation. "My point is, we need to play this right, which means you can't go in as the Cordovas' Hound. You need to be—"

"Yours."

His calm declaration robbed her of air, and all she could squeeze out was, "What?"

"I need to go in as yours. We go in as a couple out on a date."

"I would never bring someone important to me here," she said before she could rethink what it revealed.

He shot her a look, and his voice softened. "I know, but if someone you trusted wanted to surprise you, you'd roll with it even if it made you uncomfortable."

She couldn't deny that.

"If we use that story, plus your concern about a new drug hitting the bar scene, we might be able to stir the pot."

Oh, there was no doubt they'd stir the pot. She was just worried about what would rise to the surface.

chapter 8

Locke

Locke stood at Isa's back as they waited for the slow-moving cars to drive past. Once they caught a break, the two of them crossed over into the sprawling collection of single and multistoried buildings in the entertainment district. The open patios were filled with patrons, and the warm night air carried music and voices. He looked back to the sprawling lot where they'd parked.

"Your car will be fine," Isa said without turning around.

"Not worried about the car."

And he wasn't. He'd picked a spot under one of the many lights. Between that and the embedded security wards, anyone stupid enough to mess with his car would quickly learn it was a bad idea. What made his neck itch was the seemingly casual group of three hanging around a tricked-out classic Impala and the way they were eying Isa. They leaned against the hood, the two doors behind them open wide as a heavy beat pulsated from the interior. They were young—mid-twenties at most—with a sketchy demeanor that had passersby giving them a wide berth.

Locke angled his position, and his movement snapped

their attention to him, which was where he wanted it. He stared them down, letting them see exactly who they were facing. Their rough edges dissolved under his baleful stare, and it wasn't long before they retreated, turning away with nervous chin jerks, hunched shoulders, and weak smiles.

"Really, Locke?" Isa chided.

He turned to see her looking up at him from where she stood at his side. "What?"

She shook her head but took his hand and crossed the street. They hit the sidewalk, and Isa's heels clicked over the pavers as she led him deeper into the plaza. They passed the milling crowd outside the multiplex theater and the green space that held scattered seating arrangements under wide umbrellas. Soaring palm trees joined the old-fashioned light posts and more modern heating lamps—currently not in use—along the wide pathways. Despite it being a Sunday, businesses were busy. The crowd was a mixed bag—families clustered by the theater while roving bands of teens moved in and out of bookstores and lively restaurants, leaving the clubs and breweries to the singles and couples dressed to impress.

Isa made a left between a rowdy restaurant and a bustling brewery, leading him farther into the complex. They passed a partially filled escalator taking patrons to the upper levels and headed down a short passage that spilled into a circular patio dominated by two fountains. Water danced under colored lights to music that was not too loud but was definitely there.

They followed the curving line of shops, galleries, and eateries before reaching a narrow staircase tucked in a shadowy alcove. Inset lights illuminated the steps, but the closer those lights got to the top, the more the thick shadows seemed to swallow them. And it wasn't just the lights. The music and voices from the plaza became muffled as if covered by a heavy cloth, and something unsettling was in the air. Locke felt like they were being watched.

Not a fan of being prey, he felt his magic surge forward as he eyed the crouching darkness above. Scents grew sharper. His eyesight adjusted, bringing further definition to the varying shades of blackness, and his hearing gained an almost painful sensitivity. A sixth sense warned of active magic nearby.

Locke tightened his grip on Isa's hand, bringing her to a stop. "Isa—"

She looked back at him with a frown that disappeared quickly when she caught sight of his face. "We're good, Locke." She tugged on his hand. "Come on."

Without letting her go, he moved up the stairs. She waited until he was a step behind her then turned and headed up. They reached the second-floor landing, and instead of going right to where a line of empty offices loomed, Isa made a sharp left. She started up another set of stairs then came to a stop near a black plaque hanging next to a heavy iron gate and let Locke go.

Crowding her back, Locke studied the plaque, but there was nothing to see, just a dull-black surface that soaked up what little light surrounded it. He peered into the concealing darkness beyond the gate, his magic stalking forward, intent on sniffing out any threat, only to draw back with a low warning growl. There was nothing natural about that darkness. Before he could stop her, Isa laid her hand on the plaque and muttered something. A flare of magic sliced through the strange atmosphere. It moved along her hand before disappearing. A dull thunk echoed through the stifling quiet.

Isa reached for the gate's handle, but Locke got there first, his hand closing over the thick metal. "I've got it."

The handle was warm to the touch. He pulled hard, expecting to encounter resistance, but it swung open easily on silent hinges, leaving him unbalanced. Isa pressed a hand against his back, holding him steady, and matched his steps as they retreated to pull the gate open.

There was an odd shimmer to the shadows blanketing the opening that made Locke hesitate but not Isa. She slid by him and moved through. Not wanting to lose sight of her, he stuck to her heels, crossing the threshold to the unknown. The gate swung shut with a dull thunk. Like a pebble thrown into a still pool, waves rippled through the shimmer, and in their wake, light began to eat at the darkness closest to them. Locke caught Isa by her waist and drew her back against his front as the illusion of an empty space began to crumble, revealing glimpses of another lit walkway hidden in the veil of darkness.

Isa shot him a look of impatience and worry over her shoulder as she batted at his restraining arm. "What?"

He shifted, forcing her back a step so he could take the lead. "Let me go first."

She gave in with an aggrieved sigh but stayed at his back, hooking her fingers through one of his belt loops.

Uneasiness clawed at his spine as the shadows continued to fracture at a faster rate, revealing more of the wide, well-lit walkway and setting free muffled conversations.

"Illusion ward?"

"Yep. Keeps the unwanted out," she said softly.

He gave the fracturing darkness another hard look then prowled forward slowly, following the retreating shadows, Isa matching him step for step. They didn't get far when the last inky vestiges faded to reveal a short line of patrons corralled by thick blue ropes strung between waist-high posts. At the head was a young woman in a glittery formfitting dress, her hair a mix of gold and brown piled in a complicated twist meant to look casual. Her long, bare legs were made even longer by needle-thin heels. She worked a phone and an earpiece as she greeted each person. At her side was a muscle-bound bouncer in a black suit, his hair shorn close to his skull and his face set in the *don't fuck with me* lines adopted universally by bouncers everywhere. He held his position in front of the entrance, clearly blocking it, his thick arms held in a deceptively informal pose as he scanned the incoming patrons.

As Locke and Isa moved into the light and out of the illusion's hold, they got some curious looks from the waiting patrons. The men taking in all that was Isa with an appreciative eye while the weight of female perusal hit Locke like an unwelcome touch. But it was the bouncer's stillness as he caught sight of Isa that left Locke on edge. If Locke hadn't been watching so closely, he would have missed it. He wasn't the only one who'd clocked it—Isa came in at his side and got close. He curled his arm around her waist, his hand coming to rest on her exposed curves in an unmistakably possessive gesture.

They kept walking as he dipped his head down until his mouth was near her ear. "You know him?"

She turned that little bit into him, her lips curving into a small smile as if he'd said something privately amusing, but her eyes were dark with worry. "He goes by Carter. Don't know if it's a first or last name."

Locke brought them to a stop a few feet from the end of the queue and angled his body so she was partially blocked from Carter's view. Her hands came up to his shirt as she held on. He cupped her face and dropped his head until their foreheads touched. "He going to be a problem?"

Her tongue came out and touched her lips in an unusually nervous tell as her gold-flecked eyes searched his. "I don't think so."

"You good, or do we need to turn around?" He offered the out but was grateful when she didn't take it.

"I'm good."

Taking her at her word, he cupped the back of her head and pressed his lips to her forehead then moved aside so they could join the end of the line. Carter followed their movement but continued his door duties. As they stood there, quiet conversations floated around them, and Locke found himself absently stroking the warm, silky skin of where Isa's waist and hip met. She leaned in deeper, one hand resting on his chest just above his heart as her familiar scent of cinnamon and vanilla curled around him. Despite her causal pose, he could feel the tension riding under her skin.

He tightened his hold and brushed his lips on the top of her hair. A ripple in the air behind him had him turning to look back just as another couple stepped out of the illusionary barrier. The man was in his early forties, with a brawler's build and thick dark hair marked by silver. He was draped in tailored linen. His companion, a honey blonde by choice, had to be half his age, wearing a slash of eye-catching crimson meant to be a dress with impressively high heels. Unexpected recognition hit, and he stiffened.

"Well, shit," he muttered, watching the couple's approach.

"What?" Isa half turned to see who had his attention. "Who is that?"

"That is the very married—and not to the young woman at his side—Beto Montenegro." The line moved forward, which gave Locke an unneeded excuse to turn back around and ignore the advancing couple. "He also happens to be one of the bigger money men behind a lot of the Valley's developments."

Isa followed his lead and turned away. "How do you know him?"

"I don't."

He tightened his hold on Isa as Beto and his companion bypassed the line and walked right up to the bouncer without even pausing. The couple spoke to the hostess with an easy familiarity.

"I just investigated him for Emilio," Locke murmured,

"and what I found meant Emilio chose not to move forward with the deal Montenegro offered. Unfortunately, losing Cordova support meant other investors who were on the fence decided to jump ship as well, and that made him very unhappy."

"So he's sketchy," she said.

He met her gaze and gave her a small smile. "Very, which is why Emilio has me keeping tabs."

"Then he should fit in just fine with this crowd."

As Montenegro ushered his companion inside, Locke felt the slow slide of Isa's hand moving from his chest to just below his ribs, where it stopped. He cleared his throat. "Makes me wonder what connections he's working to earn VIP access to an underground social club."

Through the material of his shirt, he felt Isa's nails press into his side, gaining his attention, as she pulled back against his hold. "Do me a favor tonight, Locke. Just stick to our hunt."

"That's my goal." And it was. If he managed to sniff out new scents on old trails, well, then, he could track those later.

Those compelling eyes searched his for a long moment, and he got the sense she was weighing his intent. When the line started moving again, she turned forward and, with a soft sigh, walked the few feet necessary. She didn't say anything more, not even when a group of chattering twentysomethings joined the line. Their excited conversation babbled behind him as they drew closer to the entry.

Then it was Locke and Isa's turn.

"Good evening," the hostess said with a professional smile that warmed as it drifted over Isa and landed on him.

He pulled the wooden disc from his pocket, held it up between two fingers, and offered it to her. "Evening."

Light winked off the small crystals embedded in the hostess's pointed, polished nails as she took the disc. A flash of blue-tinged orange magic swept over the disc and winked to gold. With a graceful twist of her wrist, the disc disappeared.

She inclined her head and motioned them forward. "Enjoy."

Locke took Isa's hand as they cleared the few steps to the entrance, but they were forced to stop when Carter didn't move aside. Stepping in front of Isa, Locke moved into the bouncer's space. "Problem?"

Carter's attention went from Isa to Locke, something working behind the stony expression as he held Locke's gaze. Then, surprisingly, without a word, the man reached back, opened the door, and stepped to the side. Lights flashed from deep inside, but strangely, no sound emerged, indicating there was more than one spell at work.

Without releasing his hold on Isa's hand, Locke ushered her forward, keeping his body between her and Carter. As they passed, a faint scent teased his nose, but he didn't have time to chase it down. Not with Carter watching them. They stepped across the threshold and into a deafening wall of music. The heavy bass line was an underlying heartbeat that seemed to sync with the flashing lights as he followed Isa deeper inside. The place was busy for a Sunday night, but then again, he wasn't sure the patrons were the typical nine-to-fivers, so perhaps the whole day-of-rest thing didn't apply.

Isa led him up a short set of stairs that opened to a wide walkway ringing the mass of undulating bodies on the floor below. As she wove her way through the club-goers, he took in the scene. There were three levels—the main floor below, the walkway they were on, and the top level above. In between the spastic lights, he made out various alcoves on the top floor, with group seating and tables for patrons to lounge at as they watched the happenings below—most likely the VIP tables. Unsurprisingly, he spotted a couple of faces he recognized by reputation.

Isa made a beeline to one of the two bars dominating the second level. Most of the seats were filled, but as Locke and Isa approached, one opened up. Isa took advantage, sliding in before anyone else could claim it, leaving Locke to wedge himself into the space next to her. Isa turned so her bare back was to Locke and crossed her legs as she waited to catch the bartenders' attention. There were two, both female, both busy as they moved in a coordinated dance along the back line of the bar. It only took a minute or two before the younger one flashed them a smile and a nod, indicating she'd be over in a minute, as she popped tops off a pair of long-neck bottles and set them in front of a customer. The older bartender was busy with a customer a little farther down.

As he and Isa waited their turn, Locke scanned the crowd, noting it was an interesting mix that ranged from discerning sophisticates to edgy unconventional people and everything in between. The music from below was loud, but considering he could still hear the buzz of nearby conversations, it was clear that whoever was running this scene didn't skimp on things like soundproofing spells—a financial layout indicating this supposed fly-by-night setup was well funded, and he couldn't help but wonder whose pockets those funds were buried in.

He noticed a handful of bouncer types positioned through the club and was on his return sweep when he saw the older bartender register Isa's presence and do a double take. As the younger one started to head their way, the older one directed her toward another customer and took her place. She stopped in front of them and wiped a towel over the bar's top before setting her palms flat so she could lean in.

"Isa, I thought you were shot of this scene." Her tone was casual but concerned. The woman's mature features had Locke putting her age closer to forty than thirty despite the trim, fit curves displayed by the triangular leather top that left her arms and back bare above her formfitting leather pants.

"Hey, Nova." Isa shifted forward so the two could talk. "Wasn't planning on making a return appearance, but my guy here"—she reached out and put her hand on Locke's chest—"got an invite and thought to surprise me."

Nova's eyebrows rose. "Hell of a surprise."

"You're telling me." Isa's response carried a guarded edge.

Nova's eyes narrowed. "Don't you have enough business at your place to keep you out of mine?" she asked with a hint of cautious teasing.

"It keeps me out of trouble," Isa said.

"Sorry to hear that."

Isa gave a surprised laugh. "Me too."

Nova's grin was a little less strained as she straightened. "Well, what can I get you?"

Isa looked at the back of the bar, where bottles were lined on lighted shelves. "How about we start with two Eagle Rare tens, one neat, one on the rocks?"

Nova shook her head. "I see some things don't change."

Isa shrugged. "What can I say? I like nice things."

Nova grinned, her gaze sweeping over Locke with obvious feminine appreciation before returning to Isa. "I can see that."

Isa chuckled as Nova moved off to get the bourbons.

Locke dug cash out of his pocket then extended it over Isa's shoulder so she could see it as he bent to her ear. "Here."

She turned and studied him, her face close to his. He wondered if she was going to argue. If she did, he'd be putting a stop to that with a kiss, considering that her mouth was right fucking there.

He couldn't decide if he was surprised or disappointed when she took the money with a quiet "Thanks."

He tucked a few more bills into the glass filled with tips then went back to watching Isa's back.

Nova returned and set a squat glass filled with golden

amber in front of him and one that included a round ball of ice in front of Isa. "Enjoy."

Isa handed over the cash, though she held on to it when Nova went to pull it away. "Just five minutes, Nova. That's it."

Nova and Isa stared at each other for a long moment, then the older woman inclined her head. "I can give you five. Go grab a table."

Isa let go of the cash, and Nova headed back to the register. Isa picked up her drink then slipped off the stool. Standing in front of Locke, she said, "Come on—let's get a table."

He picked up his drink and stayed at her side as they moved through the crowd. Finding a table on the second level wasn't easy, as they were few and far between and in high demand. He spotted a group near the back wall that looked as if they were getting ready to leave, and he touched Isa's spine to silently guide her over. They were almost there when Locke slid past Isa to intercept an incoming trio and set his drink down on the tall table. The trio moved on.

Isa joined him and made room for their drinks by nudging the empty glasses and flameless candle to the side. He put his back to the wall then looped an arm around Isa. He pulled her in until she stood in front of him with the high-top table next to them. With one hand at her hip and the other around his drink, he settled in to wait for Nova. Next to him, Isa sipped her bourbon, her body stiff with tension. He picked up his glass and brought it to his nose, where he caught hints of toffee and orange and something sweet.

He leaned into Isa, ignoring how she stilled as he put his mouth near her ear. "Relax, *reinita*."

Her glass froze halfway to her lips, and he heard her breath catch as she turned to give him a startled look.

A little amused at her reaction to his endearment, he touched the rim of his glass to hers. "*¡Salud!*" He held her gaze as he took a sip, and she did the same. A bold blend of candied almonds and rich cocoa hit his tongue. He murmured, "Nice."

Isa slowly lowered her glass, her lips curving up, and a bit of her stiffness drifted away. The urge to bend in and taste the bourbon glistening on her lips beat strong and hard in time with the music. Without breaking eye contact, he set his glass down then cupped his hand around the back of her neck to bring her closer. Anticipation thrummed through him as an echoing desire darkened her eyes, her tongue darting out to swipe over her lower lip, her drink caught between them, the spicy bite of her natural scent deepening. He dipped his head and subtly inhaled the heady aroma of vanilla-touched cinnamon, letting it twine deep in his core, where a dark hunger woke on a growl. Her lips parted, offering an invitation he was all too happy to accept, but before he could, the moment was broken.

"Should I come back?"

Unable to stop a frustrated snarl as color rose under Isa's cheeks and her lashes swept down, Locke moved just his eyes to see that Nova had joined them. The woman stared unapologetically back, her eyes wide with faux innocence.

"No," Isa said huskily as she pressed the hand with the glass against his chest.

He heeded her silent request, letting her go and giving her room.

Nova watched the interplay with unconcealed amusement. She set a glass with ice water on the table and took up a position on the other side. "You wanted to talk, *chica*. Talk quick because Mandi can get pissy if I leave her alone too long."

Isa turned to him. "Babe, can you give us a few?"

Not the question he'd expected. He studied her and caught the warning in her eyes. To get Nova to talk, Isa needed privacy, but he had no intention of missing a word. He dipped his chin in silent acknowledgment, picked up his drink, and moved off to the side just far enough to preserve the illusion of privacy. Then he let his magic off its leash. With the ease of practice, he split his attention between the movements of the roving bouncers and those of the surrounding crowds, while his magic shifted the air currents to filter out unnecessary background noise until the conversation at the table took center stage.

chapter 9

Isa

ISA WATCHED Locke move a few feet away and take a seemingly casual position as he watched the crowd.

"Girl, where did you find that?"

Locke's drink paused halfway to his mouth, and behind the flimsy cover of the glass, his lips twitched before the bourbon continued on its journey. Isa decided to ignore the fact that he was listening in on her conversation.

She turned back to Nova. "He walked into my bar."

"Lucky you."

Sure, if luck is a cosmic cat and I'm the idiot mouse. She picked up her drink, wondering if the result would be indigestion. Or better yet, heartburn.

Before Isa could spin further down that rabbit hole, Nova continued. "Though if I were you, I'd convince him to check out another hot spot tonight."

The warning struck like lightning, freezing her in place and squashing her momentary levity. "He's here?" She was proud the question came out sharp instead of shaky.

Nova shrugged, her gaze shifting beyond Isa before coming back. "Your guess is as good as mine, but considering the amount of muscle being flexed..." She paused as one of the bouncer types strode by, his attention on the floor below. Once he was out of earshot, Nova studied Isa, twisting her glass of water absently, and continued. “What I can confirm is he’s got eyes and ears all over this place.”

That news wasn’t unexpected. Neither was the prospect that Isa might already be in trouble. She figured the minute Carter had caught sight of her, he’d told the powers that be about her presence, which meant she was on the clock, especially if Angel was in house. It also meant Nova would be her only chance at useful information.

“Then I’ll make this quick. I heard some things and figured since I’m here, I might as well ask.”

Interest sharpened Nova’s attention as her fingers curled around her glass, holding it still. “Might not have your answers, but you’re free to ask.”

“There was this guy who popped up on the scene a few months back and hooked up with someone I know. I don’t have much on him, but he made it sound like he had connections, big ones, and lately, he’s been flashing this new product around. He tried to get her to try it, swearing it would rock her world, but since that’s not her thing, she declined. The other night, he tried again, but this time he decided to show instead of tell, and it did not go well for him. Whatever he took messed him up.” She held Nova’s gaze, leaned in, and waited until the woman did the same before adding in a quieter tone, “And by that, I mean *messed him up*, Nova.”

Nova studied Isa for a long moment, lines creasing her forehead and bracketing her mouth as she played with the straw in her glass. Finally, she murmured, “That sucks, but in this scene, that shit happens on the regular.”

“True, but not like this.” Isa sat back without losing eye contact. “This girl, she was freaked right the fuck out because whatever he took *changed* him.”

Nova seemed to think it through. "What do you mean, 'changed him'?"

Sharing might not be wise, but she couldn't see another way to get the information without giving more away. If Locke didn't like it, she had no doubt he'd shut things down, but until he did...

"He was throwing around power that wasn't his to play with."

Even with the candle's muted lighting, there was no missing the way Nova's face blanched. "That's impossible."

Isa raised her brows. "I'm just sharing what she told me, and she's not one to lie." She gave Nova a minute to process before adding, "She also said he was sharing this pill with others, and, girl, if this does to them what she said it did to him, unwanted attention is going to be beating down our doors."

Nova's attention shifted to the crowd as she picked up her glass and took a healthy swallow.

Unwilling to let her wiggle off the hook, Isa dug in a little deeper. "I have to know, Nova."

Nova flicked her a glance. "Know what?"

"If this is a one-off. If so, then I can relax, but if not, I need to be prepared because I'm not willing to lose my business over someone's Frankensteined party favors. So, from one friend to another, do I have reason to be concerned?"

Nova set her glass back on the table and met Isa's gaze. "You know I stay out of that shit, Isa."

Something in Nova's voice made Isa's pulse tick up. "I know, but that doesn't make you deaf or blind."

Nova's lips tightened as she drummed her fingers against the table. "Haven't seen anything, but I might have heard a couple rumblings about something new," she said, her voice tight. "But you know how it goes." She gave an uncomfortable shrug. "Some stray comes in looking to make a name by showing off a juicy new bone—it doesn't take the big dogs long to catch a scent. And once they do, they're all over it."

At Nova's roundabout confirmation that Leo had been playing well above his level, the knots in Isa's gut tightened. "And the strays?"

Nova's fingers stilled as she stared at Isa intently. "You know how territorial he can be."

Isa fought her flinch and swallowed down the resulting nausea. "Yeah, I know."

Nova folded her arms on the table's top and leaned in, her grim gaze searching Isa's face. "So, again, *chica*, may I suggest, highly, you grab your treat and beat feet before he catches wind of your scent and latches on?"

Gods, I want to. Unfortunately, the reason she couldn't was counting on her for some answers. "I intend to, but whatever this product is, it's dangerous. I don't want it in my bar, especially if he's got anything to do with it."

"You can't take him on, Isa. You tried that, remember?" Nova snapped, fear and frustration breaking through her thin layer of callousness.

Through sheer will, Isa held her casual pose even as a little voice in the back of her head urged her to run fast and hard. "You know me—I can't exactly stand aside and do nothing. Not if he's setting something loose on these kids."

Sympathy flickered through Nova's face. "They aren't your responsibility."

"They belong to someone."

"Then let someone deal with it."

Isa winced.

Sighing, Nova reached across the table and squeezed Isa's fist. "Girl, your heart is in the right place, but be smart. You barely got free last time. I'm not so sure your luck will hold a second time around."

Neither am I.

Nova held Isa's gaze. "Let it go." She paused for a heartbeat. "Don't make the mistake of walking back into his web."

The problem was, Isa wasn't sure she'd ever really escaped Angel—not when those sticky ties kept dragging her back in. But Nova was waiting.

"I'm not planning on it," Isa said.

Relief swept through Nova's face, easing the worried lines. "Good." She let Isa go and moved back, preparing to leave. "Now, as much as I loved seeing you, I gotta get back to work before Mandi comes looking for me."

Isa dredged up a smile. "Thanks for making time."

Nova's smile turned surprisingly sweet as she picked up her glass. "It really was good to see you, Isa. Maybe next time, I'll take a seat at your bar."

"Looking forward to it."

With that, Nova lifted her chin at Locke then turned and headed back to the bar.

Heat hit Isa's back as Locke moved in, crowding close as he reached around to set his now empty glass on the table. He braced his hands on the table on either side of her as he bent his head close. "Get ready, sweetheart," his voice rumbled against her ear.

Caught between him and the table, the only thing she could do was turn her head toward him, which put her lips temptingly near his jaw. "For what?"

He dipped his head closer until mere inches separated them, and she could see the light of sardonic amusement burning deep in his eyes. "We're about to have company."

She didn't have time to do much more than blink before one of the bouncers took Nova's place. Slowly, Isa turned toward their unwanted visitor. Big and broad, dressed from head to toe in black, he was focused on Isa, stupidly dismissing Locke.

"Ms. Serrano, Mr. Herrera would like to invite you and your friend to his table for a drink."

There was no way to get out of the invitation, but she still tried. "Appreciate the offer, but we're good."

The bouncer's attention went to Locke then back to her. "He insists."

She opened her mouth to respond, but Locke got there first, his hand drifting down her spine and setting off a shiver. "I could use another drink."

She pushed her drink away as resentment curled through her. She wanted to rail at him for dragging her here, even though it had been her decision. It wasn't fair, but then, none of this was.

So instead, she crammed all the messy emotions into a familiar box and locked that bitch down tight. "Fine."

Leaving her half-finished drink on the table, Isa followed the bouncer across the walkway and up the stairs to the third floor. Locke stayed at her side, close enough that their bodies brushed but not so close that she felt crowded. They hit the third level, and the club noise took a step back, adding to the ambience of importance. As they walked by the shadowed alcoves, the brush of invisible eyes was nearly physical. Her skin crawled with each step as the weight of unwanted curiosity joined the sticky strands coiling around her, pulling her deeper into the darkness. It was as if Angel's presence crawled through the club, slipping along the emotional threads emanating from those gathered and tightened around her until breathing was difficult.

Unsettled, she played with the Zemi charm bracelet at her wrist, and the constricting bands eased enough for her to rediscover her balance. She snuck a look at Locke. In between the dance of shadows, she could make out the tight line of his jaw and the feral intensity as he scanned their surroundings, his body coiled and ready.

She caught his hand and laced their fingers together. He looked down at her, and she mouthed, "You good?"

Locke angled his head to her, his lips curving not in humor but in predatory delight. He brought her hand up and brushed his lips across her knuckles.

Right, okay. So the unseen threat she'd felt was just her freaking out. Something she couldn't afford to do because her emotions would only feed the monster lying in wait.

She pulled in a breath discreetly and refocused, herding her apprehension over to the box she'd shoved her other emotions into and coaxing it inside. Once it joined the others, she proceeded to bury it deep. By the time the bouncer came to a stop outside one of the larger alcoves, she was comfortably numb.

"Ma'am." The bouncer turned sideways and waved her toward the recessed booth, where a petite blonde in a sparkly sheath snuggled up to a man in all black and, to their right, another couple lounged.

Anchored by the weight of Locke's palm at the base of her spine, Isa glided up the two steps and into the web.

chapter 10

Locke

LOCKE STUDIED the man holding court in the center of the curved, cushioned seat that made up the alcove. He wasn't quite sure what he'd expected, but it wasn't the urbane sophisticate dressed in tailored black, untangling from his blond companion to get to his feet as Isa moved up the two steps into the alcove. Any lingering signs of the streets that had spawned the man were hidden under a slick veneer of charm as he threaded his way between the legs of the couple sitting to the side and the low round table cluttered with drinks and half-finished appetizers.

"Isa, lovely to see you. Thank you for joining me."

Isa stepped onto the floor of the alcove and stilled. "Not sure we had much choice." Her voice remained coolly polite, though under Locke's palm, he could feel the tension singing through her spine.

White teeth flashed in Angel's dark, close-cropped goatee as he closed in and caught her hands in his. "The choice is always yours."

He went to lift her hands, but she pulled them away, turned deeper into Locke, and placed her palm against his chest. Without hesitation, Locke adjusted his hold, his hand sliding down from her back and around to her hip, where he could tuck her into his side.

Based on the quick flash of fury in Angel's eyes, Locke's message had made it through loud and clear. Angel's attention centered on Locke, and his charming smile sharpened. "And you are...?"

"Hers." The blunt truth served the dual purpose of claim and challenge, neither of which would sit well with Isa but would land him on Angel's radar as a rival.

"Is that so?" Angel studied him for a long moment.

The hair on the back of Locke's neck rose as something unseen sniffed around him, bringing with it a skin-ruffling scent. Uneasy, his magic stirred, ready to snap its jaws at the threat. Remembering Isa's earlier warning about Angel's siphoning power, he played possum, letting his possessive side rise to the fore and take center stage.

Angel turned to Isa and murmured with a hint of menace, "Interesting pets you're keeping, *chiquita*."

There was an actual temperature drop in the air around Isa. Locke was surprised when she didn't default to her typical cutting rebuke but instead simply watched Angel as if he were nothing more than a curious, potentially dangerous insect.

"I am surprised to see you here." Angel's voice had cooled. "I thought you didn't do this scene anymore. Too—what was it you called it? Problematic?"

"It wasn't the scene, Angel," she said without inflection. "It was you, and that hasn't changed."

Something flared deep in Angel's eyes, and for a moment, the monster peeked out from behind the charm. "Yet here you are."

"My choice, not hers," Locke said, wading through the treacherous currents lapping around Isa.

Angel's attention snapped back to him. "Is that so?"

Keeping his tone dismissive, Locke drawled, "Heard about

this place from a friend, got an invite, decided to surprise her." He looked at the woman in question and squeezed her hip. When she turned her face up to his, he said, "Surprise."

That got him a small smile.

It also earned him an irritated huff from Angel. "Please."

They turned back to see he had an arm raised and was motioning toward the empty seat on the curved couch, where their silent audience watched the unfolding drama.

"Sit." It was no less than an order gritted out through a forced smile.

Isa led the way to the booth. As they got closer, Locke recognized the male half of the couple sitting on the end nearest to them—Janek Healy, deep-pocket investor in Signature Enterprises, an investment firm Emilio had gotten Locke to dig into over a year ago when the Delphi serum first came to light. Interesting to find the man here with someone like Angel, but considering that the woman at his side was too young to be his wife, maybe it wasn't so surprising. There couldn't be many places Healy could indulge his adulterous intentions without gaining public scrutiny. And the gods knew no one here would risk themselves to expose someone else's misdeeds.

Healy and his companion shifted over, making room on the couch, while Angel rejoined the now pouting blonde, who alternately glared at Isa and eyed Locke with speculation. Isa did that female thing of smoothing a hand over her rounded ass before taking her seat and crossing her long legs. Whatever material her pants were made of was light enough that the movement caused it to ebb and flow like water. She left room for him, but instead of taking it, he braced a hand just behind her head on the edge of the seat. He had no intention of being caught unawares or trapped in the narrow space. She looked up at him in silent question.

"I'm good," he said.

A server moved in and quickly cleared the glasses before taking requests. When she got to them, Isa did a repeat of their earlier order and the server glided away.

"Everyone, this is Isa and her pet." Angel wrapped an arm around the blonde. "Isa, pet, everyone."

Locked was amused by Angel's continued condescension, a clear sign that Locke's mere presence was providing enough of a threat to make the man defensive.

"You look familiar," Healy said, studying Locke. "Have we met?"

"No, I don't think we have," he lied. When Healy's jaw tightened and his gaze narrowed with speculation, something told Locke to step carefully. "But it is possible we crossed paths at some point."

"What is it you do?" Healy asked.

"Acquisitions." It was a vague but accurate answer Locke often used and one that would work easily in this crowd. Especially as money appeared to be a factor in, well, everything. It also appeared to appease Healy's rising suspicions.

Conversation halted as the server returned with their drinks. When she left, Angel eyed Isa over the rim of his glass. "I remember when such things bored you."

Isa paused with her drink halfway to her lips, her eyes sweeping over the young blonde before landing on Angel. Her voice, when it came, was dismissive. "Much like a good whiskey, some tastes improve with age."

A strange relief bled through Locke. The acerbic witch he knew and adored had finally made an appearance. Considering how Angel's knuckles whitened around his glass, he was less impressed.

"It's good to see your palate has... evolved," Angel said. When Isa simply sipped her drink and didn't bother to hide the small, secretive curl of her lips, he tried again. "Isa was one of my more popular bartenders once upon a time, back before she decided to try her hand at running her own place. Well, not really on your own, as you have—what, two?" He flicked a look at Locke. "Or is it three partners now?"

Unruffled, Isa balanced her glass on her knee. "Just the two."

"Well, should you ever need another, I'm always looking to expand."

Not batting an eye, Isa drily replied, "I don't think Wonderland would fit with your portfolio."

"That's where I've seen you," the woman at Healy's side said then blushed when attention turned to her. "Sorry. I've been sitting here trying to figure out why you seemed familiar. I've been to Wonderland a couple times. Mainly after work with friends. We love it. It's such a cool little place to hang out at." She sounded sincere.

"Thank you," Isa said. "I always enjoy hearing that kind of feedback."

Locke wasn't surprised when Angel once again grabbed control of the conversation. "I'm curious, *chiquita*—now that you've been on the other side of the business, what do you think of your old stomping grounds?"

Isa's eyebrows rose. "They've certainly changed."

"How so?" Healy asked.

"It appears Angel discovered how to attract a more selective clientele."

"Oh, I've always been highly selective about who I let through my doors, but to your point, we have become more discerning of late," Angel drawled.

Isa lifted her whiskey. "It's definitely working for you. Business appears to have picked up."

"That's due in part to the generosity of people like my business partner here." Without looking away from Isa, Angel indicated Healy, who winced. A pulse of spite soured the air around Angel as his smile sharpened. "Their investments have allowed us to expand our amenities."

"Is that so?" Isa sipped her drink.

"As I explained when you mentioned wanting to branch out on your own, never underestimate the influence of a good professional network, as you never know when those connections will prove useful." There was a hint of a threat in Angel's statement. "It's why so many independent businesses fail."

Seeing Isa's fingers whiten on her glass made Locke want to wipe the smirk off Angel's face, but this was a verbal battle —punches weren't allowed. "Not something Wonderland has to worry about." Locke waited for Angel to look at him then issued his own threat. "There are quite a few names invested in its success. That's what happens when established locals decide to crown a neighborhood favorite." He held Angel's dark gaze, and the man's features tightened.

Before Angel could resume his game, Healy cut in, asking Isa questions about Wonderland. She answered, and the conversation drifted into shallower waters. Angel continued to watch Locke with obvious calculation, but Locke refused to look away. He knew the minute he and Isa left the club, Angel would go on the hunt, trying to discover who those local investors were and how they connected with him, Wonderland, and more importantly, Isa. The predatory part of Locke studied Angel with anticipation while Angel's eyes glittered with an answering malice. Only when the blonde at his side demanded his attention did he finally break off their staring contest.

Locke's lips curved at the small win, and he sipped his drink as he let Isa's conversation with Healy and his companion wash around him.

The blonde finished speaking to Angel and rose, murmuring, "Excuse me," before slipping out of the alcove.

Angel rejoined the conversation, but a discordant note of

awareness brushed against Locke's magic, jarring the prowling power that had remained on wary alert ever since they breached the illusion barrier. Trusting Isa to fend off Angel's verbal swipes, he tuned in to the advancing threat. The strange current of energy buzzed against his senses, like the leading edge of a breaking storm.

Locke tilted his head toward the alcove's opening just as two people filled it. One was a bouncer, and the other was Beto Montenegro.

The bouncer wasted no time. "Sir, sorry to interrupt—"

"Herrera," Beto said, rounding the bouncer to move up the steps. "We need to talk." His flat gaze swept over the other occupants and paused on Healy with a short nod of acknowledgment before going back to Angel. "Now."

Locke noted Isa's minute stiffening, but his magic demanded he keep his attention on Angel.

The air around the club owner darkened as Angel's charm evaporated, his lips thinning, his eyes hardening. He slowly waved his drink at the table at large. "I'm busy at the moment."

Beto didn't back down. "Get unbusy."

An oppressive weight filled the alcove as Angel set his drink on the table, got to his feet, straightened his cuffs, and murmured to Healy, "Excuse me." He turned to a watching Isa. "I had hoped to speak to you further, but it seems business has other plans. Perhaps I will see you when I'm done."

"Unfortunately, I think it's time to call it a night."

Angel's smile was sardonic. "Of course. Well, then, until we met again, *chiquita*." With that, he turned to Beto. "Shall we take this in my office?"

A muscle worked in Beto's jaw, but he spun on his heel and stormed down the steps. Angel followed, his bouncer at his back. The men made their way to the elevator and disappeared inside.

Isa set her drink on the table and got to her feet. She turned to the other couple. "It's been lovely, but as I told Angel, it's time for us to call it a night."

Polite goodbyes were exchanged, then Locke was following Isa down the steps and along the wide walkway, his hand once again resting against the warm skin at her spine. He stood with her as the elevator slid back down from an upper level and the doors glided open. They stepped inside. Once behind the closed doors, Isa surprised Locke by turning into him, sliding her hands up his chest, and linking them behind his neck. Her move pressed her soft curves against him, igniting an inconvenient response. But that didn't stop him from gently gripping her hips and tugging her close.

Awareness flared in her eyes, leaving small gold sparks behind. Her lush lips parted as a delicate shiver ran through her and color swept over her cheeks, her delicious scents curling around them. "Play along," she murmured.

Oh, he was more than happy to follow that order. He spun them around and crowded her against the back wall, giving in to the hunger that had waited not so patiently to play. He wanted to growl at her small, excited gasp but managed to refrain.

He dipped his head until mere inches separated them. "What are you up to?"

Her gaze drifted to his mouth then came back up. The gold glints in her eyes were brighter and hotter, and her tongue darted out to touch her top lip. "I want to check something out, and with Angel holed up in his office, now works."

He took in the determined glint under her desire and recognized it for what it was—a need to best the monster. "You like to live dangerously."

Those fascinating lips curved into wicked temptation. "So do you."

Since actions spoke louder than words, he took her mouth

in a kiss. Despite the need clawing through him, he kept it gentle, brushing his lips against hers once then twice before she let him in. The minute the sweet and spicy taste of her exploded against his tongue, his hunger went white-hot. It was the wrong damn time and definitely the wrong damn place, but he couldn't have stopped even if he'd wanted to. He swallowed her soft moan, his hands tightening as she pressed closer, her grip on the nape of his neck pulling him down as she kissed him back.

Feeling the elevator slow, he somehow managed to catch hold of his badly frayed control and ease back. The prick of her nails against his neck made him smile as he slid his lips from hers to whisper next to her ear, "Later, wildcat."

He wanted to laugh when she stiffened and unwound her arms from his neck so she could push against his chest. Heeding her silent request, he pulled back as the elevator stopped and the doors opened on a soft ding. "Lead on, my lady."

She shot him a glare before smoothing it away and stepping beyond him. He caught her hand in his and let her lead. In the short time they'd been upstairs, the crowd had grown. Under the flashing lights, Isa wove her way through the bodies.

As they worked their way to the darker edges of the floor, Locke flexed his magic, slowly cloaking their presence from watching eyes. Magic settled over him like a second skin, and with a thought, he expanded it to encompass Isa. A form of magical camouflage integral to Hounds, bolstered by his natural air mage abilities, utilized the deep shadows and made it easy to blend in. So long as she continued to hold his hand and stay close, maintaining the masking would remain instinctual.

Clearly, Isa had a destination in mind, because she moved resolutely toward the staircase. For a moment, he wondered if she was going to head back up, but then she turned toward a door partially obscured by the stairs. When she came to a stop, she tugged her hand free and grasped the knob. A small red flare indicated a lock charm.

"Dammit," she hissed.

Standing behind her, he put his hands on her hips and nudged her aside so he could examine the charm. His magic prowled forward and nosed the charm, drawing in the magical scents of its caster.

Flat. Tasteless. Generic. Cheap. So much for investing in security.

He gave a derisive snort and unraveled the charm quickly, using the stored magic in the silver signet ring on his right hand. When the red light flashed to a steady green, he twisted the knob and pushed the door open to expose more darkness.

Isa blinked at him. "How—"

"Bastard never reprogramed the lock." He stood sideways and motioned her forward. "Go."

She shook her head and slipped inside.

chapter 11

Isa

DEATH'S insistent call tugged at Isa with painful intensity, prickling her soul with impatience as she waited for Locke to join her in the darkness. As much as she wanted to dash through the thick shadows that greedily sucked the illumination from the flashing lights of the dance floor behind them, she wasn't a complete moron. She dug out her phone to use the built-in flashlight. The door clicked shut, locking them inside, and low floor lights sprang up like fireflies, illuminating a claustrophobic narrow space.

"What is this?" Locke asked, his voice pitched low.

"A utility hall." She shoved her phone back in her pocket and started down the hall. "It leads to the service areas."

"Service areas?"

"There used to be an industrial kitchen on the third floor, but by the time Angel added this place to his rotating roster, it had been gutted." She shifted her weight to her toes, trying to soften the sound of her heels against the concrete floor. "Back when I worked the bars here, they would dump their stuff in the old chill units upstairs."

"So we're going to go check out—what? Their alcohol inventory?"

"No, the kitchen wasn't the only thing on that level. There were other spaces." Memories clawed against the locked doors in her mind. The coppery scent of spilled blood and the sound of anguished cries wafted through the cracks, and she pulled the icy cloak of her magic close, freezing them out. "Spaces with limited accessibility."

"Do I want to know what happened in those spaces?" An edge of heat ran through Locke's voice.

I didn't want to know. "No."

He caught her wrist, bringing her to a stop. She stiffened but refused to look back. His thumb brushed against her inner wrist, the gentle touch at odds with the harsh note in his voice. "What are you chasing, Isa?"

That chill holding past horrors at bay deepened. "Death." She twisted her wrist until he let her go, and she started walking again, a little faster than before. She didn't get far before she felt him at her back, matching her step for step. "There may be cameras watching up there, so if you have some nifty way to deal with that..."

"It won't last long."

Before she could decide whether to take his presence as a threat or a comfort, a glint of metal in the darkness indicated they'd reached the end of the hall and the door that led to the service stairwell. She reached for the cool metal bar as ghostly fingers tore at her mind, clawing for a hold. The unearthly touch had her sucking in a sharp breath. She shoved it ruthlessly away and added another layer of emotional ice between her and the essence desperate for acknowledgment. This was not what she wanted to deal with tonight, but whatever had happened left her with no choice—not when it was so close and so raw. It was like waving a dangerously juicy steak in front of a starving woman, and she knew stuffing her face would hurt, but she was a glutton for punishment.

Unfortunately, Locke was about to take a seat at the table

—he just didn't know it. Her hand met cool metal, and she realized she wasn't comfortable leading him into this without giving him any warning. "I don't know what we're walking into, but whatever it is, it's fresh."

His light eyes fairly glowed in the dimness, but instead of apprehension, what stared back looked disturbingly like anticipation. "Lay on, Macduff."

She gave a near-silent huff of amusement before pushing through the door and into a light-filled space. When no alarm sounded, she led Locke up the steps, trying not to wince at the overly loud echo of their passage. She kept expecting someone to burst through a door and catch them, but the incessant hum from the overhead lights was their only witness. The lure of recent death dragged her up the three flights of stairs. At the top landing, she reached for the door, breathing hard. Heels and stairs made for a hell of a workout.

"Wait," Locke said.

She stilled, her hand poised in midair.

Locke glided in front of her, forcing her to step back as he took her place. "Give me a second."

He turned, keeping his body between her and whatever lay on the other side. His magic swept past her like an invisible brush of fur and claws, raising the hair on her arms, as an unearthly glow seeped from under his lashes. He lifted his head as if catching a scent while one hand hovered over the metal push bar. A heartbeat passed then a second before he carefully depressed the metal bar on the door, and the latch released with a soft click.

Tension trickled down her spine as Locke eased the door open. Heavy silence wound its way out of the narrow opening. It was stupid to do this blind. They had no idea who or what was up here. Piercing threads of panic, confusion, resentment, fury, and—under it all—a nasty miasma of fear anchored Isa, refusing to let her go.

Locke crept through the door. Despite her driving need to push the Hound aside and charge forward, she stuck to his heels as they moved from the stairwell into what remained of the old kitchen. Moonlight squeezed through the small, grime-covered windows set high in the walls and glinted off the metal vents and broken fluorescent lighting hanging from the water-stained ceiling. Fortunately, that wasn't their only light. Spelled lanterns were on either side of the room, showing them a walkable path through what was clearly being used as a storage space. Stacks of glassware and other supplies were shoved into the doorless lower cabinets of what used to be the main pass. Tall tables, like those used on the second floor, were piled two deep against the wall on the far end. Nearby, a large swinging door hung precariously.

In a blue aura, Locke moved deeper into the room, searching out potential threats, his magic circling him and Isa like a protective wolf. Caught in death's thrall, Isa headed to the left, where three large metal freezers lined the wall, leaving him behind.

There, at the far end. She ignored the first two walk-in units, one half blocked by a jumble of metal, the other a yawning pit of shadow, and went straight to the third, which still had a metal door intact. She stood in front of it and cocked her head, listening to the soft rush of air as it twisted into whispered screams. Images played through her mind in a dizzying macabre dance. Ominous emotions flew around like carrion birds eager to feast, and the pendant resting just below the hollow of her throat started to warm. The drifting shadows crept steadily closer, chilling the air even as they gained weight and settled around her to form the familiar folds of the Reaper's cloak, catching her in death's embrace. The world around her crystalized into a pitiless clarity where compassion and empathy couldn't exist.

She grabbed the handle and pulled. The door swung

toward her, forcing her to step back into Locke, who was at her back. He caught the door before it could close and shoved it against the wall. Light from the lanterns failed to pierce the darkness inside. She started to walk in.

He took hold of her arm, forcing her to stop. "Hold up."

She was about to argue when a small glowing ball burst into life.

Locke let her go and motioned with his hand. The orb zipped inside and came to an abrupt stop in midair. "Well, shit."

"Who are you?" The wavering form of a young man glared at Isa and Locke.

Ignoring him, she joined Locke, who was staring down at a tarp-covered bundle on the floor, his hands on his hips.

"Guess this is why Montenegro wanted to talk to Angel." Locke's voice was tight with fury. He lowered himself to his heels and braced his arms against his knees. "Can you find out who she is?"

"Actually, it's not who you think." She moved to the other side of the body, crouched down, and started to work at the duct tape holding the tarp in place. It didn't take her long to peel back the heavy plastic and reveal the face underneath.

"Hey, lady, what kind of sick game are you playing?" The young man's voice broke.

"That's not a woman," Locke said.

"No, it isn't." Isa stared down at the blood-smeared face that mirrored the panicked soul remnant pacing back and forth as it made ever shriller demands.

As the specter started to fray, another remanent wavered into being, this one darker, heavier, and fueled by fury. She could feel it growing stronger by the second. She kept her focus on Locke, which enabled her to hold back the echoes battering at her psyche.

"I've got something to work with, but it's not going to last."

Grim-faced, Locke nodded. "Do what you can, I'll keep an eye out."

Trusting him to watch her back, she gathered the Reaper's magic close, feeling it fall into place. The starlight bursts of magic gathered into the familiar form of the staff. She leaned into its warm weight and straightened, finally turning her attention to the echoes currently losing their shit.

"I don't understand. Who are you? What is this place? What's happening?" the first wailed.

"That bitch. I knew she'd screw me over," the other snarled.

The two echoes wove around the body in a confusing, mirrored dance, their ragged edges tangling then untangling as they moved. The panicked one stared in horrified fascination at the body at its feet, pulling at its hair, while the other glared malevolently between Isa and an unsuspecting Locke, the promise of retribution burning deep at its core. Their voices overlapped, creating a confusing resonance of the emotional currents gathering around Isa. Her magic expanded, sweeping the spirit's chaos into its arms, tightening its hold with merciless bands until there was no escape. Then she dragged the pieces toward her.

They didn't come easily, twisting and turning in an attempt to get loose as she used the staff to stitch the remnants into one ragged cloth. Threats and pleas turned into screams as she forced the tattered remains together. She was relentless, knowing time was of the essence and she and Locke needed answers.

When she was sure the rushed stitching job would hold, she started in. "Name."

"Owen Havers." The reluctant admission was half sobbed in fear, half hissed in fury.

"What happened?"

The facial features contorted, shifting from panicked to sly and back. "I don't... I don't know."

The undercurrents said otherwise. There was confusion, yes, but of the kind that suggested Owen wasn't convinced of his current unalive status, and that feeling was drowned out by an unmitigated fury. If his anger continued to gain strength, she'd end up with a vengeful wraith on her hands—not something they had time to deal with. She dug her skeletal fingers into the ephemeral cloth, straining the newly set bindings, and began to slowly shred the threadbare spirit.

Black bled through Owen's eyes, his scream thin as he bucked uselessly against her hold.

Unmoved, she asked again, "What happened?"

"She was mine first, not his." He sounded petulant, like a child deprived of a toy. Owen's anger and resentment churned through the weaker waves of guilt and empathy, dragging them under until only his darker desires remained. "But as soon as she realized who he was, she dumped me. Gold-digging bitch."

Noxious as the venomous bitterness was, her magic fed on it, and the Reaper's cloak changed from starlight and night skies to an ominous stygian pit. Images flashed through Isa's mind sickeningly fast, but she got the gist. The woman on Beto's arm had been with Owen first—had, in fact, sought him out one night at another club. Like many twentysomething males, the low-level Charmer had been easily enraptured by her wiles and had stayed that way until she told him they were better off as friends. That was when Owen realized her approach had been calculated. As Beto's assistant, he was just a stepping stone to someone with deeper, older pockets. It hadn't taken long for hurt pride and dented ego to shift to fury-driven blame, and he decided she had to pay. Then he worked to make it happen. With access to Beto's schedule—

the one the businessman didn't share with his wife—Owen had known the illicit couple would be here tonight, so he'd made his move.

"An email? Really?" Isa asked dryly when a memory flicked past of Owen drafting an email and then scheduling it to go to Beto's wife.

"What?" The question was an irritating whine heavily seasoned with malicious resentment. "She deserved to know who's in her bed. If she decides to take the asshole to the cleaners, that's just karma, right?"

That was not quite how it worked, but Isa wasn't up to having that discussion. Instead, she focused on what had happened after. She saw Owen on the second floor of the Den, waving a nearly empty glass toward the dance floor below as he whined to some faceless guy about how he'd been screwed over but had a plan to make that bitch pay. As he continued to expand on his revenge plan, his mysterious companion leaned in and offered him a helpful boost in the form of a pill. The unexpected offer had Isa trying to make out the man's indistinct features, but between the dizzying dance of the flashing lights and the swirling shadows, she got nothing.

"What is that?" she asked.

A flare of insecurity, edged with guilt, pierced the shade's bitterness but disappeared quickly under sly consideration. "It's just something to keep me level."

"Lie." With one word, she tore away his self-preserving pretense, exposing his brittle, battered vanity.

The echoes contorted in her grip, trying to evade the metaphoric mirror she held up, but no matter how Owen twisted, the unvarnished truth stared back. He finally relented on a pained sob. "Fine! I needed a boost so she wouldn't ignore me. He promised it would work, and it did."

The memories rushed forward, and Isa let them lap around her, watching as he rode the high of his magic. How he unapologetically lured the woman upstairs into one of the rooms Angel's VIP guests used to conduct private meetings while fantasies played out in his mind, each more profane than the last. How the woman spiraled deeper and deeper under his magic until she was nothing more than a breathing doll. Drunk on the unexpected power trip, Owen didn't notice when his magic turned on him, feeding his depraved hungers until they were all-encompassing. He didn't clue in when the woman shook off his unnatural thrall and started to fight back. She threw a spell, and the air around him thinned, choking him. He struck out, knocking her into a wall. The spell shattered, and blinded by fury, he attacked, both physically and magically. Unfortunately, whatever he was on interfered with his magic but didn't lessen the brutality of his fists.

"That's not me. I'm not like that."

Isa almost missed the horrified whisper. As the memories played out, she could see Owen trapped inside the monster wearing his face as he viciously continued his attack. Somehow, the woman managed to get to her feet long enough to use her magic to pick him up and slam him so hard into the drywall he left a body-sized dent in it and a crimson smear along the framing underneath. He hung there, pinned by her air magic, and she rushed for the door and got out while she could.

Owen writhed against her invisible hold as his innate power turned inward like a ravaging fire, searing away everything he knew. The pain was relentless, leaving no way to escape. It was everywhere, burning him, burning his mind and his world, and it hurt, hurt, *hurt*, then...

Nothing. Everything stopped for one breathless second.

Isa witnessed how Owen's decisions played out—how he'd chosen to put his needs first. How his callous disregard for the woman as a person had only deepened his depravity, how the ember of outrage smoldered until it caught fire in a blaze of retribution. In this in-between world where the Reaper reigned, a scale formed.

In what used to be Owen, realization dawned. "It's not my fault! I was out of my mind! It's her fault! If she hadn't used me—"

Tuning out the excuses, Isa snatched Owen's hastily stitched spirit and shoved it onto one side of the scale. Magic locked him in place. On the other side, his intentions and decisions piled up until the unevenly weighted side tipped and slammed down. Within the consciousness that used to be Isa, the firestorm of judgment twined into an unrelenting gale of merciless reprisal she couldn't stop. Not that she had any desire to even try. It swept through the remnants of Owen and seared away the soul stitching. His mouth yawned open in a soundless scream as the dark flames of the Reaper engulfed the shredding spirit, leaving nothing but ashes to drift into the ether.

chapter 12

Locke

LOCKE BRACED as dark tendrils slithered from Isa's feet and coiled around the tarp-wrapped body like some grisly phantom anaconda, carrying hints of ash and smoke. His magic, cautiously curious, settled in to watch her work. A chill entered the air. He could scent it under the other smell, like a storm on the horizon, and his skin prickled under the ghostly touch but remained warm. His attention shifted away from the body lying between him and the woman standing, still and distant, on the other side. The weirdly skeletal mask was back, complete with the unsettling ink slithering over her eyes, swallowing the hints of gold and brown.

Yep, the Reaper was back behind the wheel.

"Name." The demand was followed by a disjointed head tilt as her attention narrowed in on something he couldn't see. "What happened?"

Even though he knew better, he waited for the dead to talk, but there was only an eerie silence filled with writhing shadows. Then, in a disconcerting voice that was deeper and colder than anything he'd ever heard from Isa, she asked again, "What happened?"

Worried her impromptu interrogation would gain them

unwanted attention, he used his magic to etch a set of sigils on the metal wall behind him. The privacy ward flared to life, trapping sound and movement within the confines of the walk-in freezer.

"An email? Really?" she asked. The amount of disdain packed into those three words made him curious. So did her curt follow-up of "Lie."

He wasn't ready for the temperature to go from uncomfortably chilly to painfully icy in heartbeat or for those smoky shadows to shift into rough black chains as a ghostly, high-pitched scream rode the edge of his hearing.

Holy shit—Isa is pissed. Clearly, whatever the kid was saying was not going over well.

Locke's magic snapped its teeth, but he'd already heard it —the sound of footsteps, faint but coming closer. He left Isa to handle whatever the hell it was she was doing and slipped out of the walk-in unit, easing the door almost closed, ensuring Isa's magic didn't venture outside the confines of the walk-in.

With one ear on the approaching footsteps, he moved quickly through the kitchen, skimming the available supplies until he found what he needed. He grabbed an oversized container of pink salt, a small spool of twine, and a squat jar that held what looked like dried flowers then headed back to the freezer. Thanks to the privacy ward, he couldn't hear what was going down in the walk-in, but he hoped there was enough of Isa inside death's little helper to understand that time was not on their side.

With the footsteps drawing close, he quickly reinforced the twine with his magic then strung it just above the floor across the narrow gap of the not-quite-closed door. With a couple of creative sigils laid in salt then covered by a layer of dried flowers and a strand of Isa's hair that had been caught in his shirt button, his trap was set. Anyone—other than Isa—

coming through the freezer door would get an unwelcome surprise, and Isa wouldn't be caught off guard. It had to be enough. He shoved his lingering worry into a corner and settled in for the hunt.

As much as he wanted to meet the incoming threat head-on, that wasn't a viable option. Defense would be his best offense. There weren't many places to hide in the exposed space, but he needed only one. He slipped into the shadowy middle unit untouched by the glow of the kitchen lanterns. With his back to the wall just beside the opening, he worked a small, lethal blade from its sheath behind his belt buckle and let his magic off the leash. It curled around him, blending his presence with the surrounding shadows until Locke all but disappeared.

A creak of hinges was followed by a soft thump as the swinging door met the wall behind it. "I'm checking it now." Footsteps moved heavily into the kitchen then stopped. "It doesn't look like anyone's here." There was a pause then an irritated, "Yeah, yeah, I'm checking," followed by a muttered, "Asshole."

The man moved farther into the kitchen, and Locke waited patiently, letting his prey come to him. He didn't need the vibrations of the heavy tread that ran through the cement to track the other man's course, because his presence rode the air like an annoying insect. Anticipation zinged through Locke, but his breathing remained steady and his mind clear as he considered his choices. Locke could take the man out before he found Isa and alert whoever was on the other end of the conversation, or he could give the man something else to chase.

Going with option one, he began manipulating the air inside his walk-in freezer, thinning it just inside the door. He wrapped an air current around a discarded piece of cardboard, ready to use it to lure the bouncer inside. From his position,

Locke could make out the solidly built security guard as his shadow darkened the doorway.

The guard jerked to a stop, put a hand to his ear, and bit out, "What? When?" Whatever response squawked in his ear had him spinning on his heel and running back the way he'd come. "Yeah, I'm heading in now." The man hit the swinging door, sending it screeching in protest.

Locke released his magic and waited while the man's footsteps pounded away. The sense of impending danger retreated, and only when the air seemed to calm did Locke drop the concealment spell and head over to retrieve Isa. He disabled his earlier trap, pulled the door opened, and came face-to-face with Isa, who was staring toward where the bouncer had disappeared with a detached curiosity that was unsettling. That strange, flat absence of scent was back too.

"Who was that?" she asked, her voice low.

He managed not to flinch as the thin line of her normal hazel slowly replaced the unnatural black. That physical manifestation of her magic, along with her bland tone, set his metaphoric fur on end.

"Security."

She stepped out of the freezer. "Is that what they're calling it. Guess Angel's still cheaping out on the important things."

"Maybe, but something's up, so we need to get out of here." He grabbed her hand, tightening his hold when it remained lax, and started for the service stairwell. "Want to tell me who the kid was?"

"Beto's assistant."

As much as he appreciated her succinct answer, a little more detail would have been helpful, but now wasn't the time to press. Fortunately, there were no alarms on the emergency-access doors, probably because this top level was used mainly for storage, and anyone entering would have to get past the lower-level security first. He pushed through the door and got both of them out on the landing. Once Isa was clear, he closed the door softly then checked the stairs for movement and electronic eyes. When things remained quiet and blind, he tilted his head in an indication to move. Together, they headed down the stairs. They'd walked barely half a flight when a door above opened and angry voices drifted down.

"This is not my mess to clean up." The irritated voice bounced down the stairwell.

"He works for you, and you brought her here." Those familiar tones belonged to Angel.

Locke crowded Isa against the wall and put a finger to his lips in warning as his magic snapped into place. The rush of power settled over them like an invisible cloak, the air dampening their own sounds even as it allowed them to listen in on what was happening above. So long as they moved slowly and steadily, stayed away from the railing, and kept to the shadowed edges, they had a fighting chance of remaining unnoticed. He craned his head to risk checking where the men were. Sure enough, both were coming down the stairs at a steady pace, accompanied by a hard-faced bouncer.

"And you promised me discretion!" snapped the first, deeper voice that belonged to Beto.

"For fucking around, sure," Angel snapped back. "But this... this will be expensive."

The pair's footsteps rang hollowly through the stairwell. Locke nudged Isa ahead of him, timing their movements to those of Beto and Angel as his magic muted their steps and smudged their images. They just needed to make it past the second-floor door.

"What a surprise," Beto said flatly.

"You and I both know nothing worthwhile comes cheap, my friend."

Locke and Isa hit the second-floor landing and stayed toward the back wall.

"Fine, I'll foot the fuckin' bill." Beto's frustration eased back, replaced by what sounded like actual concern. "I need to get her out of here."

"Will she talk?" There was a hint of menace in Angel's question.

The footsteps above stopped abruptly. Locke grabbed for Isa, who was in mid-step, and yanked her back. She gave a soft, surprised gasp, but fortunately, it didn't travel far.

"Not your problem, Herrera."

"No, I can guarantee it won't be."

"Don't be a dick," Beto growled as a series of beeps sounded. "I don't know what got into the little shit, but she said he attacked her. It was clearly self-defense."

A door was pulled open. "That should be easy enough to verify."

"I'm going to want that recording," Beto said.

"I'm sure you are. Let's go see how your companion is doing." There was a pause, then Angel added, "After you."

There were the sounds of movement. Locke waited for the definitive clunk of the door closing. It didn't come. Isa went to move, but he pressed her harder against the wall and shook his head. Someone was above them. Listening.

"Dutch, you coming?" a voice called out.

After a heavy pause, a gruff "Yeah" came from directly above them. Finally, the door closed, and silence resettled in the stairwell.

Locke put his mouth near Isa's ear. "Haul ass, babe. We need to get out now."

She didn't need more prompting. They hustled down to the first floor.

He reached for the push bar on the door only to stop when Isa seized the back of his shirt and pressed against his back. "If we can get in without being spotted, head to your right. There should be a fire exit at the end of the hall by the restrooms. Don't forget the cameras."

He nodded and cracked the door open. The pounding swell of music rushed in. Locke's magic slipped through the opening, sniffing out the electric buzz indicating active surveillance. With skillful ease, he separated the competing scents of bodies, alcohol, and noise and locked on to the telltale hum of security cameras. His magic slid along the nerve-tingling scent and struck out, interrupting the digital feed so they wouldn't be spotted. He nudged Isa in front of him, opened the door just wide enough for her to squeeze through, then followed her into the flash of dizzying lights.

It took a second for his vision to adjust, but Isa had already grabbed his hand and started pulling him toward to the restrooms. He scanned the crowd and spotted one of the bouncers a few feet away, his back to them as he looked out over the crowded dance floor, one hand at his ear, clearly talking to someone.

Isa squeezed his hand hard in warning, and he saw another bouncer winding his way through the dancers, coming closer. Locke thickened the air, pulling the shadows around him and Isa, blurring their images until they were just another couple out to make the most of the limited privacy offered by the restrooms. He crowded Isa's back, blocking as much of her as he could from the bouncer's attention, but even as they kept moving, he could feel the man watching them hustle down the hall. He braced for the inevitable confrontation and was almost disappointed when it never materialized and the sense of being watched faded away.

Isa turned toward the women's restroom, using Locke to block her as she looked behind them. "We're clear."

"Go," he urged, nudging her farther down the hall, where the red glow of a fire exit taunted them.

They rushed forward, and Locke hastily etched a rune,

using the residual magic in his signet ring, and disarmed the alarm, clearing the way.

Thank the gods for shitty security.

They pushed through the door and onto a narrow walkway at the back of the building.

Isa grabbed his hand and looked to the left then to the right. "Come on, this way."

Figuring she knew where she was going, he followed even as he kept an eye on their back trail. He was a little concerned about the apparent lack of security. It seemed too easy to get out of a club that required secret code words, passing through illusions, and a mute, stone-faced bouncer to get in. He would have thought they'd be a little more invested in keeping unwanted attention at bay.

Am I missing something?

Unease crept over him, but no one popped out of the door or around a corner to stop them. They got to the end of the building, where a covered walkway led off to the left and into a lighted parking garage. Two flights down an open stairwell later, they were back on the main side of the mall. They skirted the outdoor lighting as much as possible as they made their way to his car. Only when they were inside his Charger and turning out of the mall parking lot did some of the tension riding his ass ease up.

"Well, that was fun."

"It was something." Isa watched the side mirror, proving he wasn't the only one who thought their escape was a little too easy.

He checked the rearview mirror. Darkness stared back. "If he puts a tail on us, we'll be able to clock them on the freeway."

"If that's the way he decides to play it." She toyed with the charm at her neck.

He considered how focused Angel had been on Isa, almost

to the point of ignoring the threat Locke presented. Someone with that kind of obsessiveness didn't like to lose. "Will he come after you?"

"Probably."

That wasn't reassuring. His fingers tightened on the steering wheel, and he fought back the possessive growl grumbling in his chest. "You're staying with me tonight."

"Um, no, I'm not."

"Yes, you are."

"No, I'm not," she shot back. "I've been playing this game with Angel for years. I'll be fine."

"Ever brought another man into his territory?"

Frustration fairly hummed in her stubborn silence.

Figuring his point had been made, he continued. "Either you come home with me, or I follow you home. Pick one. Because if that dick is stupid enough to come after you, he'll have to get through me."

He could literally feel her rolling her eyes as she said with exaggerated patience, "It's not like you can be with me twenty-four seven."

"Wanna bet?"

"Oh, come on, Locke. We both have lives, jobs, responsibilities—"

"You get what I do, right?" he asked, unrelenting. This was too important. *She* was too important.

"You go after prey and bring them back to your master." Her familiar derisive edge was back in full force.

He let her resentment of the Families roll off him because whatever her issues were, they would deal with them later. "I take care of threats before they become problems, and Angel is more than a problem."

"You can't go after him."

He caught the worry underneath her statement. "Can't I?"

Her lack of faith was easy to ignore, considering he knew his own strengths. Besides, one narcissistic asswipe would not be much of a challenge. Even if he was a magical leech.

"Oh my gods! Whatever. It's your funeral."

"Won't be mine, babe." He turned onto the exit to the freeway. "Now, your place or mine?"

She didn't answer right away, but he waited her out. Finally, she gave in. "Yours, but you'd better have clean sheets for your bed."

Content that she was coming back to his place, he drawled, "Why? You planning on sharing it with me?"

"Asshole," she muttered, and he tried not to grin.

Over an hour later, Locke pulled his Charger into his garage and hit the button to bring the door down behind him. Isa, asleep in the passenger seat, didn't stir. He released his seat belt and turned so he could study the woman next to him. Events from the last two days had obviously caught up with her. Ideally, whatever respite she found during the ride would help lighten the smudges under her eyes.

She shifted in her seat, and a lock of hair fell over her face. Her nose wrinkled, and her hand went to bat it away, but he was already there, drawing her hair back gently. As their hands met, her lashes rose, revealing a mesmerizing mix of green and gold that stared at him in sleepy confusion.

"Locke?"

"Hey, *reinita*, we're home," he said, matching her quiet tone. He trailed a finger along the side of her face and over her jaw.

She turned into his touch as awareness sparked deep in the drowsy gold, exposing a rare vulnerability normally hidden by mile-high walls. "Why *reinita*?"

Caught in his little queen's spell, there was no room for games, only truth. "Because it fits."

He wasn't expecting the flash of insecurity that wiped away her last vestiges of sleep. It didn't last long. Familiar emotional walls rose fast and hard even as she pulled back, lashes lowering as she started to fumble with her seat belt.

"What time is it?" she asked.

Going along with her ploy, he let her go. For now. "Just after two."

Her seat belt zipped back, and she reached for the door. "I'm going to need to pick up my car from Wonderland by eight."

Sighing, he got out and waited for her by the back door as she came around the hood. "Is there a curfew I need to know about?"

"What?" Isa played with the beaded bracelet on her wrist, her brow furrowed. "No, it's just that parking enforcement does their rounds at eight, and I don't need another parking ticket."

He disarmed the security ward, opened the door, and waved her inside. "After you."

He followed her into the laundry room, where the washer and dryer sat next to a deep sink on one side and a bench with cubbies on the other. A couple of lightweight jackets hung on the hooks above. She didn't go far and instead stopped in the middle, the glow of the floor-level recessed lighting pooling at her feet. He stepped around her and hit the main switch. The soft lights blinked off, replaced by the brighter illumination of canned lights above.

"Welcome to my never-ending DIY project."

"DIY project?" She peered out the door and down the shadowed hallway.

"Yeah." He moved into the hall, hitting light switches as he went. "I've been working on rehabbing this place."

"By yourself?" Her question was accompanied by the click of her bootheels on the wide planks.

"Except for where I need a second set of hands, yeah."

"Huh." She followed him into his most recently finished project, the kitchen. "Oh wow."

She gazed at the deep-blue cabinets topped by gray-veined quartz that ran down the left side and jutted into a short breakfast bar. Under more canned lights, the upper white cabinets and stainless-steel appliances gleamed.

He tossed his keys on the pub-style table to their right and headed to the refrigerator. "Did you want something to drink? Water? Tea? Coke?"

"Water works," she said as she ran a hand over the countertop. "This is beautiful, Locke."

"Thanks." He pulled a glass out of the cabinet. "Ice?"

"Please." She moved through the kitchen and into the great room.

"Light switch is to the right. Just watch where you step."

She flicked it on, revealing a large room stripped down to cement flooring, drywall, and framing. Incongruously, a deep-seated coppery-brown sofa sat off to one side, facing a flat-screen TV perched on a wood-topped worktable that served as a makeshift console table.

When the ice dispenser was finished, she asked, "How big is this place?"

He pulled the water pitcher out of the fridge and poured. "It's a two-bedroom, two-bath, just over seventeen hundred square feet. The main bath, my bedroom and bathroom, and the second bedroom that's currently holding all my tools are all down that hall."

"Wow," she repeated, stopping in front of a half-framed wall. "Are you putting in a fireplace?"

Locke poured a glass for himself. "A gas one."

"That'll be nice."

He brought over her water and handed it to her as she studied the two openings to the left. One was clearly a door. The other looked like it should hold a window, but it was looking into a room. "What is that?"

"When it's done? My office." He motioned to the mock window opening. "I'm trying to decide if I want to close that up."

Isa sipped her water as she took in the large windows covered by dark shutters on the far side of the office, visible through the opening. She turned back to the unfinished living room. "You'll lose some of the light in here."

She wasn't wrong. "Not if I replace the sliding patio door and that window with floor-to-ceiling glass doors."

She walked over to the patio doors, pulled back the cheap vinyl slats, and tried to peer out into the night-shrouded yard. "Are you backed up to a mountain?"

"One of the preserves, actually, so I don't have to worry about neighbors popping up in my backyard." One of the reasons he was so keen on this house. "When the sun's up, I'll show you the covered patio. You can almost believe we're not in a city."

She let the blinds fall back into place and shook her head. "I was so out of it. I don't even know where we are."

"Northern Scottsdale, just south of Cave Creek."

She looked over her shoulder and shot him a frown. "This isn't a flip for you, is it?"

It was a legit question. Real estate in the Valley continued to be a hot commodity, especially in this particular area. "No, it's not."

She studied him over the rim of her glass, and he wondered what she was thinking.

"This wasn't what I was picturing when you told me you were bringing me here," she said.

His constant curiosity with this woman had him sticking

with the conversation when there were more important topics to discuss. "Where did you think I lived?"

"Somewhere on the Cordova estate?" It came out as a question. "Or in one of the high-rise condos they own." She gave an uncomfortable shrug and looked away. "I figured you'd get a good deal on the rent, considering your job."

He watched her every move, noting—and liking—the hint of nerves she revealed. "If I wanted to go that route, I'm sure Emilio would be more than happy to cut me a deal. But I like my own space." Plus, it kept him close, not only to his job but to his parents' home in Scottsdale as well.

"If it's anything like your kitchen, it'll turn out really great." She wandered over to the hall that led to the other side of the house and flicked on the lights.

He wondered at the hint of melancholy running under her sincere statement. "I hope so." It was late, and she wanted to be at her car at the ass crack of dawn, so they needed to talk. "Isa."

She stopped and looked back.

"We need to figure out what the hell went down tonight."

She grimaced. "I know."

He moved to her, his voice softening. "Either we can talk in the kitchen, or if you'd rather change into something more comfortable, I can get a T-shirt and shorts for you, then we can talk."

"Can I grab a shower? I won't be long, and I can just use that bathroom." She motioned to the main bath.

Unable to resist, he let his fingers drift down her exposed spine before settling at the small of her back, then he gently nudged her toward his bedroom. "I'm in the middle of retiling the tub surround, so it's out of commission. Use mine."

She moved down the hall in front of him. "Never mind. I can take one in the morning."

"No, go ahead." He got them into his bedroom and hit the lights. "I'll get you set up, get my shit, and leave you to it."

He moved past her and into the bathroom, where his walk-in closet was. He tossed his sleep pants and a T-shirt over his shoulder before gathering a pair of basketball shorts, an old concert tee, and a clean towel. Back in the room, he found her sitting on the end of his bed.

Locke stopped in front of her and handed over the borrowed clothes. "I'll meet you in the living room, okay?"

She watched him with a mix of exhaustion and wariness as she took the towel and clothes from him. "Okay."

Standing over her with mere inches separating them, he was struck full force by the implication of their positions. He didn't stand a chance in hell of keeping his body from reacting. With a formidable effort, he took a step back.

"Right. Good. See you in a few," he muttered before hauling ass away from the temptation she presented.

chapter 13

Isa

ISA TUGGED on the T-shirt Locke had given her and pulled her wet hair free. She was twisting it up when the woodsy scent of Locke's shampoo teased her nose. With no one around to witness her weakness, she brought the wet strands up, closed her eyes, and took a deep hit of the comforting scent. It curled in her chest, nudging out the frigid residue of death that the hot shower hadn't been able to touch.

Freed at last, the emotions she'd held at bay all night charged forward, threatening to swallow her whole. Seeing Angel again had reopened old scars, allowing his poison to once again seep into her veins. Tainted memories roused the ugly fears and self-doubts she had never been able to conquer, shredding her clarity and leaving her confidence shaken, but wrapped in Locke's scent and clothes, she found a tentative foothold and held tight to the reminder that she'd survived.

He won't let you go a second time.

She didn't bother to argue with the experienced voice of logic. There was no point. The fact was irrefutable—Angel would come for her. It was just a question of when. And knowing just how much he enjoyed his games and got off on her pain, he would do it when she least expected it, and it would result in hurting someone she loved.

Like Locke.

Her world rocked under the quiet declaration.

No. She didn't love Locke.

But you could.

She stared unseeingly at the half-fogged mirror, curiously numb. Her hands moved by rote, clipping her hair in place, as her mind and her emotions battled it out. She couldn't be falling for the infuriating man. She knew better. He was always on her ass because nothing she did measured up to whatever impossible expectations he had. And why in the hell did he even think he was entitled to have any expectations when it came to her?

She didn't answer to him. Hell, she chose a long time ago not to answer to anyone, especially not to a Family-made man. And Locke Turon would always belong to the Cordova Family. It was an inherent truth of the nature of Hounds. Loyalty, once given, was hard to break. That depth of commitment, she knew better than anyone, could leave you bloodied and broken if you landed on the wrong side—which she would because following someone blindly was not in her character.

It was just the attraction that raged between them that was messing with her head, driving her to challenge him, to see how far she could push before he snapped. Unfortunately, he got off on her defiance, acting as if it was something to be admired, not cursed. Even worse, it was doing a hell of a number on that stupid unloved girl that she tried so hard to bury, tempting her with some silly hope that she could change his perception of her, become something important to him.

"Why *reinita*?"

"Because it fits."

Does he really believe that, or was it just a line?

She ignored that last, knee-jerk thought. Locke didn't need lines. Hell, he just had to touch her, and she could create a world of excuses to fall into bed with him. It was hard to keep him at arm's length, but she was determined. Hence, her continual verbal swipes. And yes, she could admit her bitchy attitude served a dual purpose. Not only did it keep them out of bed, but no man would put up with shit like that for long. Eventually, he'd give up and walk away just like everyone else.

As rational as those arguments were, she couldn't ignore the visceral hunger to claim Locke as hers and have him regard her as his—to have one person who saw all of her, from the fragile, barely hanging-on shards to the jagged scars reshaped by darkness. She knew she was an emotional nightmare most men would shy away from, but at Locke's core was a relentless resolve—a critical necessity for whoever chose to stand beside someone like her.

But it had to be his choice, not her risking everything to ask it of him. The phantom dream of having him as a partner drifted just out of reach, tempting her to give him the slightest opening, knowing he'd sweep in and take it. He was all about besting challenges, and when he looked at her, she had no doubt that was exactly what he saw—a challenge.

She wanted to be something more, something cherished, especially by him. It was why she played with fire, never quite slamming the door of chance closed. If he managed to get through and claim his prize, would he even understand what she was offering, or would he see only the darkness that stared back?

It's not like he's all light and rainbows.

But she and death—they were interchangeable, a truth not a lot of people could handle. Maybe not even someone like Locke. There were risks to being a Reaper. Each time she and death danced, it took longer to discard the Reaper's mantle and reclaim Isa. How long would Locke be willing to deal with that? There could come a day when Isa put on the cloak and forgot to take it off—or even worse, chose not to remove it.

He wouldn't let you go.

It was a lovely thought. Too damn bad she couldn't trust it, because she knew damn well everyone walked away eventually. Maybe not Cass and Des—not yet—but that was because she refused to let them go. Everyone else, though? Her father, her stepmom, and her extended family were all quick to believe Angel's lies. They had barely blinked at his twisted version of events and had all but abandoned her, leaving her alone to pick up the shattered pieces he'd created.

And speaking of Angel...

If he learned that Locke meant anything to her, he'd go balls to the wall to use Locke against her. She could admit, at least in the privacy of her own mind, that if that happened, Angel's chances of getting his claws into her would skyrocket. And as inconvenient as it was, on some level, she considered Locke hers.

But it wasn't just Angel she worried about—there was the Cordova Family, who held more sway with Locke than she ever could. They had money, power, influence, and Locke's loyalty. All she had to offer was... well, just her.

It could be enough.

But it won't be. Family first, chiquita.

Sounding a lot like Angel, that second voice had been quiet for so long she'd almost forgotten it existed. But thanks to Angel's reemergence, it was back, mocking mercilessly as it tore through old scabs and straight to the heart of her worry.

It all came down to trust. Could she trust Locke to stay and not betray her, even to his Family?

Among the powerful and monied Families, the skills of a Hound and a Reaper were in high demand. Who couldn't use a Hound who never lost a scent and could track down anyone or anything? And gaining access to a Reaper who could reach beyond death for damnable secrets... The image of greedy-faced people rubbing their hands together in glee flashed through her mind. It might be paranoia, but she was well aware of how far Families would go to keep someone like her on tap. She'd witnessed horrific deals that swallowed unique magics into unfathomable corporations and left behind broken lives, all to feed someone else's greed. It was a reality she fought against constantly, not just for herself but for Cass and Des too. It was why Wonderland existed. Someone had to step in and help those who couldn't stand alone. And if she allowed Locke to be part of her life, how long would it be before the Cordovas pressured him for access to her or her small family?

How long before Locke starts to bend and so do I?

If she let herself fall all the way with Locke, she knew with sickening certainty she would rationalize the risk of bending, even knowing it would break her beyond recognition.

A knock at the door and Locke's voice snapped her out of her dismal spiral. "Isa, you good?"

"Yeah, I'll be out in a minute."

She stared at her reflection, searching for answers, the caustic mix of unresolved emotions leaving her raw and on edge. It might be too late for her heart, but no one else needed to know that. With as much painstakingly care as someone handling a live grenade, she tucked away the messy truths to deal with later. For the moment, she needed answers from Locke because the more she knew, the better equipped she'd be to ward off Angel's manipulations.

"So, no chance that it was Leo who handed Owen the pill?" Locke watched her, his hands behind his head as he stretched out his legs and crossed them at the ankles on the far end of the sofa. His well-worn shirt rode up just enough to flash an intriguing glimpse of flat abs.

"No." Curled up in the opposite corner, Isa kept her attention on the borrowed T-shirt she fiddled with. "The face wasn't clear, but it was someone older than Isaiah. Honestly, the way the whole deal played out, I'd say it was one of Angel's crew."

"Because...?"

Sighing, she gave him a look before pointing out the obvious. "Because Angel wouldn't let anyone else deal on his territory."

"Yeah, I could see that." He scrubbed a hand over his face, his exasperation coming through loud and clear. "Why in the hell did that kid take something from someone he didn't know?"

It was a good question. Too damn bad there was no good answer. "I don't know, but considering how things went down, I feel pretty confident saying it was the same drug Leo took." When Locke remained quiet, she decided it was time to push. She studied him. "What are you really chasing, Locke? Isaiah or this drug?"

For a long moment, he stared at his feet, his hands laced over his flat stomach. Finally, he asked, "Does it matter?"

Her stomach knotted because she knew this was a test she couldn't afford for him to fail. "Yes."

Without lifting his head from the cushion, he turned to her, his gaze drifting over her face, his thoughts veiled behind a remote mask, but something burned deep in those eerily light eyes. "Why?"

She held that uncomfortable gaze with a hard practicality, refusing to allow even a shimmer of her emotions to surface. "Because I need to know where your priorities lie and what they're going to cost me."

There was a shift behind his mask, something she couldn't quite catch, and she waited for the inevitable claim that there was no price to be paid. Instead, he surprised her with a truth. "Finding Isaiah is the priority right now."

Her mind spun with his admission, and she finally started thinking. The last couple of days, she'd been twisted up in her worry about Angel and hadn't taken a breath to examine the pieces and put them into a larger picture. Even worse, she'd followed Locke's lead blindly instead of asking more pointed questions, specifically about the unknown drug.

She set aside her concerns with Angel and focused on what she knew. The only reason a Family would use a Hound of Locke's caliber on a runaway teenager was because that runaway was a threat to them. And what could threaten a power player? Secrets. Like, say, the existence of an unknown, lethal drug designed to unleash magic in nonmagic users or boost the existing power in a mage. She could imagine a hundred different ways a powerful Family would benefit from such a thing, especially if they held complete control over its existence. And if someone else controlled it, they'd stop at nothing to change that.

"You think Isaiah can lead you to whoever is dealing the drug that killed Leo and Owen." It wasn't a question, so she wasn't surprised when Locke remained silent. More pieces fell into place, creating a twisted picture she prayed was wrong. "This drug—where did it come from?"

If Locke was working to cover up some kind of Family scheme, it would make her decision about trusting him a no-brainer—though, granted, it would be painful as hell.

This time, his pause was longer, but he didn't look away. "You understand that there are things I can't share with you."

Her heart dropped at his nonanswer. "Can't or won't?"

"Can't." He dropped his feet and pushed up to a seated position, his arms braced on his knees as he kept his attention on her. "Not because I don't trust you but because there are some situations where I don't have a choice."

"You always have a choice, Locke, but I get it. Family comes first." She couldn't keep the bitter bite out of her tone. "And I'm definitely not Family." He was making that abundantly clear.

He dragged his hands through his hair and snapped, "That's not what I said."

"Isn't it?" Something tight was wrapped around her chest, squeezing it painfully. Feeling inexplicably betrayed, she shoved off the couch and watched Locke do the same. "I asked you a question, but you dancing around the answer is an answer in itself. Somehow, someway, the Cordovas are mixed up with this drug. Either they created it, or they want to own it, but either way, they have their own agenda. One you'll make sure happens."

A muscle jumped in his jaw. "Gods dammit, Isa. Is that what you think of me? That I would—what? Blindly follow orders or something?"

"I think if it comes down to a question of Family priorities, the Family wins." She knew she should let this go—that what was growing between them was too new for such demands—but she couldn't seem to stop pushing him. "You want to protect your precious Family? Fine, but don't ask me to do the same."

"Oh, trust me, I'd never make that mistake," he shot back, his verbal knife finding its mark.

She winced.

Instantly, some of his anger faded and remorse moved in. "Dammit, Isa, that's not—" He shook his head. "Look, I don't know which Family fucked you over and why, but the Cordovas aren't like that. They're trying to stop this thing."

Clearly, he believed that. Too bad she didn't, which meant she had to see this through, not only for her own peace of mind but also to make sure the Cordovas didn't screw over Locke or, eventually, her.

"All Families are like that," she said, resigned. "It doesn't matter how big or how small they are. If they see a threat to the status quo, they'll eliminate it."

Hell, it was true for her own small family of Des and Cass. If anyone threatened them, Isa wouldn't hesitate to take them out. *Can I really stand in judgment of Locke for feeling the same?* Since the answer to that was an uncomfortable no, she decided to guide them back to safer waters. "It doesn't matter where it came from. What's important is that it's out there and it needs to be stopped. Can we agree on that?"

For a moment, it looked as if Locke was going to push the issue, but whatever he saw in her face had him changing his mind. "Yeah, we can agree on that."

"Okay," she said, strangely relieved and little bit sad. "We know Angel's involved somehow, since it's being dealt at his club."

"We need to figure out how he got a hold of it."

"That won't be easy." She sank back down onto the couch. "He's got connections everywhere."

"We can start with Beto and Healy."

She looked at him. "I'm not sure either man would just willingly meet with you and answer your questions."

He headed over to the breakfast bar. "Maybe not me, but I'm sure they'd make time to meet with the Cordova Family representative." He grabbed his phone and started to type.

A little concerned, she asked, "Who are you texting?"

"Zev." He finished up his message and set the phone back down on the counter. "After we pick up your car, I'll need to fill him in on what went down tonight."

She knew who he was talking about. The tall, dark, intimidating Hunter had been in Wonderland with his girlfriend, Rory Costas, more than once. "Why?"

He leaned back against the bar's edge and folded his arms. "Because he's been working the drug angle while I've been focused on tracking Isaiah. Now that we know for sure the two are connected, we need to combine our efforts." He studied her. "What's on your schedule for tomorrow?"

"Kelly's meeting with River at eleven. Des and I promised we'd be there. After that, I need to deal with an inventory order that's coming in at one, and payroll is due by three." It didn't take a genius to follow Locke's thoughts. "I'll be fine. Des will be with me, and Angel avoids Wonderland."

"Why?"

Amusement bubbled up. "Because last time he set foot inside, Des sicced a poltergeist on him, so Angel believes the place is cursed."

"Cursed?" he asked with a raised eyebrow. "Seriously?"

She gave a shrug. "He's a superstitious son of a bitch. Plus, it took months for Angel to get rid of the spook, and it cost him quite a few business deals, since he couldn't seem to get through a meeting without shit happening." Des was nothing if not inventive when it came to retribution. "Ever since, he steers clear of the bar."

Locke's frown indicated he wasn't as sold on the idea that Angel would stay away simply because of a haunting. "Can you get Des to stay with you until I'm done meeting Zev?"

"No." She didn't need a babysitter. "I'm not dragging his ass out of bed after he worked closing for me. Besides, it's only a couple of hours. I'll be fine."

"Isa—"

"No, Locke," she repeated, firmer this time. "You can drop me off then go meet up with Zev."

Still unconvinced, he tried again. "That won't take long. I can make it a phone call."

She was already shaking her head. "Stop. You go do your thing and let me do mine." As much as she appreciated his protective streak, she was torn between exasperation and amusement. "Do your meet with Zev. Chances are I'll be picking up Kelly to take her to River's office by the time you finish up. Since you obviously can't come to that meeting, we should just plan on meeting at Wonderland afterward, and you can spend an exciting afternoon watching me do paperwork."

He continued to look at her with a deep frown. His obvious concern softened her misgivings, and she found she was tired of holding the line. Hell, she was just tired period. Knowing they could continue this argument until the sun came up, she decided to do the unexpected. She got up, crossed over to stand in front of him, and placed her hands over his crossed forearms.

With a gentle squeeze, she repeated softly. "I will be fine."

His moody gaze drifted over her face, but he finally, reluctantly gave in. "Fine, but you'll text me when you leave your place and when you get to River's office, then—"

Without even thinking it through, she leaned down and stopped his words with a kiss. When she pulled back, they were both breathing a little heavier. She stared into the hot, electric blue eyes, unable to escape the swirling mix of heat and hunger that promised all sorts of temptations.

The urge to give in was strong, but somehow, she managed to shuffle back from the edge. "I'll be fine, but thank you."

He uncrossed his arms, dislodging her hold as his hands went to her hips and held her in place. "You'll be careful."

It was almost enough for her to believe she mattered to him. "I will." And she would. It just might not be enough.

chapter 14

Locke

THE NEXT MORNING, Locke pulled into Wonderland and parked next to Isa's modest four-door sedan. "Looks like we beat the ticket."

"Nice." Isa undid her seat belt and let it zip back. "Thanks for the ride." With her phone in hand, she reached for the door but turned back when he shut down the car and opened his door. "What are you doing, Locke?"

"Coming with you."

Her sigh was exasperated as she shoved open the passenger door. "I told you—"

"I heard you, Isa. But I'm still walking you inside." He got out and shut the door behind him then waited for her.

She came around the Dodge's hood and headed straight for Wonderland's entrance, leaving him to follow. His lips twitched as she all but stomped her way across the cracked asphalt lot and slapped the security ward. He didn't care if his presence pissed her off. It made him feel better. The previous night, Angel had been too focused, too intent on Isa, and that didn't sit well with Locke. Especially after how simple it had seemed to drive away from the Den. He'd worked with

Hunters like Zev for too long not to understand how predators lulled their prey into a false sense of security before attacking. And when it came to Isa, Angel was definitely playing the part of a predator.

Isa yanked open the door and slipped inside. He caught it before it closed and followed her down the stairs and into the main area. She stomped over to the bar, set her phone down hard, and then turned, her hands going to her hips as she faced him.

"You walked me in. I'm fine. Now go."

Ignoring her bad-tempered demands, Locke closed in and set his hands on either side of her, trapping her against the bar.

Stubborn to the end, she tilted her head back and narrowed her eyes as she glared at him in feminine affront. "Locke…" His name came out like a warning.

He ignored it, dipping his head down as she tried to lean back. With the bar behind her, she didn't get far. He stopped with only a few inches between them and was gratified when color rose under her skin and her lips parted.

"Text me," he said.

Those long lashes drifted down then up, dark amber swirling with emotions he really wanted to explore.

A door hit a wall.

Isa jumped and turned her head, the move causing her loose hair to brush against Locke's jaw. Locke didn't move away as the silky strands caught on his stubble. He simply shifted his gaze from her flushed face to the amused man walking in from the back, an empty coffee mug dangling from his hand.

"Morning, Des."

The other man gave him a grunt of acknowledgment before turning to Isa. "Thanks for letting me know you were alive." Sarcasm was alive and well in his voice.

"Shit, sorry," she said with a wince. "Did you stay here last night?"

"Yeah. Used the couch in the office." Des turned Locke. "I'm guessing, from your presence, Angel's going to push his luck."

"No."

"Yes," Locke said at the same time.

Her head whipped around so fast he barely avoided getting clocked. "No, he won't," she enunciated, glaring at him.

"Yes, he will," he shot back, frustration rising at her stubborn refusal to see the threat. "Which is why you promised to be careful."

Her hands went to his chest, and she shoved, trying to force him back. "And I will be."

He didn't move. "Yes, you will."

"What happened?" Des stood at the complicated-looking coffee machine, which was quietly whirring away.

Isa shot Locke a wary look.

He eased back, resigned. "Go ahead and catch him up."

Her eyebrows rose. "Really?"

"Like you wouldn't spill it all the minute I'm gone."

A glint of humor peeked through, and her lips curved up. "Well, yeah."

He shook his head. "Text me when you're back here, okay?" Ignoring her rolling eyes, he turned to Des. "Angel's jonesing for her, so don't give him an opening."

"I'm right here," Isa muttered as she went through the pass to join Des. "And I can take care of myself." She grabbed the empty mug from Des, pulled the carafe out, and started to pour. "And I told you, I'll be busy most of the day."

Des took the creamer from a small chiller and handed it to her. He turned to Locke as she finished doctoring her coffee.

"For what it's worth, Angel tends to avoid this place like the plague."

"So I heard," Locke said. "But shit went down, and I don't trust him."

"Yeah, neither do I," the other man agreed. "I've got her covered this morning."

"I heard." Locke looked at Isa, who sipped her coffee. "I'll be back after I finish up with Zev."

"Don't rush on my account," she drawled.

It was all he could do not to round the pass and kiss that arrogant smirk off her face. Instead, he gave Des a nod, turned on his heel, and reluctantly left Isa behind.

Twenty minutes later, Locke was sitting at a kitchen island in a downtown condo, enjoying his own cup of joe.

Zev closed the dishwasher and then dried his hands. "Rory got Montenegro to agree to meet at Haven's Corner in an hour."

Rory Costas, Zev's girlfriend, was sitting on the couch to Locke's left, her foot braced against the low coffee table as she laced up her boot. Locke raised his cup to her.

"Thanks," Locke said.

"Not a problem," the dark-haired woman replied, tying off the laces then tugging down the leg of her equally dark slacks. "Though, got to say, he didn't strike me as the underground-club type."

"Me either," Locke said as she wove around a couple of unpacked boxes. "I'm thinking that was more the side piece's decision than his."

Rory grimaced as she joined them. "Beto being a dick—that is something I can totally believe." She set a hand on Zev's back then reached around to grab the to-go cup he'd brought her, sliding him a telling look. "Maybe someone should tell his wife about his after-hours entertainment."

"Could we maybe not piss off every-fucking-one in the Valley, babe?" Zev drawled.

"I don't know. It's been—what, a month without anyone gunning for us?" she said with a small smirk. "I'm starting to get bored."

"Maybe we should warn Mari she's about to put in some serious overtime," Locke suggested.

With how often the independent Transporter got into hot water, a heads-up to Mari would make sense. Not that she would mind. She got off on all that legal stuff, which was why her main client was the Cordova Family. Until Locke met Rory, he'd never realized how dangerous transporting magical items could be. Then again, for Rory, danger was par for the course.

"I heard her thanking Rory the other day for her contribution to her shoe fund," Zev told Locke with mock seriousness.

"She actually picked up a new pair yesterday." Unusually enthusiastic, Rory set her mug down, took out her phone, thumbed the screen, then turned it around to share a picture. The screen showed a pair of black sky-high heels with bloodred soles and a line of silver crawling up the needle-thin stilettos.

Locke leaned in, looking closer. "Are those daggers on the heels?"

"Yep." Rory pulled her phone back, enlarged the picture, and turned it back around. "And check out the cool-ass black lace pattern."

Now that Rory mentioned it, he had to agree—they were definitely cool as shit. He sat back and teased, "Never thought you were the heel type."

"I like them as much as the next woman," she said, setting

her phone down on the counter. "I just wouldn't pay four figures for them."

That he could believe. When Rory and Zev first met, she had been working under the aegis of the Western Arcane Guild, a kind of magical mercenary storefront. And everyone knew the Guild took a hefty cut of earned fees. After her role in retrieving Emilio's nephew, she turned fully independent, hoping to minimize that cut. Then she caught the attention of the Arcane Council, in part because of her connection to the legendary Sabella Rossi-Giordano, a matriarch of one the original Arcane Families. As Sabella's niece, she carried a sort of curiosity cachet, but her bigger draw to the Council was her Prism ability. Being able to negate magical attacks made Rory a magical unicorn with one of the most powerful entities in society. The Arcane Council was keen to acquire her talent and then lock that shit down. Unfortunately, that kind of focus left Rory facing a higher-than-normal amount of danger. In an effort to keep breathing, the intrepid Transporter had turned down the Council's recent contractual offer, hoping to sidestep the attached exclusivity clause in favor of cultivating her own resources. Zev and Rory were still braced for the potential fallout that came with rejecting the Council.

"Hey, been meaning to ask, how's business?" Locke asked.

"Better than I thought, actually," Rory said.

"Yeah?"

She nodded. "At first, I was worried I'd shot myself in the foot by turning down the Council's backing, but demand is starting to pick up. I even snagged a couple of contracts out of Vegas and California, which means longer runs for me, but the money's good."

"And the Council? Are they pulling any shit?"

"Not yet," she said blandly, though her eyes betrayed a flash of unease. "They've actually reached out with a couple of routine jobs, which went fairly smoothly. For now, I'm taking their requests on a case-by-case basis."

"Smart."

"I try to be. Speaking of..." She turned to Zev and covered his hand on the counter. "I know I said it earlier, but it bears repeating—be careful with Beto. I get the impression he really likes his position as Mr. Moneybags for the Filthy Rich, and so long as he swings clear of any troubling implications, he won't be in any hurry to cut himself loose."

Zev reversed his grip and brought Rory's hand up so he could brush a kiss over her knuckles. "We just want to tug on a few lines and see what rises to the top. I'll be fine. Promise."

Hearing Zev echo Isa's favorite refrain reignited Locke's irritation. Maybe it was due to lack of sleep or simply the fact that Locke was still stewing over their early-morning conversations, but either way, he couldn't suppress an annoyed snort.

Rory shot him a look. "Anything happens to him, it's your ass, Turon."

He lifted his hands from his cup and held them, palms up, in mock surrender. "Like Zev said, we're just going to ask him a couple of questions." He reclaimed his cup. "Besides, Maeve doesn't like shit going down at her place."

The Transporter frowned. "You know, I could always ask around, see what I can find out about this Angel guy. Might be safer than getting into it with Beto."

"No!" The denial erupted in stereo.

She rolled her eyes. "Chill. Jeez, you two. Fine."

Disgruntled, Locke looked at Zev. "You told her?"

"You wanted a meet with Montenegro," the other man said, clearly unrepentant. "She could get us one but wanted to know why, so I told her about your run-in at the club."

"The guy sounds like a douche," Rory added.

"Oh, he's definitely a douche. He's got a hard-on for Isa, but it's not like she takes it seriously." Locke caught Rory's repeat of Isa's name and Zev's responding nod but ignored both as his resentment and frustration boiled over. "I swear to all that's holy and unholy, for a smart woman, she's being pretty fucking stupid, thinking I'm going to—what? Just leave her curvy ass out there so that dick can tag it? As if that was a fucking option."

"And yet you're here and she's... where?" Zev's voice was carefully neutral as he let go of Rory.

"Back at the damn bar with Des. Telling me she'll be *fine*," Locke snarled—he was coming to hate that word—"when I know damn well she's just waiting for me to walk away."

"And will you?" Rory asked, her dark eyes on him, deadly serious, as she stood next to Zev.

Something in her face had him checking his temper. "No, but getting her to believe that is next to impossible."

Rory's lips twitched. "Of course it is," she said with a whisper of amusement.

He narrowed his eyes. "What?"

She continued to study him, the hard edges fading. Finally, she shook her head. "Nothing, just putting some pieces together."

"Rory," he said through gritted teeth.

"Locke," she shot back in the same aggrieved tone before sighing. "Look, seriously, it's really nothing. Though I have to admit I'm super surprised Wonderland is mixed up in this at all. I mean, Cass is all about staying out of shit." Rory grimaced. "Correction—she'll stay out of shit, but she won't hesitate to stir it up."

"Cass is in Vegas, dealing with a family thing, and Grayson's with her," Locke told her, not wanting to get into the death of Cass's grandmother. "And Wonderland is not mixed up in this." If that rumor got off the ground, Isa would never forgive him. "I needed insight into the club scene, and

Isa could provide it. That should have been the end of the story."

"But...?" Rory prompted.

"But she refused to back off, and now she's back in that narcissistic asshole's crosshairs." *And it's my fault, gods dammit.* Unexpected guilt socked him in the gut, leaving him winded. It didn't matter that Isa wouldn't have stopped digging into Leo's death. Locke could have made her, right? He muttered a curse and rubbed a hand over his face.

"I know that look," Zev said.

Locke dropped his hands to look to his friend. "What look?"

Zev motioned to his face. "That one." He folded his arms as he leaned a hip against the counter. "I don't know Isa well, but she doesn't strike me as the shrinking-violet type."

Rory's snort had Locke switching his glare to her. "What?" he snapped.

She pressed her lips together and shook her head, amusement dancing in her eyes. "Nothing." When he continued to glare at her, she added, "Honestly, I didn't say a word, Locke."

"Your face did."

Emotions washed through Rory's eyes, too fast to follow. She looked at Zev, brows raised. He tilted his head and shook it.

The entire silent conversation took a matter of moments, then she turned back to Locke. "All right, I'm going to be brutally honest here because I like Isa and I like you, but I know you and can only guess about her."

He did not like where this was headed.

"I don't know her history, but chances are she grew up like I did—no family, no real support, only herself to rely on. Which means trust and loyalty are not given—they're earned, and not easily. My guess is only Cass and Des have managed to win that prize, but everyone else?" Rory shook her head.

"They have to prove themselves. Prove that they won't eventually turn and stab her in the back."

He really didn't like how uncomfortable this made him feel. "I'm not going to fuck her over."

"No, not intentionally," Rory said. "But can you admit you might?"

Isa's words from the previous night settled like a stone in his gut: "I think if it comes down to a question of Family priorities, the Family wins."

Didn't I already choose Family needs over hers when I pushed her to use her magic to question Leo, and again when I took her to the Den?

Rory kept going, mercilessly driving her point home. "I've met your parents. They adore you, and for the most part, you've always known who you were and what your place was. Which is why when you commit to someone or something, your loyalty is incorruptible. That's a hell of a thing, and for someone like me or Isa, it'll never happen. At least, that's what we believe. We've grown up being told we're less than, that no one values us because we have nothing of value to offer. Or that our only value is what we can give someone else. That constant doubt, it's corrosive, and when someone finally dares to tell us we are worth the risk, it scares the shit out of us because if we let them in, all it will take is one perceived rejection or betrayal to destroy what we managed to salvage. So when someone like you, who enjoys the chase, decides to run us down, as thrilling as it is initially, the reality is we're all about self-protection, which means we'll fight tooth and nail to keep you out."

Aching and angry at himself and the whole fucked-up situation, he snapped, "So I should just walk away? Wouldn't that just reinforce all the twisted shit she believes?"

"Is that really an option?" Zev asked.

"No." Locke didn't even have to think about it.

"Okay, then," Rory said. "So, say she lets you catch her. What happens next?"

"I don't know, but I want a chance to find out."

"She might not give it to you."

"Then I'll have to earn it."

"I hope you get that chance."

So did he. "I'm not sure I like you right now, Rory."

"That's okay. I still like you." On the counter, her phone vibrated. She picked it up and checked the screen. "Shit, I've got to go." She turned to Zev, gave him a quick kiss, then told him she'd text him later. She gave Locke a finger wave, then she was running out the door.

In the quiet that followed her exit, Zev asked, "Want some advice from someone who's been there?"

Emotions churning, Locke managed a short nod.

"Be patient," Zev said.

Locke waited a beat. "That's it? That's all you've got?"

Zev shrugged. "You want her to let you in, so you need to show her you're willing to do the work to be there. That you see her as an equal, not someone to fix or save. And heads up, it'll be a lot of work."

Of that Locke had no doubt. "But it will be worth it."

"Definitely," Zev said.

Locke settled into a chair across from Zev at a table in Haven's Corner. The small, witchy café was nestled in a strip mall up in the Camelback Corridor. From her stool behind the counter, Maeve, the owner, was armed with her ever-present knitting needles as she kept a benevolent eye on the customers. Her current project was an eye-searing collection of greens and yellows.

"Who suggested meeting here?" Locke broke off a piece of crumbly scone and popped it into his mouth.

"Me." Zev's gaze roamed over the midmorning patrons. "It's not his normal scene, so less of a chance of running into anyone he knows."

"It's also not exactly the best place to discuss business, and I'm assuming that's how Rory got him to agree to this meet."

"She may have mentioned that Emilio was considering expanding his portfolio."

Locke's brows raised. "And he believed that?" Construction projects weren't a Cordova Family interest—never had been.

"Never underestimate the self-deluding power of greed." Zev eyed Locke over the rim of his cup as he sipped his coffee. "He's not going to be happy you're here."

Locke leaned back in his chair, unconcerned. "If he recognizes me."

"You think he won't?"

"I think we have a fifty-fifty shot. He was pretty worked up when he confronted Angel."

"Speaking of..." Zev settled back in his seat. "How dirty do you think this Angel is?"

"Fucking filthy. From what Isa shared about how he came up, it's no surprise he's got his hands in this mess."

"You mentioned trafficking and drugs." When Locke nodded, Zev said, "Those two interests tend to land high on the authorities' radar."

"Not if your 'talent agency'"—Locke formed air quotes around the last two words—"is part of a larger enterprise fronting a criminal syndicate. And given that Angel's a Harvester, it's not hard to believe he's got his fangs in quite a few key people."

Zev studied him. "I had Roxy start running information on Angel or any known members of the Idyl Devils."

Tension zipped through Locke. "And...?"

"And it's slow going. Those that aren't dead or in jail have buried their identities deep." Zev drummed his fingers on the table. "And whoever Angel used to cover his tracks did a thorough job, because Roxy's still untangling the knots."

"Nothing that connects him to the Forge Foundation?"

Zev shook his head.

Locke wasn't surprised. Nothing could ever be that easy. "Well, if Montenegro doesn't give us anything, we need to hit up Janek Healy."

Zev's attention sharpened. "Healy? From Signature Enterprises?"

"Yeah, he was there last night too." Locke rubbed the back of his neck. "I thought I told you that."

"You didn't."

Locke winced. "Shit, sorry." There was something in Zev's expression that had him asking, "What?"

Zev gave a half shake of his head. "Maybe nothing, maybe something." He took out his phone and sent off a text as he kept talking. "It's just that the Thatchers were angel investors with Healy's Signature Enterprises."

"Are you serious?" A sharp sense of anticipation woke, as if Locke had caught the faintest hint of a revealing scent.

Zev nodded as he set his phone aside. "They weren't the only ones, but..."

"But it's a link." Dubious as all hell, but it was something.

Back at the start of this mess, two rival Family companies, LanTech and Origin, were chasing the formula Emilio's sister-in-law had created, the same one that would become the Delphi serum. Keith Thatcher had kept LanTech's books and used insider knowledge to blackmail his way to a very violent death.

"You would think after Emilio got done with decimating

LanTech and Origin, that would've been the end of it," Locke said.

Zev's expression darkened. "It would've been if not for Jude Novak."

"Got to admit, I never really thought the whole Cabal story was real." The traitorous councilman had been a player in a shadowy group of disenfranchised fringe mages and twisted scientists intent on gaining both political and financial power from the Families. "Now I've got to wonder just how deep their rot runs."

"Deep," Zev said grimly.

A ring of bells drifted over the din of conversation and background music. Zev's gaze sharpened on something behind him, so Locke twisted in his seat as Beto shouldered his way through the door. Dressed in a bespoke suit, he stuck out like a sore thumb. He pulled off a pair of sunglasses and scanned the room. His gaze landed on Zev then flared just a bit when it encountered Locke. Beto frowned.

"Yep, he saw me," Locke said under his breath as he twisted back around, giving the financier his back as he took another sip.

Zev tilted his head toward the counter where Maeve sat, a silent indication for Beto to order something. Locke maintained his casual pose as he watched Zev track the other man's movements. Silent minutes passed as they waited for Beto to join them.

"Aslanov." Beto's voice was surprisingly relaxed but carried a hint of something darker.

"Montenegro." Zev motioned to a chair. "Have a seat."

Beto set a glass of iced tea on the table then settled his thick body into the chair, taking a moment to smooth out the lines of his slacks. He watched Zev activate the privacy rune etched into the table's wooden top, ensuring that their conversation would not be overheard. Only then did he turn his attention to Locke.

"I didn't catch your name last night."

Locke curved his lips, more in warning than welcome. "I didn't give it."

Beto's mouth tightened, and irritation flared deep in his eyes. "Why am I here?" he asked Zev.

"We have some questions."

"About...?"

"Your assistant," Locke said.

chapter 15

Isa

WORRIED AND ON EDGE, Isa fought for patience. “Just drop me off first,” she repeated as she finished her one-word text to Locke. “Wonderland is closer. Drop me off, then take Kelly home.”

Des stood in front of her, arms crossed, eyes hidden behind sunglasses, expression unyielding. “We can wait at Wonderland until Locke shows up.”

The last twenty-four hours—hell, the last forty-eight—had been a nonstop pressure cooker, and Isa’s rising frustration threatened to blow the lid right off her churning emotions. She locked her jaw, determined not to let it spew all over Des. She understood he worried, but for fuck’s sake, she was a grown-ass woman who did not need a babysitter.

“No, you can’t. You need to get that girl home, and I need to get back to the bar,” she said.

As if it wasn’t enough that the meeting with River had gone long, Wonderland’s alcohol delivery was running early, leaving Isa with just enough time to get back to the bar to accept it. If Des stopped playing overprotective brother.

“We can wait.”

Isa went toe-to-toe with him. “No, you won’t.” She

grabbed Des's chin and forced him to look to where Kelly stood a little ways down the sidewalk, talking on her phone, shoulders hunched, arms wrapped protectively around her stomach. "She needs to get home to her mom, where she feels safe." Under her fingertips, a muscle jumped in Des's jaw.

"Fine," he snarled as he circled her wrist and pulled her hand away from his face. He lowered his head until he could glare at her over his sunglasses. "You will set the security ward and keep it active until Locke shows up."

Under her skin, irritation simmered, making her twitchy and bitchy. She twisted out of his grasp. "Fine. Whatever." She pulled her sunglasses off her head, grimaced when they took a couple of strands of hair with them, and shoved them in place. "Delivery's only fifteen minutes out." And if they weren't there to accept it, a reschedule would cost extra.

She caught Kelly's attention and pointed toward Des's SUV. When the younger woman held up a finger, indicating she wouldn't be long, Isa started over to the car. Des followed, muttering. She had pulled open the passenger door when her phone vibrated with an incoming text. Knowing who it was from, she sucked in air, hoping patience would follow, and checked the message.

CU in 30.

She got into the SUV, slammed the door shut—harder than necessary—then gave Locke's response a thumbs-up instead of the middle finger before dropping her phone into the console cupholder so she could fasten her seat belt.

The driver's-side door flew open, and on a wave of irritation, Des got behind the wheel. His silence was loud as he started the engine and hiked up the AC. It grew louder as they both stared out the windshield at Kelly. Isa wasn't surprised when Des broke first.

"Dammit, Isa." His rough voice held anger and fear. "This isn't good."

"I know."

And it wasn't Angel they were talking about but what had gone down in the lawyer's office. Even though River tried to put a positive spin on things, the more he spoke, the more Des and Isa could read between the lines, and what they detected made them edgy. Based on the preliminary police report River had gotten his hands on, the scene supported Kelly's self-defense stance, but if push came to shove and they ended up with a trial, it would come down to a he-said, she-said situation, with the *he* in this case very much dead at Kelly's hand, something a jury might not look on favorably. River explained that he was "fairly confident" the incident wouldn't make it as far as a trial, but just in case, he went into detail on a couple of defense approaches, one of which involved Isa.

"If it comes to it, I'll do it," Isa said. By "it," she meant hosting Leo's soul and basically giving voice to the only other eyewitness to his death.

Des's fingers flexed against the steering wheel, a muscle jumping in his jaw. "If you can even call him back."

"If it keeps Kelly out of jail, I'll drag his ass back one piece at a time." And she would. It would just be... difficult.

"And then what, Isa?" Des finally looked at her. "You told me he was already fragmenting. That was almost two days ago."

"It can be done."

"I'm sure it can, but should it?" he asked. When she didn't answer, he went for the kill. "It's not like it's floating around, waiting to be called back. Say you find enough pieces to patch that soul together and you are able to weave him back into some sort of reflection. How warped will it be?"

Isa winced. Des's assessment was spot-on. Whatever remained of Leo's soul would be reshaped by the judgment it was enduring, and the result could be dangerous.

Des didn't give her a chance to respond. "Then there's the

legality of it all. Say the judge allows it and the defense doesn't scream 'bias'? Then the judge is going to hex you so you can't interfere. Which means there's shit all you can do if the little fucker decides to turn."

And based on her first encounter with Leo, the odds of that happening were high. Not something she wanted to admit to Des.

He didn't need her to. "Exactly," he said.

She turned away and saw Kelly heading toward them.

Des did the same. "You need to get Locke to share whatever the hell is happening with River." His voice was tight and hot.

Des's order just added pressure to the weight of guilt she already carried.

"And how do you propose I do that, Des?"

Because whatever was going down with that damnable drug wasn't something the Families wanted out there, which left Kelly as nothing more than collateral damage.

"I don't know, but I'm sure you can figure it out," he said.

She wished she had his faith in her persuasive abilities.

Kelly reached the car and pulled open the back door. "Hey, sorry about that. My mom said she'll meet us at my place." She hopped into the back seat. Kelly kept talking as she got situated and pulled the door closed behind her. "She wants to stay with me. Says she'll help me finish packing up."

"I think that's a good idea," Isa said.

"I don't know," Kelly admitted in a low voice. "Maybe I should call my new boss and ask if I can delay my start."

"No," Des said. "You heard River. He told you the investigation is going to take some time, and if the police have more questions, you can always come back." He put the SUV in gear and headed for the bar.

"So they can arrest me," Kelly said softly.

"They aren't going to arrest you," Isa said, turning so she could see Kelly.

The young woman was staring out the window, her face pale, her hands knotted in her lap. "Not yet."

"Hey." Isa's sharp voice had Kelly turning to her, eyes wide. "Enough, Kelly. I know you're scared, and you have every right to be, but you did nothing wrong."

With uncharacteristic bitterness, Kelly snapped, "I killed him, Isa."

"In self-defense," Isa shot back, refusing to let the other woman see how much it hurt to push this. "You think your mom, me, Des, Cass—any of us—would rather be attending your funeral right now?" Kelly blinked, her mouth forming a small disbelieving *oh*, but Isa refused to back off. "You didn't start the argument. You didn't hit him. You walked him home, and he attacked you. His choice, Kelly. Not yours."

"He was wasted." Guilt trapped the girl in her corner.

Not about to let her get stuck there, Isa said, "And whose choice was that?"

Tears welled in Kelly's eyes, and she pressed her lips together. She dropped her gaze to her lap, where her fingers were twisted together so tightly her knuckles were white. "I should've just got out."

"You tried."

Tears spilled and trailed down Kelly's cheeks.

Isa softened her tone. "And when that didn't work, you did what you needed so you could get away. You have the right to defend yourself, Kelly. Especially when your life is at risk—and it was."

Kelly gave a hesitant nod.

Isa sighed, knowing it would take time and tools for Kelly to work through things. Since she had no idea what those tools were, she made a mental note to give Kelly's mom the number of a therapist who had worked with some of Wonderland's after-hours clients.

The rest of the short ride passed in quiet, each rider caught up in their own thoughts. By the time Des pulled up in front of Wonderland, Isa was sick of hers. They kept tangling up in useless circles. She exchanged subdued goodbyes with Kelly and an abbreviated one with Des that included another annoying reminder by him to set the security wards. Then she was free, at least momentarily. She could feel Des watching her cross to the building, undo the security, and slip inside. As soon as the door closed, she reset the damn wards. Only then did she hear the faint rev of Dev's engine as he left.

She checked the time and hurried down the stairs to the main floor. The delivery would arrive at any minute. She made her way across the bar's main floor by rote, barely taking the time to flick on the lights above the drinking well before pulling up the inventory spreadsheet on her phone and shouldering through the door to the kitchen. She hit the kitchen lights, and the fluorescents stuttered to life. Blinking her vision clear of white dots, she made a mental note to have Des check the overhead bulbs. She double-checked a couple of items on her list, verifying that the numbers were right, then headed to the dented metal door at the back of the space that led to the service elevator. It was the one thing she, Cass, and Des had agreed to sink money into when they'd taken over the bar. In this part of downtown, the streets were narrow, and with Wonderland's main structure sitting at basement level, having an elevator that opened into the alley was the easiest way to get deliveries without going up and down the steep stairs in front. She hit the button, and it flashed red in warning.

Shit, right.

She reset the security ward to Standby, irritated all over again with the over-the-top requests from the males in her life. When the security light went to a steady blinking orange, she jabbed the button again. This time, the door slid open. She rode it up to street level and got out to wait at the curb. A boxy white paneled truck proclaiming Spirits and More was turning in to the alley.

Perfect timing.

The truck made its way over and lumbered to a stop. The driver got out and came around, his hat pulled low, his sunglasses dark, and his smile white against a tawny, weathered face. "Hey, afternoon. Got a delivery here for..." He checked his phone. "Wonderland?" He looked up, his smile notching up a bit. "Says to ask for a Des Ward or Isa Serrano. I'm guessing you're Isa."

"You guessed right. And you are...?"

"Mitch."

"Nice to meet you, Mitch." She started for the back of the truck, letting him fall in beside her. "Is Georgie off today?"

"Yeah, he's currently riding the waves of the Caribbean. Anniversary thing with the wife." They got to the rear of the truck, where Mitch unlatched the ramp, pulled it into place, then shoved up the rear door. "Hey, thanks again for being so flexible. I hope I didn't mess anything up for you."

"No, you're good. Just glad we were able to connect."

They stood inside the back of the truck, going through the order, stacking items on the handcart, loading them into the service lift, and then doing it again. There was a bad moment when it looked like a scotch order was missing, but fortunately, Mitch found it buried near the back.

He added it to the other boxes, his grin a little rueful. "Sorry about that. Must have set it over there this morning to get it out of the way and forgot to move it back."

"No harm, no foul," Isa said, checking off the last of the order on her spreadsheet as she followed him down the ramp.

They got to the elevator, and Mitch set the last of the boxes next to the others. He shifted his handcart back out and pulled his phone from his pocket. “Okay, I think we’re good. If you could just sign here.” He turned the phone to her, and she initialed the receipt. “Thanks.”

“Welcome,” she said as he started to turn away. “Enjoy your afternoon.”

“You too,” he called with a wave.

Isa waved back then hit the button. The elevator’s door slid closed, and it made its way back down. After setting it to hold its open-door position, Isa started hauling the wine and beer to the walk-in cooler. During one of her many back-and-forth trips, she tied her phone to the Bluetooth speaker they kept in the back, queued up her favorite playlist, and let the music fill in the space. It made restocking less of a workout and more of an enjoyable time-out.

She was up on a step stool, arranging bottles on one of the cooler’s top shelves, when she thought she heard something over the music. She set down the bottle she held, climbed down, and stepped out of the reinforced-metal-walled walk-in. The instant temperature change between the cooler and the kitchen pebbled her skin.

“Lower volume.”

The music took a step back. Rubbing her arms, she crossed the kitchen and caught a glimpse of a steadily flashing orange near the elevator. Isa winced. *Des is going to kill me.* She had forgotten to reset the security ward after the delivery, and it was still in standby mode.

A muffled thump came from the main floor.

The endless warnings from Des and Locke returned, rattling her nerves. Her gaze skittered to the clock set on the wall as she noted the time. It was probably Locke. He’d said thirty minutes, and it was now closer to thirty-five.

“Locke?” she called out.

No one answered.

Unnerved, she moved to one of the last cartons sitting

open on the counter and pulled out a thick bottle of gin. Maybe she was overreacting, but better safe than sorry. She adjusted her grip until she was holding the bottle like a makeshift hammer. Her magic pooled under skin, wanting to be let out to play. She held it back as she moved toward the door.

"Locke, is that you?"

She took a second to hit Pause on her phone, which lay on the counter. The music cut out abruptly, heavy silence taking its place. She waited a heartbeat then two. Everything remained quiet, almost too quiet. Instead of calming, her breath sped up, and she could feel her skull light up with tension. She set her back to the door and, with her free hand and shoulder, pressed it open, bottle held at the ready. She had a momentary regret at not turning on more than the light above the bar, because the faint glow from the sigils buried in the mural along the back wall wasn't enough to beat back the varied shadows filling the floor. She stared into the murkiness, wanting to call Locke's name but unable to get it out past her tight throat. She swallowed hard and stepped fully through the door.

Something moved to her left. She turned, swinging out with the bottle. It hit something, the impact rattling up her arm, and a pained grunt sounded. She went to swing again but was too late. Magic punched her, searing across her senses. She stumbled back. Somewhere far off, glass shattered, but she was gone, swallowed by the sudden dark.

chapter 16

Locke

"I'm so glad we took your car, because odds are she's going to puke any minute now."

Locke grimaced at Zev's dry but potentially accurate comment. Through his rearview mirror, he checked on the moaning girl slumped in his back seat. Not that he could see much from this angle, just a tangle of brown shoulder-length hair matted around a wan, green-tinged face, bruised eyes barely slitted open as she rolled her head against the seat.

"You hurl in my car, Paisley, you'll be cleaning it up."

Her response was another whimpered groan.

"Mari says she's got medical on standby, so once we get to the clinic, we can hand her off," Zev said. "You know, it's going to take a few hours before you can get anything out of her."

"Yeah, I know. Hopefully, she'll be more useful than Beto."

Zev gave an annoyed grunt. "Yeah, that was kind of a bust."

The financier hadn't known jack shit about the drug, other than that his assistant had inconveniently overdosed on it, which threatened to expose his double life to his wife. He was not happy to discover that despite paying Angel for his "discretionary silence," his plan to quietly sweep Owen's death under the rug was in jeopardy. Zev and Locke banked on that paranoia to get Beto admit that his relationship with Angel was a fairly new development. They also got him to agree, reluctantly, to keeping them informed of his future dealings with Angel.

"At least we know it was Angel that reached out to him and not the other way around."

"I'll have Roxy shift her focus, see if she can figure out how someone like him came into money like that." Another groan came from the back seat, and Zev did a quick visual check then shook his head as he turned back to face forward. "If Mari finds her parents, you might get stonewalled."

Locke gave a disgusted snort. "Maybe, maybe not." They'd found Paisley dressed in club wear and passed out in an apartment that appeared to serve as a crash pad for free-roaming teens, so he wondered just how concerned her parents could really be. "If they do try to block me, I'll sic Mari on them. I'm sure she can find plenty of ways to encourage them to let me talk to her." He checked the time and winced. "Dammit."

"What?"

"I was supposed to be at Wonderland, like, five minutes ago."

The call that linked Paisley to Isaiah had come in as they finished up with Beto, along with Isa's text that the meeting with the lawyer was running long. It made his decision to run down the fresh lead on Isaiah fairly simple. Finding Paisley had been easy. Unfortunately, getting her to talk coherently—not so much.

"Need me to text Isa?" Zev asked.

"Yeah. Let her know I'm running late."

Zev grabbed his phone, held it up so it could read Locke's face, then quickly shot off a text.

Within minutes, Locke was turning into the quiet parking lot outside a private clinic. The Cordova Family lawyer, Maribel Ortiz, was waiting for them out front with a scrub-wearing twentysomething manning a wheelchair. After pulling up to the curb, Locke got out and helped Zev guide the still-groaning teen into the wheelchair so the PA could whisk her away.

"Her parents?" Zev asked Mari.

She shook her head. "We've left messages at the numbers on file. Nothing yet."

"I need to know as soon as she's able to talk," Locke said.

"She's a minor, Locke."

"I'm aware, but right now, she's the best link I have to tracking Isaiah down." And something told him Micah's brother was running out of time.

Mari worried her bottom lip.

"You asked for Emilio's help," Zev reminded her.

"I know." Mari blew out an aggrieved sigh. "I'll make it work. Once she's sober, I'll tag you."

"Thank you." He quickly took his leave and hopped back into his car, impatient to get back to Isa. He checked his text and frowned when it showed that it had gone unread. An uneasy prickle raised the hair on the back of his neck. He thought about calling her, but considering Isa's escalating irritation with his so-called hovering, he decided against it. Besides, Wonderland was only fifteen minutes away. He'd be there soon enough.

Locke pulled into Wonderland's empty lot, that unease

slithering down his neck and knotting his shoulders. *Where the hell is Des's SUV?*

The thought had barely formed when the vehicle in question turned in. As it came to a stop, Locke saw that Des was alone. His hands fisted, and he barely waited for the man to get his door open and step out before snarling, "Where's Isa?"

Des's dark brows rose above the edge of his sunglasses as he threw his door closed. "Inside." He started for the entrance. "You're late."

"And you left her alone," he snapped as he matched the other man step for step.

"I had to run Kelly home." Muscles coiled and bunched, indicating that Locke's barb had found its mark. "It was a rough meeting."

A pinch of empathy pierced Locke's frustration, and he forced his hands to uncurl. "She going to be okay?"

"Depends on how far the police want to push things." Des reached the door, yanked his sunglasses off, and shot Locke an assessing look. "It would help if someone could provide proof of how that jackass was suddenly able to throw around magic."

"I'm sure they have their theories." Reassurance was beyond Locke, because if things got truly dire for Kelly, what got shared with whom would be up to Emilio.

Des's lip twitched with ill-disguised disgust, but he turned away and reached for the door only to stop and mutter a low curse.

"What?" Locke's question was a sharp bullet of sound.

"The security is on standby." Des yanked open the door, and the two men rushed down the stairs.

Nebulous shadows filled the space, distorting the normally friendly floor into an otherworldly maze of unseen threats. At the far end, a light burned over the bar, and just beyond that was the soft luminance of the graffiti art along the back wall.

Des didn't slow as he navigated through tables and booths. "Isa?"

There was no answer.

"Isa?" Locke called, his magic pushing forward, whining to be used.

Still nothing.

Des went to the far end of the bar, just beyond the pass, and hit a switch. Harsh illumination burst into life, wiping away the shadows.

Locke blinked away the small stars as his vision adjusted. At first, everything appeared undisturbed, but a bitter bite rode the air, and it took him a second to place it. "Is that gin?"

Des didn't answer but shoved through the pass. A small shot glass rolled off the counter and tumbled to the floor. "What the—" His gaze went to the right and landed on something behind the bar. He froze.

"What?" Alarmed, Locke rushed forward, his magic settling around him like a second skin, the predator at its heart, yanking at the leash.

"Stop!" Des's sharp command and upraised hand stopped Locke in his tracks. "There's broken glass back here." He moved carefully into the narrow space behind the bar then dropped into a crouch, disappearing from view.

Locke cleared the last few feet, pulled open the swinging half door, and stood just inside the pass. Isa was gone. Taken. He knew it down to his bones. Just like he knew who was behind it. The ugly mix of fear, worry, and underlying frustration surged, but he shoved it all into a box and slammed the lid closed. He would deal with the emotional shit later. Getting Isa back was primary, and to do that, he needed to focus.

Des was frowning as he held up a chunk of green-tinted glass, mindful of its ragged edges. "That smell is definitely gin."

Locke took it from him. It was a thick piece from the

lower half of a bottle. He let his magic snap free, and it surged forward, eager for the hunt. Smells sharpened, scents separating into concise strands. He brought the chunk up to his nose and inhaled. The bite of juniper filled his nostrils. Under it was a barely-there hint of musk he couldn't place.

He looked at the shards between him and Des. "Where's the rest?"

A small ball of light popped into existence and hovered over Des's shoulder. He waved it forward, and it cruised low and slow over the floor. It pulled up short near the well.

Des found a safe spot to brace his hand then leaned forward and pulled out the other half of the bottle. "This is what's left of the top half." The still-sealed cap clung to the squat neck, and one jagged shoulder remained intact. The little ball of light zipped back to Des as he rose to standing. He twisted the glass shard, his frown darkening. "I think there's blood on this."

"Let me see it."

Locke took the piece from Des, his magic cataloguing the visual clues with rapid-fire sequence, the details burned into his brain. It was easy to miss—a single drop with spines and satellites, dry and dark, erupting from around the nearly perfect circle, with a brighter center. He brought the piece of glass up to his nose, careful to avoid smearing the small drop near the label, and drew the scent deep. The bite of iron was there, not faint but not strong, and under it was the barest hint of cinnamon. His heart stuttered.

"Is it Isa's?" Des asked.

"Yeah."

He focused on what wasn't there. No blood patterns indicating repeated violent blows, no alarming smears to signal a struggle or cleanup effort, so a single blood drop could be nothing more than a minor cut. He took in the rest of the scene. The residual liquid dripped from a low shelf just above the floor, splattering over the shards of glass scattered along the aerated mat and seeping through to the cement floor. His magic ruffled the air, collecting the scent of herbs and spices accented by a dry pine-like hint. The gin had sprayed outward, raining over the tight space. But the way the pieces lay…

"Back out carefully," he ordered Des. "Try not to step on anything."

He waited for Des to move out of his way, then he stepped in and noted a void in the mess of glass and gin. Small indentations in the aerated mat created an abstract pattern. He let his magic extract the pieces and reshuffle them. A partial shoe tread came into focus. "Someone, likely male, stood right here."

He held his position and studied the rest of the story. A hand towel was crumpled on the floor near a box of glasses on a low shelf, but up on the counter, the only thing out of place was an off-kilter drying mat. He started toward the other end, and Des, who had his back to the door leading to the kitchen, shifted out of the way, causing the door to open inward. Bright light spilled over the concrete floor, revealing more clues.

"Hold that door," Locke said.

Des went still, keeping the door open.

Locke sank to his heels, his magic zeroing in on the faint scuff marks that filled the area near the kitchen and the pass. "Another one was here, waiting." There was a heavier scrape just on the other side of the pass. "They drew her out, ambushed her." It played out in his mind.

The light brightened as Des leaned back, forcing the door wider. He looked into the kitchen then back at Locke. "She knew someone was out there because she brought the bottle with her." He motioned into the kitchen. "Open box on the counter, which means she was here to get the inventory delivery."

"And she managed to get at least one hit in." Locke straightened. "Not sure what damage, if any, it did, because there're no other signs of blood."

"Just hers on that one piece," Des said grimly.

"Which came after the bottle broke."

Des kept one hand on the door and leaned forward into the kitchen, reaching for something. When he straightened, he had a phone in his hand. He held it out to Locke. "Isa's."

Locke took it. The lock screen showed a paused playlist and, under it, a text notification. The box holding his emotions at bay rattled. He ignored it.

"We missed her by fifteen, maybe twenty minutes." Locke scanned the bar's ceiling. "You have cameras?"

"Two inside, four outside," Des said, turning to the kitchen and leaving Locke to follow as he talked. "We can access the feed in the office. I can use my phone, but the desktop gives me multiview options." He started off down the hall.

Locke took in the quiet kitchen—the stack of boxes and crates near the back metal door, empty boxes flattened and piled up near the half-open door to the walk-in cooler, and the security ward flashing a steady orange. Isa's impatient voice floated through his mind—"I'll be careful." He stalked after Des.

The man was looming over the desktop, his face thunderous. "Motherfucking pissants fucked with my security."

Locke came around the desk to see six security feeds, each filled with static. "Electro mage."

Fury pulsed off of Des. "It has to be, to mess with the cameras without interfering with the security wards." Any halfway decent electro mage would hex all nearby cameras, so there was no use in requesting to pull video from neighboring businesses.

"So we've got nothing." Exasperation tore at Locke's self-restraint.

"Not quite." Des straightened, his face set in hard angles as he walked over to a dented filing cabinet in the corner. He pulled out a drawer—which gave an ear-splitting squeal—reached in, and came back out with a small zippered pouch. He slammed the drawer closed and stormed past Locke. "Come on."

Curious, Locke followed. Des went back out to the main floor and straight to one of the high-top tables. He set the pouch down and then worked off a heavy silver ring from his left hand and two from his right before holding them out to Locke.

"Hold these for a second."

Locke took the trio of rings. "What are you doing?"

"Finding out what happened to Isa." From the pouch, Des pulled out an unlabeled bottle, uncapped it, and poured a small amount of what appeared to be oil into his palm. "Take those rings—don't let them go—and go sit in that corner booth."

As he talked, he dipped his finger into the oil and started trailing it along one of the intricate tattoos winding its way over his ring finger and up his left forearm. A pungent mix of citrus and soap drifted from Des's skin, chased by the near-electric zing of magic.

Locke drew back as the combination seared across his enhanced senses. "Is that rue oil?"

"Yep." Des continued tracing the pattern etched into his skin. The dark lines of the tattoos sharpened and emanated a faint glow. "Now, so long as you don't draw attention to yourself, you should be good, but if things take a turn, a standard protection ward should be enough to discourage any leeches."

Locke had started to move to the booth but on that last word stopped and turned to pin Des with a look. "Leeches?"

“Yeah.” Des shook the excess oil from his palm then wiped it on his pants. “Some of these spooks can be stubborn assholes. The last thing you want to pick up is a rider.” He plucked a piece of chalk out of the pouch. “I can pull them off, but it’ll take time we don’t have.” He turned on his heel and started to shove tables off to the side. Before long, he had an open space in front of the graffiti-laced wall.

Sliding into the booth, Locke rolled the three heavy rings in his palm. “What’s with the rings?”

“They’re hexed,” Des said with a disconcerting casualness as he lowered to his heels then started drawing on the concrete floor. “Specifically, so ghosts will leave me the hell alone.”

Locke opened his palm and studied the rings. Sure enough, he recognized some of the symbols. He looked back to Des. “And those wards you’re drawing…?”

Without looking up, Des said, “Ensuring that the uninvited don’t crash our meeting.” He got to his feet, tucked the chalk into his back pocket, and looked at Locke over his shoulder. “Ready?”

“Ready.”

Des turned back, took a breath, and, in a disturbingly deep voice, commanded, “Wake up.”

The soft glow along his left arm flashed bright, burning white, then settled into an unearthly haze as the overhead lights flickered for a long moment before steadying. His power washed outward, touching the walls then climbing it like ivy. A breeze swept through the room, bringing the scent of fresh-dug dirt marred with bone dust and an unnatural chill that raised every hair on Locke’s body. It twined around Des like a devoted pet, demanding to be acknowledged.

Locke held still as his magic stalked silently forward, curious about the phenomenon. It stayed back but not far enough. Des’s head turned, giving Locke a glimpse of his profile. His familiar features blurred into a ghastly mask.

Though similar to the one Isa wore as a Reaper, Des's had a savage undertone—a warning that universal rules would not apply.

Des's mouth moved, and with a bone-rattling boom, he warned, "Back off!"

Locke called his magic back. Like the hunter it was, his magic eased reluctantly away from the threat and settled warily between the two men.

Des's power continued to spread behind him then slid through the urban art to spill into the interspersed sigils until they writhed, shifting to form a decorative arch. Des turned back and fed more power into the wall until the space within the arch shimmered. Then it settled into an inky black pit.

"Alphonse Magariue, come forward."

The empty doorway quivered, and deep inside, a haze brewed, gaining form as it drifted closer until a thin man wearing a cowboy hat, a tattered long-sleeved chambray shirt, and jeans—the kind in sepia photos of the Old West—stepped out of the archway.

He stood—well, hovered—there, glaring at Des, his weather-worn face screwed up in a scowl. "Why you calling me, boy?"

"Tell me what happened to Isa."

"Hell if I know. Ain't like I hang around watching you idiots."

"You watch Isa all the damn time, Al. And I know you were watching her today. You left your damn shot glass on the counter."

A crafty look slid over the phantom's face. "That ain't mine."

Magic surged, and the room took on a menacing stillness. Then Des moved almost preternaturally fast, snatching the phantom's shirt and dragging the spirit close. He loomed over the old cowboy, his head passing through the brim of the hat as he snarled, "Tell me what happened, Alphonse."

Locke never thought a ghost could pale, but Des must have scared the spirit shitless. The cowboy's hands fluttered uselessly against Des's hold. "Don't git yourself all riled up, boy."

A low, unearthly moan seeped out from the spectral doorway, and Alphonse twisted in Des's grasp, his eyes wide with terror as he stared into the writhing pit behind him. He turned back around.

"All right, all right," he said, his voice high with panic. "She was back in the kitchen, putting stuff away. I just wanted a taste. Figured if I left it out, she'd share. She does that sometimes. Then these two dress-suit burglars slid on in, one of 'em throwing magic around like tossin' lightning. The other can't stay on his feet, stumblin' like a one-eyed drunk—nearly took out one of them tables. She must've heard him 'cause she came out, but they jumped her. She managed to get one in the gut with the bottle, but they got her trussed up good then dragged her out."

"Describe them."

"I don't know." Alphonse kept trying to pry Des's hands off his shirt with no success. "One was taller than me, the other wider than me. The clumsy one, I mean." He stopped struggling and hung from Des's grip, resigned. "The silent one, Tall Man, he was definitely in charge and mean."

Wanting to join the interrogation but knowing he couldn't, Locke clenched his teeth and fisted his hand, Des's rings biting into his palm.

Des cocked his head. "Mean? What did he do?"

"Nothing to the woman. He even told the other one that the boss wanted her unmarked. It was just..." His hands fluttered then dropped. "He carried the dark with him, you know?"

The muscles in Des's back went rigid, but he let the ghost go. "They say anything else?"

The ghost shook his head so hard his face blurred. "Nothin', just in and out, slick as shit. This ain't the first rodeo for those two. They're old hands." The phantom drifted carefully back, as if trying to stay out of Des's reach. "You know I like that girl—she's good people. I'd've tried to help, but not much I can do. You've got us locked down so tight I can't even get a tick in here without you. Maybe you might want to consider letting us help now and again."

Des's hands fisted on his hips. "Don't need your help, Al. Bad enough you like breaking my stock when you throw a hissy fit. I don't need the added aggravation of keeping you off my customers."

The old cowboy managed to look affronted. "If they didn't want people gawking at their illicit activities, they'd take themselves elsewhere, garner a little privacy. Besides, ain't like I can do anything but watch anymore."

Clearly deciding the conversation was done, Des flexed his magic, and dark tendrils emerged from the archway to coil around the phantom's form. "Leave, Alphonse Magariue. Go back to sleep."

For a moment, something ugly rose behind the cowboy's amiable features, but the inky ribbons coiled around him and pulled him slowly back into the shadowed depths. When the last hazy fragments dissipated, Des's magic surged forward, crawling back through the archway, moving in the reverse of their original path until the sigils were once again buried within the urban art spanning the back wall.

Locke got out of the booth and moved toward Des, who turned. Locke held out the rings. "Angel took her."

Des's mouth tightened into grim lines as he took the rings. "No, he sent two of his crew to take her because Angel likes to play with her."

"Isa's not a toy." The words came out on a vicious snap.

"No, she's not," Des said. "But she knows his game better than anyone. She can hold her own."

For how long, though? He tried not to let the fear rise, but it was there. "I need a starting point." He wasn't asking.

Des slid the sliver rings back into place then flexed his fingers. "I'll get you one, but it's not going to be fast."

Cold determination settled deep in Locke's gut. "Let's see what we can do to change that."

chapter 17

Isa

"I TOLD you she wasn't to be hurt."

That voice crept into Isa's mind, slithering along pain-ridden paths and tripping old triggers. The resulting quake widened the scar-covered fissures until panic seeped through in a corrosive slow-moving leak. The driving instinct to claw free was held in check by heavy, unresponsive limbs.

"It's just a knockout spell. She should wake up soon." That voice was unfamiliar and too close for comfort, but the words... She grabbed hold of their meaning, piecing together why everything felt wrong.

"Give her to me."

There was a sense of movement, as if she were floating, then a slight jolt as she stopped. Noxious dread sank through her skin like invisible tentacles that latched on with a terrifying speed and strength.

"Get out, both of you."

That hated voice, way too close now, resounded through her aching skull. A nearby door shut, and the anxiety deepened, sharpened. A subtle inhalation echoed around her, followed by a hum of dark satisfaction. For a moment, time slipped, and she was back at the beginning, trapped in Angel's grasp, her sense of self shattered beyond recognition and reality a grotesque play of twisted half-truths and cruel manipulations. She started to slide back into old nightmares, but something deep inside refused to fall. Other memories rose, giving her a way out of old horrors. There was Cass and Des moving behind the bar, the sound of their shared laughter and good-humored teasing drowning out the hateful whispers. Behind that came Locke's face, creased in irritation and concern as he demanded, "You'll be careful." Then it was Des's worried frown as he handed her the Zemi charm. "I'd feel better if you wore it tonight."

But they weren't enough to hold the darkness at bay as more memories spun out, bringing Kelly's traumatized shock, Leo's maddened fury, Owen's guilt-ridden anguish, and Nova's anxiety, all chased by the eager predatory light in Angel's face as he watched her. The chaotic mix spun tighter and tighter, threatening to pull her under, when something brushed along her neck, just under her ear, and a low, masculine hum brought her mental world to a jolting stop. It was chillingly familiar.

"And you are...?" The question asked by the arrogant, entitled, hated voice echoed in her aching head.

"Hers."

She held tight to Locke's unshakable response and reached for more fragmented memories. They came in ragged bits, but faster now. Receiving the inventory delivery, putting it away, the noise from the front of the bar, the looming figure, her swing of the bottle, then...

A groan escaped her as the final pieces fell into place. Knockout spell. Angel.

She sensed something plucking at her emotions, examining them as if searching for the perfect piece of fruit. Her pulse kicked up. *Asshole.*

She reached for her magic but came up short. The pain in

her head built. The magic hadn't gone far. She could feel it just... there. She dug deep and stretched her metaphysical hand out, power teasing her fingertips.

"I know you're awake, *chiquita*," the asshole crooned as he set her down.

There was a sense of weight settling close to her, then something brushed against her face. Her skin crawled with instant revulsion stronger than the ache reverberating through her muscles and bouncing in her skull. It was hard, but she got her arm up and feebly batted away the unwelcome touch.

"Don't." It came out slurred.

"Now, don't be like that."

The patronizing tone grated on her nerves. She forced her lashes to rise, and light stabbed into her brain, eliciting another groan. Her lashes fluttered back down as she tried to turn away, but fingers dug into her chin, forcing her still. Faced with the choice of jerking out of the hold or opening her eyes—either of which would add to the pounding in her head—she went with the less violent option and forced her lashes up to find Angel sitting next to her, a calculating light in his dark eyes as he studied her face. Dressed in a button-down shirt, a loose tie, and linen pants, he was the epitome of a charming businessman. But the hunger in his gaze revealed his true nature.

Unease rippled as phantom power whispered around her, circling her like a shark scenting blood in the emotional waters. Doubts she'd thought long buried rose, rippling outward from the darkest recesses. She slammed up a wall, holding them back. For now.

"Let go," she said, stronger and clearer this time.

For a moment, she wasn't sure he would, but then his lips curved with a familiar cruel amusement, and he slowly let her go. "You left so quickly last night that I didn't get a chance to finish our conversation." He braced his hand above her, trapping her against what she realized was a couch.

Not keen about being on her back with him, she dug her heels into the cushions and pushed herself up, careful not to touch him. The movement didn't come easy, and a thin line of sweat broke out along her hairline, but between her shaky arms and leaden legs, she managed to sit up, her back to the couch's arm. She dug her nails into the cushion under her hips. Her head spun, but she breathed through it.

When the dizziness finally settled, she lifted her head. "There was nothing left to say."

Angel's arm bent as he leaned in close enough that she couldn't avoid the dark, spicy bite of his cologne. "Now, that's a lie, Isa."

He's too close. Her pulse skittered as she suppressed a flinch. Barely. "Believe what you want, Angel. You always do."

His gaze sharpened. "So bitter, *chiquita*. It's almost as if you're the injured party."

The implication that she was in any way to blame for this current situation had fury, honed and bright, searing away the cloying vestiges of old fears until the only thing that remained was the vow she'd made years before: *Never fucking again.*

An unholy light gleamed in Angel's eyes as he dragged in a deep breath and straightened as if catching some delicious scent. "Oh, you don't like that, do you?"

The taunting reminder of who she was dealing with had her lunging for her power. The essence that made her a Reaper swept through her, freezing out every emotion until all that was left was a ruthless practicality.

"I don't like you." Her voice came out colder than the ice wrapping around her soul. She pulled the Reaper's magic closer and cocked her head without breaking their staring contest. "Is that a lie?"

"No." His malicious satisfaction was replaced by a smoldering ember of something darker as their powers rode the air between them. "Yet you still came into my territory." Without moving the hand braced against the back of the couch, he crowded her, his voice dropping, the circling predator tightening the noose. "Asking questions of my people. Interesting questions that make me wonder what games you're playing." He raised his hand and trailed his finger along the side of her face.

Underneath the Reaper's mantle, Isa was repulsed. Her skin crawled at the unwelcome touch, but strategies she'd learned years before came back with a vengeance, and she buried that which made her Isa deep, deep inside. *Ignore the bait.* It was hard not to slap his hand away.

Her nails dug into the couch even as her voice remained flat and empty. "Your games never interested me."

He stilled. A hint of rage flickered before he made a mocking pout. "But you played them so well." He dropped his hands to either side of her, caging her against the cushions, his voice sliding into that insidious tone he used like a scalpel. "With your dear papá, my lovely mamá, and me. Playing us against each other with your pretty crocodile tears and pitiful accusations." He leaned a little deeper, the darkness inside spilling out to erase the charming businessman, revealing the insatiable Harvester. "*Pobrecita*, no one believed you, and instead, you ended up all on your own. Just like you always wanted."

Rage, bright and deep, rose in her, but it remained distant, as if it belonged to someone else.

It does.

The cold voice didn't bother her. It was hers, after all—a reminder of who she was, what she was.

With a flex of will, she caught her magic in an unrelenting grip and wrapped it close, embracing the void that swam in the midst of her power. As her magic deepened, so did her awareness of his—the oily darkness slithering around, consumed by endless hunger. She could almost see it, like some tentacled beast flailing around her. She discovered that a couple of those venomous tendrils had found purchase. Instead of panicking, she was mildly curious.

Interesting.

She wrapped her power around one, and the air shifted, carrying a lethal chill matched by her voice. "What I wanted was to get away from you, and I did."

Avarice bloomed in Angel's face, but keen on the hunt, he didn't back down. "And yet here you are."

"Where you brought me. So who is really the one unable to let it go?"

With a covetous gleam, he pulled back. His power, on the other hand, kept testing her, trying to find more cracks to exploit. Not interested in playing cat and mouse, she sent a shock of magic through the tendril still caught in her grasp. Power burned through the unholy tie, and Angel's face tightened. The magical tendril recoiled, retreating to the edge of hungry magic looming just beyond her reach. The tendril waited, watching for another chance.

Angel got to his feet and walked away, his steps muffled by the large patterned rug covering the hardwood floor. He stopped in front of a smooth stone fireplace topped by a mantel of thick wood. He picked up an abstract statue and turned it over and over in his hands. "Why are you nosing around my club, Isa?"

She wasn't fooled by his apparent retreat, but she didn't waste her chance either. She carefully swung her legs around until she was no longer reclining. When her feet hit the floor, she felt steadier, as if that small movement grounded her. "I told you, it was a spur-of-the-moment decision. I didn't know he was bringing me to the Den."

As her gaze swept over what appeared to be a staged living

room decorated with bland artwork, something brushed against her awareness. She glanced around. Through the opening to her right was a kitchen and, next to that, a narrow entry table holding a tall vase of dried flowers and a notepad. On the other side was another opening, this one leading to a hall. She could make out a partially open bedroom door and, through it, the gray corner of a bed. But to get to any of that—including the front door, which was right there, next to the blind-covered window—would require getting past Angel. Those blinds were angled to let in light, but she could make out a front yard with a thick-trunked tree and just beyond it, across the narrow street, a square cinder-block home.

An older neighborhood, then. "Where are we?"

"Somewhere we can talk without being interrupted." Angel set the statue back in its spot and braced his arm along the mantel as he watched her.

"And if I want to leave?" There was nothing close by to use as a weapon but that damn statue.

"Worried your little pet won't be able to find you?"

Oh, she had no doubt Locke was already on the hunt—probably Des, too—but admitting that to Angel would just make him more insufferable. Instead, she met his mocking question with icy contempt. "Ask whatever you want to ask, but make it quick. I have a business to run."

A muscle in his jaw twitched. "I asked you a question."

"You've asked a couple. Which one do you want me to answer?" She was poking a dangerous snake, but fuck that noise. She wouldn't let him sink his hooks into her again.

Once more, that unknown presence brushed against her awareness.

Angel studied her for a long moment then moved to one of the nearby chairs. He sat and rested his arms on the chair's edges as he set his ankle on his knee. "Who sent you after me?"

Isa felt some satisfaction in his barely concealed paranoia, but she didn't have time to enjoy it. She needed to get away from him. Cautiously, she let her magic ebb outward. It lapped around something hovering near the fireplace just behind Angel.

When it came back to her, it carried a dark, driving compulsion aimed at the man watching her with unsettling intensity. *Make him pay. He has to pay.*

The gathering storm of vindictive need called to the magic she harbored, and Isa quashed her spark of anticipation before it could fully form. She crossed her legs and laced her fingers over her knee as she let her magic pool around the spirit, offering it a chance to feed from her power. It was a dangerous ploy, but if it worked, maybe she'd be rid of Angel once and for all. The spirit leapt at the unexpected gift, drawing the offering deep.

She kept her attention on Angel and not the vengeful wraith coalescing behind him as she answered his question. "No one sent me after you."

"Bullshit." A thin line of anger rode under his voice, and his magic whipped out, found the tiny fissures she hadn't been able to seal closed, and burrowed in.

Pain rippled along her nerve endings, but she embraced it, used it to fuel the cold rage simmering deep in her heart. Isa met his unrelenting hunger with merciless fury, and neither of them was able to gain ground. She touched the charm at her neck, and her magic deepened, forcing the invading power back a step while the world around her shifted.

"You're entitled to your opinion," she said.

Her small movement drew Angel's gaze, and his lip curled. An invisible band snapped around her throat, tightening in a blink. He wiggled a finger at her. "Uh, uh, uh. This is just a simple conversation. It doesn't need to get messy."

Air was trapped in her chest, but she held still, refusing to show even the smallest hint of fear. Not that she could feel any.

Logically, she knew it was there, but it was distant, as if it belonged to someone else. Instead, an affronted rage dominated, with her magic not so willing to play prey. It reached into the inky, emotionless void that was Angel and hooked its claws in his spirit.

"Release me." The demand wasn't vocal but echoed on the spiritual plane. She flexed her magical claws, her threat very real. "Or I will shred you to nothing."

On the mortal plane, Angel's lips peeled back in a grimace, his face paling, his fingers digging into the chair's arms. "You'll kill us both."

Black edged her vision. She didn't blink but simply let her lips curl up. "Your point?"

A heartbeat, two, the black seeping closer. Then the collar around her neck loosened.

Without breaking eye contact, she drew in a subtle breath. Behind Angel, a woman, maybe in her early twenties, with dark hair and eyes, crept closer, her need to exact vengeance filling Isa's nose like an irresistible perfume and forcing her to function on two levels at once. She held Angel's gaze for a long moment, knowing he had pulled back his magic as she had pulled hers, leaving them in a standoff.

Angel broke the heavy silence first, his voice flat, like the reptilian sheen in his eyes. "You were asking questions of Nova. Why?"

Still feeding on Isa's magic, the wraith's form took on depth, inching closer to Angel. Isa tried to watch it without being obvious. "There have been a couple of incidents. I wanted to know if they were one-offs or if they were something to be worried about."

He cocked his head. "And how would these incidents be associated with me?"

The wraith was right behind Angel now, still invisible to mortal eyes, but that wouldn't last. Needing it to stay unseen,

Isa locked her magic down, cutting off its food source. The wraith's head whipped up, and its fathomless eyes latched on to her as the mouth twisted open in a silent, furious scream.

Isa slowly got to her feet. "I didn't say they were."

Angel matched her movement, rising from his chair. "Where do you think you're going?"

She motioned to the kitchen. "To get some water."

"*¡Siéntate!*" He watched her sink back down to the couch. "I'll get it." He swept past her to the kitchen.

She eyed the front door as she listened to a refrigerator open then close. Meanwhile, the agitated wraith spun through the living room, working itself into a frenzy.

Enough. She flexed her power, forcing the wraith to slow.

"Go ahead, *chiquita*." Angel appeared in the opening and leaned a shoulder against the wall. The wraith zeroed in on him, forgetting Isa for the moment. He held out a plastic bottle of water. "Try it."

The door is spelled. Good to know. She stood and walked the few steps necessary to take the sealed bottle from him. Her fingers wrapped around the cool plastic and tugged.

He didn't let it go. "What? No thank-you?"

The plastic creaked under her fingers, but she stared into his smug face and stayed silent, waiting him out. A long moment passed, his amusement replaced by a flash of irritation before he let the bottle go. She took it, turned away, and unscrewed the top then dropped it on the entry table. She turned back to see that Angel had moved back into the living room. She watched him reclaim his previous spot at the fireplace as she sipped the water, letting the cool liquid ease the ache in her throat.

He turned to her, keeping his body between her and the front door. "If you didn't think these incidents, as you call them, were my doing, why ask my people questions?"

The wraith drifted in that space between Isa and Angel,

twisting back and forth, torn between its need to get to Angel and its craving for the power Isa could feed it. "I took advantage of an unexpected opportunity." It was hard to work on two levels at once, but she managed to keep the strain from her voice. "I had no idea he was going to take me to the Den. However, since I was there, and so was Nova, I figured I might as well see if she'd heard any rumors about a new drug."

Her magic wrapped around the agitated wraith, shifting through broken memories with an unnatural speed. The details came together in a violent snapshot. The woman, Caro, arguing with him. Angel losing his temper, striking out. Then Caro stumbling back on her heels, balance gone as she fell, her head hitting the mantel's edge with a sickening crack, and then the world fading as she crumpled into a boneless heap.

Isa concentrated on not crushing the plastic bottle in her hand as she raised it to her lips.

"A new drug?" His voice yanked her attention back to the room. "Why would she know anything about a new drug?"

Isa held the bottle partway up. "She's a bartender. I'm a bartender. Something new hits the scene, it tends to spread."

He canted his head. "And you thought that it had spread into my place?"

She shrugged and took another sip. In her mind, Caro's demands were getting louder, crowding out Angel's voice, a distraction Isa couldn't afford. But she needed the wraith. Luckily, the wraith needed her. To get to Angel, Caro needed a physical body, and Isa had one to offer.

Bargain.

Caro stilled, her demands going silent as she considered Isa's offer. Meanwhile, Angel drummed his fingers on the mantel. "You tried this before, *chiquita*. Remember how that ended?"

Holding that reptilian gaze without flinching, Isa set her

plastic bottle carefully on the table. "How you set Danny up for the fall? Yeah, hard to forget."

Cruel amusement flickered over his face. "There was no setup involved. Danny admitted it was his idea to run those drugs out of that business. He even shared how he lied to you to get you turn on me." His fingers stopped, flattening out against the wood. "Which you did, breaking your father's heart, my mother's heart, and mine." The last words carried an unmistakable threat.

Soul-deep aversion stripped her voice of pretense. "You don't have a heart."

"You know that's not true." Angel advanced with a predatory deliberateness. "I'm not the one who betrayed everyone, *chiquita*." He closed in, his magic coiling around her, tightening with each step.

She held her position, refusing to bend or retreat. It was what he needed from her, and she wasn't about to give him shit.

He came to a stop in front of her, leaving only a few inches between them. "That was all you."

Bargain. Caro's voiceless agreement vibrated in the air between them, carrying the weight of a magical oath given and accepted.

The Reaper pulled Caro's spirit closer in an unholy embrace. Vengeance, cold and unyielding, filled her, erasing everything but the craving for retribution. Isa reached out and wrapped her fingers around the loose tie hanging from Angel's neck as her lips curved into a cruel smile.

"That's funny," she said. The flash of uncertainty in his eyes pleased her. She tightened her grip on the tie, closing those scant inches to whisper into his ear. "I remember it being all you."

Then she struck.

chapter 18

Locke

"How good is this source, Des?" Locke raced through the narrow streets, just a bit too fast for the older neighborhood. Normally, he wouldn't chance speeding, especially since residents liked to park on the street, but it was midafternoon, and most of them were at work, which cleared a few extra feet of roadway.

"Rock-solid." The Tracer's voice was tight as he gripped the handle above the passenger window with one hand and thumbed his phone with the other. "We're not the only ones interested in Angel's business."

As Des had worked his mysterious sources for leads on where Angel would have taken Isa, Locke used his time to badger the nearby businesses for security footage. A few creative threats later, he spotted the SUV that peeled away from Wonderland as it headed south along Seventh. He tagged Roxy to do her thing with the traffic cameras and was waiting impatiently for an update when Des barged back in, saying he had an address. Locke had not thought twice before getting into his Charger and heading out, especially since that address was in the same general direction the SUV had taken. Long shot or not, it beat the hell out of twiddling his thumbs.

The Charger hit another thick traffic bump, and Des sucked in a sharp breath as the undercarriage scraped along the humped asphalt. "You're going to ruin your car."

"It's fine."

"We need a plan."

"We have one." Locke barely slowed as he took the upcoming left. "We're going in and getting Isa."

"Not much of a plan."

"You got something better?"

"Yeah, and part of it includes not tearing through the neighborhood until someone calls the cops on us."

It irked the shit out of him, but Des was right. The neighborhood might wear its age with fading dignity, but the fairly new apartments and cleared lots around the original homes showed it was trying to make a comeback.

Locke eased his foot from the gas, the Charger immediately dropping its speed to something passably legal. "Fine. Happy?"

"No." Des released his grip and started working his phone. "You need to take the third right then the first left. It'll take us to an alley that runs along the back side of the street. There's a lot next to a hostel. We can leave the car there."

"Why not park in the apartments over there?"

"Because I know the hostel's manager."

Good enough. "And the house?"

"About a half block away."

Following Des's directions, he slid his Charger into an empty spot. The minute he stopped, Des had his door open. "Where are you going?" Locke asked.

Des leaned down, one hand on the door, one on the roof. "Want to make sure you don't get towed, especially if we need to haul ass. Don't worry—Henry'll keep his mouth shut." He slammed the door and then jogged along the alleyway.

Locke unsnapped his belt, grabbed his keys and phone,

and shoved out of the driver's side. His magic yanked hard against his restraint, wanting to track Isa, but he held it in check. He strode down the side alley, dust and fumes filling his nose as the dry air shifted around him. The excited chatter of birds fell from the twisted, spindly branches of nearby palo verde trees before being drowned out by the roar of jet engines overhead as a commercial airliner made its approach to the nearby airport.

Out on the street ahead, a dust-encrusted silver sedan drove by, the bass so heavy the street vibrated underfoot. Locke slowed, giving Des time to rejoin him. As the noise from the jet faded, his ears picked up the hum of the electrical lines tacked to the wooden poles along the street. Somewhere close, a one-sided conversation in Spanish was going down. A burst of childish laughter and the clink of dishes drifted over the cement dividing the hostel and an older home with a minivan in front of it.

"Thanks again." Des's voice drifted to him, and then a door closed. Heavy footsteps crunched down a path, then came the squeak of metal. Des pushed through the gate set in the low wall and joined him at the curb. "We're good. Here." He thrust his phone at Locke, talking low and fast. "We're here." He ran his finger along the screen. "The house is here."

Locke took in the details. "We could've parked in the apartments, hopped the fence there." He pointed at a short wall running behind the apartment complex's parking lot and a home.

"And been caught." Des pinched the screen, bringing the image closer. "See? Cameras."

Sure enough, there were cameras positioned along the complex's back side.

"We go in this way." Des traced the route. "Hop this fence, which puts us next door. We go in through the back here."

"Got it." Locke handed the phone back to Des. "Let's go."

They crossed the street, threading past tipped-over garbage and recycling bins, and jogged down a narrow asphalt path winding between the tightly clustered properties. Des stopped under a tree that towered over a cinderblock fence. A low warning bark started up behind it.

Locke came up to him. "Here?"

"Here." The barking intensified. Des shot him a look. "You got this?"

Locke didn't bother with a response. He did a small hop to grab the top of the fence then hauled his ass up and over and landed in a crouch in the dirt. A chain rattled as the barking turned frenzied. Locke's magic stalked the thick-chested dog. Recognizing he was outmatched, the poor boy stopped in mid-bark and, with a whimper, lowered slowly to the ground, his attention on Locke. Locke moved to him. Easing his magic's hold, he ran a hand over the quivering mutt.

His magic sniffed the air and tasted it on its metaphorical tongue as he scanned the yard and house. Dark windows, no cameras, lots of dirt, patches of dried grass, and cracked pavers. The air carried the flat stillness of an empty place, so no one was home. Good.

Behind him, Des landed with a thump. Locke gave the dog one last pat, then he and Des headed toward the last fence separating them from Isa. Or so Locke hoped. Towering pink bougainvillea bushes filled the narrow space between the house and the fence, and another palo verde tree sat in the back corner. The two men picked a spot near the tree at the back end to make their entry.

Locke grabbed hold of the top edge and pulled himself up. He hung there for a few seconds, taking in the yard, then dropped back down. "Not much cover, but there's a straight shot to the back door. Could be an issue."

"Then we split. You take the back. I'll take the front."

"Works for me." Locke worked a ring off his finger, activated the embedded rune, and handed it to Des. “Use this. If it flashes once, hold. Flashes twice, go.”

Des took it. “One, hold. Two, go. Got it.” He turned and headed for the side gate.

Locke waited for him to clear the gate before he once again played leapfrog with the fence. Tapping into his air magic, he stilled the branches’ movements and muffled his landing as he dropped into the yard. He held his crouch for a long moment as the slight breeze whispered to him.

Not all Hounds carried the same abilities, but most tended to fall under the Elemental mage classification instead of Mystic or Divine. Having an affinity with earth, wind, fire, or water tended to give a Hound a unique advantage when hunting prey. And at that moment, Locke’s affinity for air was telling him all sorts of interesting things. Like the fact that active magic was at work, creating a barrier of artificial silence around the house. He dialed his magic in, like tuning into a radio station, until he could pick up the faint sounds coming from inside the house. A conversation between two voices, one low, one high. Male and female. He could feel Des’s presence working around to the front yard and sensed when he stopped.

Using that as his signal, Locke made his way along the fence toward the porch that ran along the back side of the house. There was a set of glass French doors, blinds drawn, on one side and a large window with square glass panes on the other. Even though blinds covered both, he kept low and avoided sight lines.

As he crept up on the window, his magic burrowed through the silencing spell and brought back bits and pieces of the conversation, including the sharp order in Spanish to sit. Inside, the air shifted as someone moved, and with his back to the wall, Locke froze. The presence moved closer, then came the sounds of a refrigerator opening and closing and the presence retreating.

The voice spoke again. "Go ahead, *chiquita*."

The endearment set Locke's teeth on edge, but the taunting, "Try it," that followed had him wondering what it was that Isa was attempting. He paused, listening for her voice. When it came, the anxiety in his gut eased a fraction.

"He was going to take me to the Den. However, since I was there and so was Nova, I figured I might as well ask, see if she heard any rumors about a new drug."

Since Locke was just as interested in Angel's answer, he waited for it and was unsurprised when the man played dumb. For her part, Isa stuck with the one-bartender-to-another angle. There was something about setting someone up, then Angel was at it again.

"The one who betrayed everyone, *chiquita*... That was all you." Something in Angel's tone set off warning bells.

But worse was the retribution in Isa's voice, signaling she was either in full-on Reaper mode or royally pissed. "That's funny. I remember it being all you."

She is definitely both.

Locke flashed Des as he got into position. He kicked out, slamming his heel just above the lock on the French door. Wood split, glass shattered, and blinds rattled. From the front came a sound of violent entry as Locke charged through the shattered remains of the back door.

He bolted through the dining room, his hip slamming into the table and sending the metal legs screeching over tile. He knocked a chair out of his way and hit the archway leading to the front of the house, only to be brought up short as his magic flared in warning. In what should have been a living room, ebony tendrils whipped around, sucking all the light deep into its dark heart, where three indistinct forms were locked in a silent struggle. Despite whatever was going down, the absence of noise was jarring. Magic filled the space like a trapped storm, churning within the confines of the living room. Flashes of power zipped through the charged air like lightning, and the bone-deep chill of power cut through the air inches away from Locke. The silent storm shredded the shadows, revealing a glimpse of Isa, her form draped in the Reaper's cloak, which shifted from black to gray to ghostly white and back. Her lips were drawn back in a fierce snarl as she lunged toward one of the figures.

"Isa!" He started to reach out.

"Locke, don't!" Des's bellow stopped him in mid-move. "I'm barely keeping this shit contained. If you step inside that mess, I won't be able to hold it back."

Only then did Locke realize Des was not one of the three figures fighting. Instead, Des was crouched near an overturned chair, magic a dull silver halo as it ran through him and into his hands, which were pressed flat against the floor to create a rough containment circle around the trio.

Questions crowded Locke's brain, but only one escaped. "What the hell?"

An unearthly scream of fury ripped through the air, and the figures broke apart, one tearing free and barreling into Des.

"*¡Muévete, chingádo!*"

Locke recognized Angel's voice even as a pained grunt came from Des. It was followed by a dull thud as Angel kicked out, sending an already off-balance Des rocking back. Power flared as he lost his hold on the magical containment.

Des snarled in frustration and tried to grab the man rushing toward the broken front door. "Asshole!"

Locke couldn't see what happened next because, free from restraint, volatile magic tore through the room on an unearthly wail. In the center of it all stood a terrible beauty, dark hair whipping around her face, her eyes disconcerting black pools, her face filled with a terrifying hunger as ragged remnants of spirits coiled around her like a beloved pet. Frenzied inky ribbons whipped out like a tentacled nightmare. Locke dodged one only to have another find its mark. Like a barbed trap, it burrowed deep with an unearthly chill as the suffocating pressure of magic tightened around him and insidious whispers tunneled into Locke's skull, shredding his sanity.

He could feel his mental grip slipping when his magic leapt forward, burning through the ice. It snarled and snapped, forcing the invading magic to retreat. As his mind cleared, he reinforced his power, holding Isa's attack at bay. When he lifted his head, he realized he had been forced to his knees by the assault. He flexed his power, searing through the tendrils anchoring him in place, then set his teeth and shoved to his feet as the last few ties frayed and fell away. Half-blinded by shadows, he fought his way toward Isa, using his affinity with air to create a shield against the storm of bone-chilling magic as the abilities that served him as a Hound helped him create a path to his target.

He broke through the dizzying dance of shadows to cut in front of Isa. She wasn't watching him but was focused on Des and Angel, who were still fighting, magic erupting like flares around them. She started forward with an intimidating deliberateness, the darkness around her hungry and focused. Locke's instincts screamed, and he reached for her, only to stop as Des's earlier warning echoed through his aching head.

His hands, just a breath away from touching her, were slowly going numb from the encroaching chill. "Isa."

She stilled, her inhuman gaze shifting to him. There was no recognition, no sign that Isa was in there, just the merciless presence of the Reaper. "Move."

He knew it was stupid to deny this creature, but he still said, "No." Power whipped around him, sinking through skin and bone to rip across his soul like vicious barbs. He hissed in pain, and his gut twisted as he fought the urge to strike out. "Stop it, Isa. This isn't you."

She cocked her head, a look of cruel amusement in her eyes. "This is all me." The silvery wisps twined tighter, momentarily warping her facial features into something unrecognizable as the wails in his head grew louder and angrier. "We will have vengeance."

We?

She turned back, resuming her measured pursuit of her prey.

He matched her step for step, reducing the space between them to mere inches before stopping. "Not like this."

She turned to him, her gaze filled with a depth of magic he didn't bother trying to decipher. "The bargain was struck. Judgment has been rendered. Recompense is due."

Questions tripped over his pulse, but they would have to wait for later. If there was a later. "We'll get it, I promise, but not like this."

He needed Isa back behind the wheel because some instinct warned him if he lost her now, it would be for good. The Reaper studied him. As close as he was to her, he could see the superimposed image of someone else's features that flickered over Isa's face like a macabre veil. It was disturbing and wrong on so many levels and left him shaken.

"Please, *reinita*."

For a moment, recognition flashed in the inky depths of her eyes, and he thought he'd gotten through, but a surge of power, followed by a pained bellow, broke the moment. Her attention flashed to the action behind him, and the traces of Isa were swallowed under by the pitiless Reaper.

"Move. Now."

The order was followed by a shove of magic, but Locke grabbed her arms, twisted her around, and dragged her toward him. An agonizing chill wrapped them both. As she struggled against him, he rode the pain, forcing her back against his chest with his arms hooked around her, trapping her against him. Locke pulled his head back as she tried to smash her head into his face, and he kicked her legs apart, disrupting her balance. He held tight even as they fell together, the bruising of his shoulder and hip lost under the excruciating cold burn as her power fought back.

At any other time, Locke would have admired Isa's tenacity as she continued to fight, using her legs, feet, and even teeth, but when his options for stopping her without hurting her were limited, it was just a pain in the ass. He was trying to use his body weight to pin her to the floor, but her movements grew more frenzied as she was reduced to furious growls.

"Dammit, Isa, come back. Stop this."

Her magic hit him like a multitailed bullwhip, and he grunted under the impact. Somehow, he managed to maintain his hold. Temper sparked, and with a snarl, he got a foot against the floor and started to force her under him. Realizing she was outweighed, she struggled harder, her embedded magic raking against his. Then Des was there, adding his magic to the fight, forcing Isa to split her attention, which allowed Locke to roll her body under his. She bucked a few more times then stilled. Not fooled by her sudden surrender, he didn't ease back.

"Let him go, Isa," Des said roughly. He lowered himself until he was looking into her face, his magic pushing against hers, as Locke tried to catch his breath. "He's not who you want."

"Where is he? The one who has to pay?" There was an unusual whine to her voice, one he'd never heard before. "Where is he?"

Des's gaze flicked to Locke, worry and a warning in his eyes. Locke braced and tightened his hold on her wrists, keeping them pinned to the floor.

Des looked back at Isa. "Angel's gone."

"No! No, no, no!" She started to struggle again, bucking against Locke's hold. "We had a bargain! You promised."

"The promise will be kept," Des said, his voice smoothing out. "Angel will pay, but we need Isa to get to him."

"She promised!" The wail contained nothing of Isa. The power around them flexed and flailed in an eerie echo of the woman struggling underneath him.

That wasn't the Reaper, and it sure as shit wasn't Isa. Understanding hit Locke like a freight train, shaking his composure, as Des tried to soothe the entity inside Isa's body. His momentary distraction cost him as Isa bucked hard, ripping her arm free from his grip and clawing out. She raked at his neck, refocusing his attention. He caught her wrist in a bruising grip and forced her back down. His mind spun with questions as Des continued to talk the entity down. Eventually, Isa's wails turned to sobs then finally fell quiet, as did the magic saturating the room.

Locke listened to Des softly cajole the entity, the tormented spirit of a murdered girl named Caro, into revealing how Isa had struck a deal with her. The magical energy eased back with each passing moment, the shadows fading away, the air resettling around them. Under him, Locke could feel the tension ebbing from Isa's body as his own aches and pains made themselves known. He stayed vigilant, not wanting to be taken off guard again, but emotionally, he was struggling. He wanted to rail at Isa for taking such a risk, even though logic argued she'd had no idea if or when help would arrive. Ceding control of one's body to a vengeful spirit was a recipe for disaster, even for a skilled Reaper. From what he was hearing, it sounded like Isa had deliberately fed Cora power, fueling the entity's fury before allowing it control. A fucking dangerous decision.

He tried not to worry as Des did his best to convince Cora

that Angel would pay and she should let Isa return, but it was taking too long. Had Cora taken too much, leaving Isa weak? Or maybe Angel had managed to do something to Isa before the bargain was struck. That last ugly fear fractured his heart, whispering he might have already lost Isa.

He lowered his head to hers. "Please, *reinita*, I need you to fight. Come back to me."

Des fell quiet.

A shudder ran through Isa.

Locke closed his eyes and sent a prayer to whoever was listening. *Please bring her back.*

Seconds ticked by, marked by the drum of his heart, and then finally...

"I'm here."

chapter 19

Isa

Isa woke with a gasp, heart pounding as she blinked into the darkness. Fuzzed by disturbing dreams, it took her a moment to realize she was in Locke's bed. His empty bed. She lifted the sheet to her nose and inhaled, taking in his familiar woodsy scent that saturated his sheets. It eased the worst of her jitters, and bit by bit, her muscles uncoiled. Still, there was a lingering sense of disconnection to her body, as if it didn't quite belong to her.

Because for a while, it hadn't.

Behind the wall she'd built, Cora's voracious need for retribution awoke and searched for an escape route. Finding none, it resettled, sullen, to wait and plot. She didn't have to be an Oracle like Cass to know it wouldn't wait for long. There would be another clash with Angel, and when that happened, the cracks would widen, and then... She forced her thoughts to go blank, not needing the reminder of the edge she skated along, but Cora's needs were not ignored so easily, lurking in the shadows like a monster.

Isa did her damnedest to ignore it. Lying on her side, she uncurled from the defensive ball she slept in and stretched out her legs. She forced her shoulders to loosen and unbent her arms, smoothing a hand over the soft cotton sheets. She stared into the quiet darkness, able to make out the nightstand and the lump of her phone in the hint of light seeping from the partially closed bathroom door as her thoughts circled like a flock of birds. For a long moment, she let them dance. Then, resigned to the inevitable, she allowed them to land.

She'd let fear and pride drive her decisions—again—and Angel had gotten away. Again. All her posturing during the last few years of breaking free from his insidious hold lay in shambles, revealing the stark truth. She had shattered his manipulative hold years ago, only to replace it with her self-doubts and debilitating fears that kept the wound open, allowing him access. And for Angel, that was akin to giving him an open vein into which to sink his poison deep, eroding her ties to everything and everyone. He'd done it before with her father and Pilar, leaving Isa with no choice but to cut ties to her old life and family, and now his venom was spreading into her current reality. She needed to grant herself forgiveness for her decision to cut those destructive ties and rebuild with a family of her choosing. One made up of people who didn't tear her apart but stood beside her, offering support when everything started to crumble.

Like Des. He'd been truly worried as he bargained with Cora. Even buried under the Reaper, Isa had felt his concern and his unshakable resolve not to lose her to the deal she'd made. He, more than most, understood how steep that price could be—how the Reaper could devour all that made her Isa. As she struggled to push past the combined demands of the Reaper and Cora, Des stayed steady and strong, his determination lighting the way back, and that journey hadn't been easy. Splitting her attention between Angel and Cora allowed Cora to feed too long and too deep, which twisted the spirit into something insatiable. Yes, she owed Cora her vengeance and had gone so far as to give her oath that it would be exacted.

That oath would bind Isa until the debt was paid. But for one heart-stopping moment, she'd almost chosen another route. A shiver crawled over her skin as she remembered how Cora's vengeance found the malicious heart of Isa's rage, how it whispered and cajoled, making dark promises. Then had come Des's voice, drawing not just her but Cora's spirit as well, pulling them away from the yawning pit atop which they teetered .

And then there was Locke. Her heart stuttered. "Come back to me." The emotion behind his plea had the hot press of tears rising unexpectedly. It wasn't condemnation or even anger but something infinitely more precious. She didn't dare name it, but she could feel it as he lay on top of her, not hurting her but shielding her as he pressed her into the floor. She remembered the raw vulnerability of his voice slipping past the storm of destructive darkness to fall like a gentle rain on her savaged heart. She desperately wished she could return his offering. She ached to be that open, to risk that much, but she wasn't sure she was brave enough. A hot tear rolled to the pillow. Would he wait for her to find the strength to shove past her self-imposed walls?

On the nightstand, her phone buzzed, and the screen lit up. Her heart gave a painful thump. No good news came in the middle of the damn night. She swiped at her face then grabbed her phone, trying not to think what calamity was barreling toward her next. When she saw the name on screen, she wasn't sure if she should be amused or terrified. Probably both.

"Hey, Cass."

"Hey, you," her best friend said. "Are you okay?"

"Shouldn't that be my question? Last time we spoke, you were worried." That was putting it lightly.

Cass had headed up to Vegas for her beloved grandmother's funeral, which required interacting with her shitty family.

Knowing what lay in wait, Isa and Des hadn't wanted her to go alone, and luckily, Locke's friend Grayson, who lived in Vegas, offered her a ride. Even better, he stayed with Cass, which Isa appreciated, since the Ambroses had behaved as badly as she'd expected. At the family's house, Cass's mother flung endless snide digs at her oldest daughter, ensuring that they drew blood, while Cass's spineless father stayed out of the line of fire. As if that weren't bad enough, Cass learned her sister, Sofia, the daughter who could do no wrong, was engaged to some desperate-to-impress idiot with his head up Cass's mother's ass, but something was off, and Cass was worried. She and Isa had discussed it a couple of days ago, and Isa had offered to help however she could. She'd meant it, even though she wasn't Sofia's biggest fan. She'd watched Cass try to salvage her relationship with her baby sister over and over again only to get slapped down.

"How's Sofia?"

"Well, the engagement is definitely off."

Concerned at the strained note in her friend's voice, Isa sat up, cramming pillows between her back and the headboard before leaning back. "Spill."

Cass recapped the last couple of days, and they were a doozy. When she finally wound down, all Isa could say was, "Holy shit, Cass. That's... a lot."

"Yeah."

"So, what now?"

"Right now? Grayson's making me stay in bed until the hospital allows visitors in the morning, then it'll be time for a family discussion."

Despite everything, Isa couldn't resist teasing her. "Grayson's *making* you stay in bed? Mmm, do tell."

Cass snorted. "That's a two-, maybe three-drink conversation for when I get back."

"I'll hold you to it."

Cass made a soft humming sound. "Let's circle back to my question. How are you?"

"I'm fine." Isa winced at the lie.

Cass's voice was gentle as she said, "Iz, it's me. Wanna try again?"

All the things swirling in Isa's head threatened to spill out, but after all that Cass had shared, Isa didn't want to pile on more. She tried one more time to dodge. "You've been talking to Des."

"Well, he needed to bitch to someone about running the bar solo."

Isa gave an amused huff. "At least it was a Sunday night." The end of the week was always slow.

"And thank the gods the weekend is over." Cass paused. "He told me what happened. Talk to me, Iz. I'm right here."

The acceptance and love crumbled Isa's already shaky composure, and her words tumbled out in a disjointed mess, yet somehow Cass managed to follow them, asking questions only occasionally.

When Isa finally fell quiet, Cass said, "I love you, Isa. You know that."

Isa's laugh was a little watery. "I hear a 'but' in there."

"Because you're not stupid," Cass said without malice. "Terminally stubborn and willing to take on more than you should but not stupid."

Thinking about her earlier realization with Angel, Isa said, "I could dispute that."

"And you'd be wrong. First, your worries about Locke's loyalties. Whether you want to admit it or not, you know that's not the issue you think it is."

Irritation sparked. "The Cordovas aren't some minor Family, Cass."

"No Family is really 'minor,' but do you honestly believe a corrupt Family could earn Locke's loyalty? Or Rory's? I mean, that girl has a damn good reason not to want to tangle with a Family, but she's all tied up with the Cordovas."

Isa had to concede that Cass had a valid point. Rory's highly coveted ability as a Prism was something of an urban legend, and the Cordovas hadn't exploited it. If anything, they'd made moves to protect her.

Cass didn't stop with her reality check. "You're using this loyalty thing as an excuse because letting him get close scares the shit out of you."

Isa twisted her fingers in the sheet *Okay, maybe she has a point.*

"Which I totally get, because Angel is a sociopathic dick who did some serious damage." There was a great deal of heat in Cass's voice. "But what you need to realize is that round one went to you, not him. When you walked away the first time, you not only injured his pride—you took away his power as well. So when you walked back into the Den with Locke at your side, Angel spotted an unexpected opportunity, and he ran with it. He thought he'd played you, but you'd known it was going to happen, and you'd done it anyway because Locke needed you to."

It sucked when your best friend held up a mirror and didn't let you turn away. "I should have left Locke behind."

Cass snorted. "Girl, please. There is no way that man would let you saunter in solo. Besides, you wanted Angel to see him, and I don't blame you. Locke on his worst day is leaps and bounds better than Angel on his best."

Isa worried her bottom lip, unable to deny that irrefutable truth. "And that was a mistake."

"Was it? You knew there was no way to stop Angel from feeding off of you. He's a Harvester. It doesn't matter how cold you go—he only needs the tiniest fissure to leech onto, and you being twisted up about coming back, about Locke, and about the situation in general created the opening he needed. That doesn't make you weak. That doesn't make any of this your fault. It just shows you're human."

"With some dangerous baggage."

"So what? We all have something we carry, Iz. Even Locke. Do you think you're the only one to struggle with letting someone in? I don't know him well, but I've watched him watch you for months, and you know what I saw? A cynical man willing to put in the time to earn a cautious woman's trust. It didn't matter how many times she pushed him away, because every time he came back, he managed to get a few inches closer to seeing the real heart underneath."

She rubbed absently at the ache blooming in her chest. "That heart is a fucking mess, Cass."

"But that's what makes it so beautiful, babe," Cass said. "Have you ever heard of Kintsugi?"

The unexpected question tickled a memory of walking through an art gallery displaying stone-fired pieces veined with precious metals. "Isn't that a Japanese art form where they use gold or silver to mend cracked teacups?"

"Any pottery, actually," Cass corrected, "but yes, that. As Grayson reminded me recently, when those broken pieces are treasured enough to be pieced back together, even as dented and dinged as they are, what emerges isn't just stronger but holds more depth and beauty than its original purpose. It's not tossed away because of a fault or two but instead is cherished for surviving the trauma and turning that damage into something better. And that *something better* should never be handed over to someone who won't value it." She took a second then landed her blow. "Is Locke the kind of person to throw something like that away?"

"No." The word was soft but heavy with truth.

Cass's tone gentled even more. "So maybe he's worth taking a risk for."

"Maybe." Her agreement was shaky but carried an edge of hope. "But, gods, Cass—"

"Stop, Iz. Be brave. Not everything ends badly." Her tone took on the vague nuances that came when Fate spoke through her. "Alone or together, find your balance and make your decision. Otherwise, it will be made for you."

After hanging up with Cass, Isa forced her way through her own protective walls to heed her friend's warning and made her decision. Her heart raced under the oversized T-shirt she wore as she padded barefoot down the hall, following the faint trail of light to the living room. She came to the archway and stopped, nerves nibbling at her determination.

Light from somewhere in the kitchen, probably the stove, seeped into the living room to reveal the man waiting in the dark. In nothing but sleep pants, Locke was sprawled on the couch, his hair sticking up as if he'd been running his hands through it. He had his bare feet propped on the edge of a box and a hand around a glass of water resting on his naked abdomen.

His gaze raked over her, hot enough to burn. "You're up."

The tone of those two words, and the way he held himself, made her feel... hunted. Her heart was a heavy beat in her chest, but a curl of anticipation unfurled and settled deep, thickening her blood. "I am."

"Did I wake you?"

"No." Excitement and dread tripped along her nerves as she took the first step then the second until she was walking into his den. "Cass called."

He watched her slow approach, the tension singing between them and tightening. "How is she?"

"Good now." She reached the couch and stopped close enough to feel the soft cotton of his pants.

He angled his head, holding her gaze with predatory patience. "Now?" He dropped his feet and leaned over to set his glass on the floor. "What happened?"

"Long story. Grayson can fill you in when they get back on Wednesday."

Locke sat back and stretched out his legs, his muscles bunching in interesting places with the movement. "Grayson's heading back to Phoenix?"

It was hard to follow the conversation when other things kept snagging her attention. Like the way the waist of his pants slipped a little lower, making her core temperature shoot up and exposing an intriguing line that disappeared underneath the material. She felt her body sway the tiniest bit as she tried to stay focused.

"Yeah. Seems he and Cass are a thing now."

Locke's chuckle was dark and male. "Damn, Gray works fast. I'll have to ask for pointers."

"Why?" The husky question slipped out before she could censor it, desire playing hell with her thoughts. "It's not like you need them."

"You sure about that?" Locke reached out and played with the hem of her shirt, his knuckles brushing against her thigh. The touch was light, but that burn in her core deepened as her skin pebbled at the near-innocent touch. Awareness flared in the bright-blue eyes, and his cheeks tightened and colored. His voice dropped to a rough purr. "I've been chasing you for a while, and it doesn't seem like I'm gaining ground."

She leaned into his touch, wanting more. "You've gained more ground than you know."

"Is that so?" He let go of her shirt to glide his palm up her thigh until it disappeared under her borrowed T-shirt. Hunger and want clashed in his icy-blue gaze as it burned into hers while he traced a toe-curling trail along the edge of her panties. Her body swayed, the tempting touch creating a slow, beautiful ache. He steadied her by sliding his hands to her hips, where they settled against her skin like brands, drawing her forward gently. "Are you still running?"

Heeding his gentle tug, she put a hand on his bare shoulder, a knee on the couch by his hip, then swung her other leg over his lap. A soft whimper escaped her as she settled against him. The evidence of his desire was unmistakable. She dipped her head, her hair falling forward like a curtain until there was nothing but the voracious hunger raging in his eyes.

Her lips were a breath away from his. "No."

Holding her gaze, he didn't hide the flare of satisfaction, and when he answered, his voice was deep and dark with intent. "Then you're mine."

For a breathless moment, she searched his face. *Be brave.* Torn between fear and hope she let go and took a chance. "And you're mine."

"Always, *reinita*." It was a vow, pure and simple.

She wasn't sure who moved first, but her lips brushed his once then twice in soft enticement. The third time, he opened for her, and she dove in. The hands at her hips tightened as he followed her lead, their tongues tangling as they tasted and teased. His hand left her hips to stroke along her spine before setting at the base to press her close to the unmistakable ridge hardening between them. Hunger, need, and instinct came together as she undulated against him, riding the edge of the storm. He bucked beneath her, eliciting a soft gasp from her.

She dug her nails into his shoulders and arched back. "Locke!"

He groaned as his hand dove into her hair, holding her in place, and spread a line of open-mouthed kisses along the sensitive skin where her neck met her shoulder. Endearments fell in a whispered rush as shudders wracked her overly sensitized body. His touch left her a mess of cravings. Her breasts ached, and need pooled at her core, hot and wet, while the urge to crawl into him became almost overwhelming. It was as if all the months of circling had been nothing more than extended foreplay that exploded into this one brilliant moment.

Her hands moved over him, learning every rise and fall, dipping below the edge of his pants to find even more temptation. She was so lost in her exploration that when the world shifted around her, she gave a surprised cry. "What—"

Locke swept her up. He held her tight as he headed to the hall. "We are not doing this on the couch."

Something about the disgruntlement made her feel lighter, younger. She wound her arms around his neck. "But we are doing this?"

He met her gaze, his eyes wild and fierce, as he carried her to his bedroom. "Hell yeah, we are."

chapter 20

Locke

LOCKE GLARED out the windshield as he navigated the morning traffic. He should have been in a good mood, considering he'd woken up with a warm and naked Isa, but his morning had quickly turned to shit. First was the phone call informing him that Paisley had finally sobered up enough to be useful. He set a time to talk to the girl, and when he hung up, Isa insisted on coming with him. Since there were still dark circles under her eyes and a worrisome paleness that had nothing to do with their lack of sleep and everything to do with Angel, he insisted she stay at his place and take it easy. She'd had other ideas, and so began their first argument—which, since she was sitting in the passenger seat of the Dodge, applying lipstick, he'd lost.

And now he was thinking about starting their second argument. They had a twenty-minute drive ahead of them, and he had questions—ones that had circled his brain the night before while Isa slept.

Did Angel hurt her?

What is the deal with Cora?

What kind of bargain has she struck, and why is Des so worried about it?

Does she have a death wish?

Okay, maybe he wouldn't ask that last one, but the others? Yeah, those needed to be asked. And this time, he wouldn't be distracted. Not like last night, when she'd stood before him, all long legs and wary eyes, battered but fiercely unbroken—an enticing mix—for the first time offering him everything he craved. Instead of talking through shit, he took what she offered, scared it was a fever dream. He spent the next few hours proving to himself she was real—soft flesh, hot blood, addicting taste. She was too much to resist, so he'd caved. And loved every minute of it. Hell, he'd be a happy man if he could keep her in his bed for however long she let him.

But reality was a bitch. Angel was still out there, still a threat, and he couldn't shrug off Des's fear from yesterday or his own worry about the shadows she still carried. He wasn't sure how to broach the topic. He didn't want to argue, but he needed to know what they were working with.

"What happened yesterday?" He did his best to keep his tone neutral.

Isa paused in mid-motion and looked away from the visor mirror. "I was careful, Locke."

"I didn't say you weren't."

"You didn't have to." She turned back to the mirror, wiped the side of her mouth, then flipped the visor up and recapped her lipstick. "Our stock delivery was arriving early, so I had Des take Kelly home while I checked it in. Afterward, I forgot to reset the security ward."

"Is that normal?" Sliding into interrogation mode was second nature to Locke.

"Is what normal?"

"Your delivery coming in early?"

She shrugged. "Not often, but the regular driver was out, so there was a new guy."

His instincts quivered. "Did you get a name?"

"Um..." She drummed her fingers on the door's armrest. "Mick? No, Mitch." Her fingers stilled. "You think he was involved."

"It would make sense." He slowed as a sedan cut across three lanes to make the upcoming left. "Changing the delivery time means you'll be at the bar at a set time."

"Which makes it easier to snatch and go," she finished in a tone of self-disgust. "I didn't even think about it."

He didn't like her self-directed criticism. "We're thinking it through now. So, you got your delivery."

"I was putting it away when I heard something out front. I thought it was you."

He ignored the flash of guilt. "Zev and I were checking Paisley into the clinic. I should have texted you earlier."

She set her hand on his thigh and gave it a squeeze. "Hey. If I can't beat myself up, neither can you."

He dropped his hand to hers and held it. Fine. He'd just keep the self-criticism quiet, then. "So you thought it was me."

"And I walked into an ambush." A fine tremor ran through the hand he held, but her voice remained steady. "There were two of them, and they nailed me with a knockout spell."

"They made you bleed." It came out between clenched teeth.

"They did?"

He managed a nod.

"Well, I managed to hit them with a bottle of vodka."

"Yeah. Found that shattered on the floor. You got one, not the other."

"How did you—" She stopped short. "I totally forgot about the security cameras."

"Wasn't the cameras. Those were on the fritz. One of your abductors was an electro mage. Des had a chat with Al."

"Al?"

"Your resident alcoholic ghost with voyeur vibes?"

She giggled. "Alphonse. I'm surprised he was paying attention."

"Seems he likes to watch you, something Des wasn't happy about."

"Des never has much patience with the dead." She resumed her story. "The two idiots dumped me at Angel's."

Locke kept his territorial anger locked down. "What did he want?"

"To gloat." She pulled his hand to rest on the console between them and threaded their fingers together. "And to find out why we were nosing around. Don't worry. I stuck to our story."

"That isn't what worries me."

She lifted their joined hands and pressed a kiss to the back of his before lowering it back down. "I'm okay, Locke."

He risked looking away from the road for a moment to find her studying him. "You're more than okay, Isa, but that doesn't mean I like his attention on you any less." He turned back but not before he caught her mysterious, feminine smirk.

"He kept asking who sent me to look into him."

"So no doubt he's involved." He let her go to hit the blinker.

"None." She shifted in her seat so she could face him more fully. "Since I didn't get a chance to tell you yesterday, thank you."

Not sure where she was coming from, he frowned. "For what?"

"Finding me so fast."

"Thank Des," he grudgingly said. "With the cameras down, I was hitting a shit ton of dead ends. I managed to follow the SUV in a general direction before I lost track. I had

Roxy scrubbing traffic cams, but it was one of Des's contacts that gave us the house. Since it was in the same direction as where I lost your trail, we decided to risk it."

"I'm glad you did."

So was he. He cleared his throat as he took a turn. "And the girl, Cora?"

Her lingering amusement faded away. "Another one of his victims."

"What happened?"

She turned to look out the passenger window. "She and Angel got into an argument. It turned violent, and at some point, he shoved her. She fell back into the mantel and hit her head. Game over."

He remembered the frenzied spirit and the spiraling madness that had tried to infect him while Isa looked at him with cold eyes. "It must have been some argument." He felt Isa turn to watch him. "She had a hell of a hold on you."

"I made her a promise," she said with resigned determination.

He remembered what Des had said when he was trying to reach Isa. "And it has to be kept."

Isa's silence spoke volumes.

He took a breath and stepped into the unknown. "What happens if it can't be kept?"

The silence grew heavier.

"Isa?" he pushed.

"I have to finish this, Locke."

His gut knotted as she continued to avoid his question, but something warned him to tread lightly. "I'm not saying you won't, but what happens if Cora doesn't get what she thinks she paid for?"

There was a long pause. "One way or another, a Reaper always pays their debt."

There was an ominous finality to her answer, and he knew

that was the only one she'd give him. Maybe it should have pissed him off, but it just left him worried.

Maribel Ortiz, the Cordovas' lawyer, accompanied a wan-looking Paisley into the small conference room at the medical clinic. Catching sight of Locke and Isa sitting at the table, the girl froze and shot Mari a panicked look.

"You said I only had to talk to him. Who's she?"

"A friend of Isaiah's older brother, Micah." Dressed in her typical stiletto heels, tailored blouse, and skirt, Mari nudged the younger woman toward a chair. "She's just here to listen." The lawyer shot Isa a warning glare as she poured a glass of water from a nearby pitcher.

Paisley took a seat. Mari set the glass in front of her.

"You remember Locke Turon?" she asked as she went around Paisley to take the seat on the other side.

Paisley cupped her shaky hands around the glass and lifted it to take a drink. A tremor hit her, and a couple of drops hit the table as she set the glass back down. She raised bloodshot eyes to Locke. "You're the one that brought me here. With the car."

"I am."

Her gaze darted to Mari then back to Locke as she moved the glass in small circles, smearing the drips over the dark tabletop. "She told me you're looking for Isaiah. For his brother, right?"

He nodded and wasn't surprised when she mimicked the gesture with a jerky nod of her own. She wiped a hand under her nose then dropped her hands to her lap.

"Isaiah won't go home. He's pissed. Said he was tired of getting his ass reamed about shit that wasn't important."

Paisley shot a look at Isa. "Maybe you can tell his brother to back off."

In the seat next to Locke, Isa shifted, the air around her filled with intent. Under the table, he put a warning hand on her knee. She shot him a glare. He raised an eyebrow. Her mouth thinned in a rebellious pout, but she sat back and folded her arms.

He turned back to Paisley and pinned her in place with a cool stare. "His brother's in a coma."

Paisley's skin turned a sickly shade of gray, and her eyes widened. "It wasn't Isaiah. He didn't do anything to him."

"Didn't say he did," Locke said, keeping his voice level. "But we'd like to know where he is so we can fill him in on Micah's condition. He's the only family left."

Paisley clutched the glass until her bones pressed against white against her skin, her throat working as she swallowed. "What happened to him? The brother, I mean?"

"He was drugged," Mari said, her tone clinical.

Paisley's mouth rounded in shock, the precarious knot of brown hair bundled at the back of her head threatening to come loose as she turned to look at the lawyer. "Whoa, no cap?"

"Truth," Mari confirmed. "Someone slipped him a drug at the Alchemist."

Something flashed in Paisley's eyes and snared Locke's instincts. Knowing if he cornered her, he'd get nothing useful, he tried to circle around the topic. "You ever been there?"

Paisley blinked at him, her brow furrowing. "Where?"

"The Alchemist."

Tension crept through the hunched shoulders as she dropped her gaze, but she managed a jerky shrug. "A few times."

He pushed back, set his foot on his knee and rested his arm on the smooth table. His fingers drummed quietly as he considered how to seed the trail. Since every time Isaiah's name was mentioned, she tensed up, he decided to try another name. "Ever meet a guy named Leo?"

A look of mild disgust flashed across her face. "Total sus."

Okay, he knew that word. Clearly, Leo had failed to impress Paisley. "How so?"

"He hangs with the elders, you know, yet he keeps trying to link up." She scratched her nail over the tabletop. "Isaiah's cool with him, even though he wouldn't leave Isaiah alone."

Elders? He shot a look to Mari, who gave an amused shake of her head. *Kelly is barely five years older than this girl, so what does that make me—ancient?*

"How so?" Mari asked.

Paisley shifted in her seat, pushing back from the table a bit. "He kept talking to Isaiah about some new gig he had going, but Isaiah wasn't buying it—said he had no rizz." She reached for her glass and pulled it closer.

Dear gods, if this interview went much longer, he'd need a translator. Based on context, he figured Leo's erratic behavior had become problematic for Isaiah, which meant he must have already been using when he hit up Isaiah.

"What about Jigz?" Locke asked.

She stiffened so fast the water in the glass sloshed. "Jigz?" Her voice pitched high at the end as her gaze went anywhere but to him.

"The truth, Paisley," Mari warned. "Otherwise, we'll be having a different conversation, one that will include locating your nearest relative."

For a moment, the real Paisley peeked out with a spark of youthful mutiny. "Good luck finding one who's sober."

A flash of pity hit Locke, but Mari didn't flinch. She simply held Paisley's stare. That cool-eyed look had Paisley's rebellion sputtering into resignation. "Fine." She shot Locke a resentment-filled glare. "Yeah, I've seen him around."

Likely used him to get her fix when needed. "He another friend of Isaiah's?"

Her nose wrinkled as she gave a snort. "Not a friend. More like a... what do you call it?" She looked to Mari.

"Acquaintance?" Mari offered.

"That." Paisley nodded and turned back to Locke. "Isaiah only dealt with him because Carter told him to." She drew her leg up and wrapped her arms around her blue scrubs–covered shin, brushing her chin over her knee.

Next to him, Isa stiffened, but he was already putting a name to the stone-faced bouncer at the Den. "Who's Carter?"

Paisley cocked her head and stated blithely, "He's my agent."

It was not the answer he'd been expecting. "Agent?"

Paisley sat up straighter. "Yeah, I got picked up by Streetwise Talent." She tilted her head and flashed a gorgeous smile that saddened him because it offered a glimpse of what she could be if not for the disease shoving her down a darker path. "Carter was getting me paid gigs, which was great, but I was already behind on my rent. I had a payment plan going with my dick of a landlord, but when he found out Isaiah was staying with me, he kicked me out."

Locke's fingers stilled. "Isaiah was staying with you?"

A hint of color stained her cheeks, more proof that they were talking to someone young. "It's not like that."

Locke lifted his hand. "I never said it was."

"But you were thinking it. Everyone always does." She spoke with a world-weary cynicism. "Whatevs," she muttered. "Look, he just needed a place to crash for a few days, to stay off his brother's radar and all, but shit changes. Besides, it wasn't like it was forever. Isaiah was going to get his own place. He just needed time to put money away, you know. Plus, having him around meant we could split expenses."

Locke nodded, feeling every one of his twenty-nine years

and then some. "And when you got kicked out, where did you two go?"

She plucked at the blue scrubs and twisted the material so it tightened around her calf then loosened. "We were crashing at one of Carter's places."

Mari frowned and sat forward. "You're living with your agent?"

"Ew, no. Carter offered to put us up in an apartment. I don't know if he owns it or if it belongs to the agency, but he said it was available. Said he'd just take a higher percentage from my bookings for the rent until I could get on my feet."

A slow kernel of anger bloomed in Locke. Considering the way Isa was white-knuckling her chair, he wasn't the only one getting pissed. This girl could not catch a break.

Paisley continued to talk. "At first, Isaiah was all, 'Man, we should think about this.'" She tried to mimic Isaiah's voice then quickly switched back. "And I was like 'Bro, it beats sleeping on the streets.' He didn't back down until Carter offered to get him a meeting with his boss, maybe to get him into some kind of entry-level job with a steady paycheck, you know?"

Locke forced his hand to uncurl and flattened it against the table as that simmering fury grew. He could guess exactly what kind of job Carter got Isaiah. But he wouldn't let his reactions seep into his voice. The last thing he needed was for Paisley to clam up now.

"And did he get Isaiah a job?"

She stopped messing with her scrubs and gave a shrug. "I guess so. He had Isaiah running laps."

What the hell? Locke frowned. "Laps? Like running around a track?"

Paisley gave a real laugh, amused and girly. "No, not that. He had Isaiah doing things for him. Like a list of jobs to do. It kept him busy and his pockets full."

"Right." A headache threatened Locke, but he kept going. "And Isaiah? Do you know where he is now?"

Her fingers returned to knotting up the scrubs as she looked from Mari to Locke. "He's probably still back at the apartment."

Even though he could guess the answer, he still asked, "The one we found you at?"

She flushed. "No, not that one. We kind of got into it because he was being a buzzkill. I had a shitty day—went in for an assignment, turned out the guy was a creeper—so I needed to blow off steam. Isaiah didn't like how that was going down and stormed off. I had a bit too much, went home with friends, then you showed up."

For the first time in the conversation, Locke thought there might be something worth salvaging in Isaiah. His reaction to Paisley's behavior spoke volumes and offered the hope that he wasn't completely lost to Angel's poison.

"This apartment you two were crashing at—you have an address?"

She rattled off a location near Seventh Street. Locke spent another fifteen minutes circling through carefully worded questions. While he confirmed that Paisley had heard rumors that something new was hitting the scene, there wasn't much more she could share. By the time he shut it down, she was gray with exhaustion and was jumping or wincing at every little noise or unexpected movement. After thanking Paisley for her help and promising not to hurt Isaiah, he rose to his feet and watched Mari hand the girl off to a kind-faced staff member, who guided her gently down the hall.

Locke pulled out his phone and texted Zev an update, including the address Paisley had shared, using the unique shorthand most of Emilio's trusted people used. He shoved his phone back into a pocket and caught Isa's questioning gaze. "Zev."

She gave a nod then turned to Mari, who had come back and closed the door. “Tell me you’ll get her help,” Isa demanded.

Mari’s eyes flashed, her jaw set in stone as she faced down the seething woman. “It’s already taken care of.”

“And after she dries out…?”

“I called in a few favors and got her a spot at Jericho House,” the stalwart justice warrior said.

Locke recognized the name of a highly successful recovery program that shied away from publicity. Isa appeared somewhat appeased as she finally rose from her seat. “Good.”

Mari eyed both of them. “How much trouble is Isaiah in?”

“I don’t know. If we’re lucky, he’s a minor player in this mess,” he said.

“If we’re not?”

He didn’t bother answering, just held her gaze.

She looked away with an irritated noise. Whatever wheels were turning in her head drove her to pace the room. When she finally stopped, she turned to Isa. “You know this Carter person?”

Isa shot him a questioning look. He answered with a raised brow, wondering if he should have warned her that Mari was a Truth Seeker. *Too late now.*

Isa turned to the lawyer. “Yes, and we know his boss.”

Mari nodded as if they’d confirmed something she already knew. “You’re going after the boss.”

Isa didn’t even look his way. “Yes.”

Mari studied Isa for a long, unsettling moment. Then a vicious smile curved her lips. “Good. When you’re done with him, I want a turn.”

Locke was still contemplating how much of Angel he would leave for Emilio—and that was if Isa gave him a chance—so he couldn’t make Mari any promises. Instead, he moved up behind Isa so they faced Mari together. "Take it up with Emilio," he said.

That cold smile warmed into a feminine one. "Don't worry. I will."

Locke almost felt sorry for the intimidating head of the Cordova Family.

Almost.

chapter 21

Isa

THE ADDRESS that Paisley had shared led them just outside the hub of downtown and into an older neighborhood where modern office buildings sat next to golf courses. Dated apartment complexes wearing new faces lined the streets. They turned off of Seventh and onto a quiet palm-lined street, where two-story white buildings with black-tiled roofs sat in the shade of mature trees.

They parked in one of a handful of visitors' spots situated outside a wood fence. Behind the fence, rising like sun-faded flowers, were umbrellas spread wide to catch the sun's rays. The entry gate was flung open in welcome, offering glimpses of the inside courtyard. Despite its modern dressings, the complex's age was still visible in the way each apartment door faced the courtyard. A sparkling blue pool, attended by the chaise lounges, held center stage. A couple of those chairs were occupied by brave residents willing to risk baring their skin to the triple-digit heat of the summer sun.

Locke turned the car off then draped an arm over the steering wheel, cocking his head to take in the complex through the windshield. "This is Angel's idea of laying low?"

"It works, doesn't it?" Isa released her seat belt as Locke

did the same. Anger churned in her gut, leaving her slightly nauseated. "No one would associate this place with him." This whole situation was riling old memories. She glared at the tranquil scene as the uglier ones replayed in her mind. "Though I'm not sure he thought it through."

"How so?"

"Think about it, Locke."

Isa could feel him watching her, seeing too much. She was struggling to get out from under old guilt. Carter was a dick—had to be to work for Angel—but the fact that he was reeling in girls like Paisley and slowly setting them up until they disappeared into Angel's network made her want to scream in fury.

"In a place like this"—she motioned to the doors lining the walkway—"you play your music too loud, someone's going to complain. There's no way people don't notice when girls move in and out. Someone has to be asking questions."

"Do they?"

Locke's solemn question cut through her rising frustration. She looked at him. He had pushed his sunglasses up, his startlingly blue eyes clear and cool.

"Think about it, Isa. Say this place is owned or rented by the agency. Moving models in and out would come with the territory. If neighbors ask, it's easily explained. Up-and-coming talent are looking to set down roots. The nature of the business is transitory. Besides, most people don't automatically go to the darkest intent when trying to rationalize things. They're happy not knowing."

Still reeling from listening to Paisley tell a story that mirrored her own, Isa was fighting to close doors she'd thought had been long locked away, as the regrets slipped free. There had been a time when she'd believed Angel's promises to help her live on her own so she could prove to her father she could do it. Even when her instincts whispered warnings, she ignored how he had chipped away at what made her *her*, reshaping her into something less. She really hoped the dark-haired lawyer would be able to rein Paisley in, because if she failed, they'd lose her. Isa could see that in the flashes of guilt and self-disgust Paisley had tried to hide. On some level, the girl knew the line she was teetering on. She just needed someone to reach out and help her find her balance.

From the busy street just behind them, a harsh blare of a horn cut through her thoughts.

"Isa, talk to me."

She turned to Locke, and because she'd made the decision last night and because she needed to release some of the poison, she told him. "I was her once, Locke." The admission came out low and hard as she tried to forgive that younger self. "Believing the lie even when I knew, I knew..." She pressed a fist against her chest. "They were lying to me. For a long time, I couldn't find a way out. Didn't want to because I believed it was what I deserved."

"But you did get out."

"Only because someone else paid the price first." Guilt dug its claws in, sinking through remembered cries for help and the stink of fear and blood. "If I'd made the decision sooner, if I'd been braver, I could have stopped him." The details of that last horrific night when she'd run from Angel—from the things she hadn't stopped—crowded her throat, leaving her choked.

Locke's eyes warmed even as he challenged her. "Could you really have helped? Be honest. You were a teen, and he was a rising member of a well-known, vicious street crew. The fact that you escaped—much less what you've made of yourself—is a minor miracle."

She didn't feel like she'd escaped. In fact, she felt like she was still running. "But he's still spreading his poison."

"So this time, we stop him."

He made it sound so simple. She just wasn't sure if her

idea of stopping Angel was the same as Locke's. She reached for the door. "Let's go find Isaiah."

They both got out, and the Dodge's doors thudded closed. Locke and Isa headed toward the open entry gate. A quick check of the property map, helpfully posted just in front of the wooden fence, directed them to the second floor of the back side of the courtyard. She started forward only to be brought up short when Locke caught her hand and tugged her gently back.

She half turned and gave him a frown. "What?"

He wrapped his other hand around the base of her neck. Her free hand came up and flattened against his chest as he leaned in. "Take a breath, *reinita*," he warned. "You can't walk in looking ready to commit murder. We're just here to visit Isaiah."

He had a point. Isa dropped her head until her forehead rested against his sternum. She drew in a deep breath, taking in his comforting scent, as she shoved all her messy emotions down. It took two more inhalations before the rigid line of her shoulders relaxed and she could curve her lips into a natural smile. Then she pulled back.

Locke studied her for a long moment before an approving gleam appeared in his eyes. He used his hold on her neck to bring her close enough to press a quick kiss to her lips, then he let her go. "Ready?"

She tightened her hold on his hand and nodded. Together, they walked in and started along the path skirting the iron pool fence. Within it, a very curvy young woman lounged on a pool float, engrossed in her e-reader. Near the shallow end, where the steps dropped into the water, a harried mother kept an eye on a couple of smaller humans intent on splashing everything, and muffled music drifted down from behind windows and plaster.

Underneath one of the umbrellas, an older woman tracked

Locke and Isa's progress with curiosity. "Hello!" she called out.

Locke didn't slow, but he did give her a charming grin and a wave. "Morning."

Isa managed to do the same, and it seemed to satisfy the woman. At the covered stairwell at the side of the building, they climbed the stairs. They walked along the second-floor walkway, crossed over to the third building that jutted away from the pool, and continued down to the far end. A sail canopy stretched over a paved area with large pots of colorful flowers surrounding a patio table, a built-in BBQ, and a stretch of artificial turf bookended by wooden cornhole boards. They passed the open door of a laundry room. Bright laughter came from inside as someone talked excitedly about a recent date, and a gust of air brought a barrage of flowery scents Isa recognized as fabric softener. Locke came to a stop and tugged his hand free, his chin angled up, his gaze sweeping around them, and the air around him sharpening.

She shot him a look. "What?"

"He's been here."

Her attention shot to the last door on the end, which belonged to Isaiah. "Shit," she whispered, dread clinging to her like a deranged monkey. She stayed behind Locke as he stalked to the door. Knowing Angel, she braced herself for what they would find inside.

Locke stayed to the side of the door and stretched out his arm, prepared to knock, only to stop and drop it. Isa realized the door wasn't completely shut, as if the latch had failed to catch. He took a step back, his gaze running over the doorframe. Whatever he was looking for, he must have found it, because his face darkened. He touched a finger to the top corner of the doorframe, and a sigil burst into silent, burning light.

It took Isa a second to recognize the silencing spell that

covered the doorway. They had no way to tell what was happening inside. Her dread froze into an icy knot. She looked behind them, where the rest of the world continued uninterrupted, then back at Locke, who had pulled a small but deadly-looking blade from somewhere. He handed it to her and motioned for her to stay put.

Even though she wanted to argue, she knew better. She took the knife from him, and her fingers tightened around the grip. It wasn't much, but it was better than going in empty-handed.

Locke put a finger to his lips and then held up three fingers, starting a silent countdown. His last finger came down. He rolled through the door, staying low.

Nerves strung tight, she stood there, heart pounding, ears straining as nothing but deafening silence answered. Time distorted, stretching interminably, as she waited for Locke's signal. It couldn't have been long before he was back, reaching to drag her inside.

She crossed the threshold, her ears popping as she stepped inside the spell. Her breath caught. The place was trashed. There was an overturned sofa to the right, and to the left, on the floor, was a flat-screen TV with a shattered screen and wires hanging out like entrails. Beside it, a listing console table was missing a leg, spilling game controllers and remotes across the floor. Behind the sofa, under the breakfast counter, a barstool lay on its side, and a cracked bowl sat in a puddle of milk and cereal. The mug on the counter was the only thing undisturbed.

Locke was already heading toward the closed door to the side of the kitchen when she heard it—a muffled groan followed by a whimper. He stopped, his hand hovering over the knob, as the air took on a sheen of blue. His magic washed over the door and seeped through the cracks. Whatever it told him had him gripping the knob and pushing in. The door moved a handful of inches before stopping. He turned sideways and set his shoulder against the door.

"Locke," she said before she could stop it. There were only so many reasons a door wouldn't open.

He turned to look at her, magic lining his iris in an eerie glow.

"Be careful."

He turned back and pushed. The door gave way, and she followed him through the narrow opening. They rounded the toppled dresser that had been blocking the door as another pained groan sounded. No one was inside the small bedroom, but there was another door blocked by a mattress hanging awkwardly off the bed frame.

"The closet," she said, but Locke was moving in that direction already. He shoved at the mattress, but the way it was positioned didn't give him much room to maneuver.

Isa looked around for somewhere to put the knife so she could help.

"Give it to me."

She handed it to Locke, who tucked it away. Together, they manhandled the mattress away from the closet door. When they had enough room, Locke yanked the door open. Inside, curled on his side in the back corner, was a young man. His eyes were wide and unseeing, his dark hair a tangled mess, his arms wrapped around his knees, which were drawn up to his chest. Clothes were piled around him, as if they had been torn off hangers or tossed inside. Boxes were tipped over as if he had managed to shove them aside only to crawl behind them like a creature desperate for a burrow.

"Dammit." Isa squeezed past Locke. "You're not going to fit in there."

His hands gripped her shoulders. "What are you doing?"

She shrugged him off. "Making sure the kid is okay." She moved into the narrow space. "Find a light switch." She pushed aside clothes and boxes until she could get to the kid and kneel next to him. She placed a gentle hand on his shoulder and crooned, "Hey, hey, hey."

Overhead, the light came to life, and the young man flinched hard enough to slam the back of his head into the wall and yank away from her touch. Scattered whimpers interrupted his frantic chant of "No, no, no." His voice was raspy, as if he'd been screaming.

"Shh... shhh." She pulled her hands back, keeping them visible as she tried to get through the panic. "Isaiah, we're not going to hurt you, okay? You're good, I promise."

Isa's heart ached at the blind animal fear that stared back. She eased back onto her heels, folding her hands in her lap, as she continued trying to reach him verbally. She took in the scrapes, cuts, and ugly bruising misshaping the left side of his face and feared there was even more damage to be found once she could get him to relax from his protective ball. A ring of what looked like finger marks sat just under the ripped sleeve of his T-shirt, and more bruising and streaks of blood covered the only arm she could see. Someone had beaten the holy hell out of him.

Seconds stretched like taffy as Isaiah fought his way back. First, the whimpers eased off, then the repetitive chanting stopped. Eventually, the blind fear receded, allowing awareness to trickle in.

Seeing it, Isa managed a small smile. "There you are, Isaiah. Welcome back." She lost his attention when his gaze darted to Locke, and he gave an involuntary jerk. Not as brutal as his initial one, but still... She moved just enough to regain his attention. "Hey, you're good. We aren't going to hurt you. We're friends of Paisley and Micah."

His attention shifted to Locke, and his eyes widened. "I... I know you."

"You do," he confirmed.

Isaiah looked back to Isa. "You're a friend of Micah? And Paisley?"

She nodded.

He straightened himself and started to push painfully to a seated position, his arm trembling under his weight, as he looked back to Locke with fear. "Are they here? Are they okay?"

"They're both someplace safe," he told the teen.

"Are you sure?" Isaiah tried using the wall to get to his feet but couldn't find enough purchase to make it. Isa caught him just before he toppled over.

Standing outside the narrow confines of the closet, Locke said, "Emilio has them both secured." His voice was firm but kind.

"Cordova?" Isaiah asked. Locke must have nodded because relief slowed Isaiah's frantic movements. He leaned into Isa's hold, and she helped him over the mess in the closet. "Okay, that's good. No way that asshole is dumb enough to take on the Cordova Family."

"Which asshole?" Locke asked.

Isaiah stumbled over a box, and a pained hiss escaped him. Isa tightened her awkward hold around his waist as he wrapped an arm around his ribs. He managed to stay on his feet.

"Carter's boss," he ground out between pained pants.

Locke had moved out of the doorway to give them room and shoved the mattress aside, gaining a few more inches of passable space. The two adults managed to guide the lanky teen out into the living room, where Locke helped him sit on one of the barstools. Isa rummaged through the kitchen and found ice and a somewhat clean cloth. She brought them over to Isaiah and had him hold them, like a compress, against the side of his face.

She took in the blood-specked T-shirt and the raw cuts

and scrapes marking what would normally be tanned skin but now carried a grayish tint. "How badly are you hurt?"

A hint of color managed to sneak into his battered face. "Hurting like hell, but I'll live."

"Ready to tell us what happened here." Locke's tone indicated it wasn't a question.

Isaiah eyed him warily and swallowed hard. "Yeah, um, sure. I was hanging out, eating breakfast when Carter came barging in, all pissed and shit. He was going off about me and Leo screwing up some deal, but I don't know what the hell he was talking about. I mean, I did their runs like they asked, and last time I saw Leo, he was crashing out hard with this girl."

Isa exchanged a look with Locke, who returned a brief head shake. He wasn't going to fill the kid in, so neither would she.

Isaiah watched them. "What?"

Lock stared him down, ignoring the question. "Tell me about these runs."

Keeping the makeshift ice pack in place, Isaiah squirmed. "Um, that was the deal, you know. I take some of Leo's runs so he can do his thing with Carter, and they leave Paisley alone. It wasn't supposed to be forever, just a temporary gig, just so I could put some cash away for a new place, but..." He looked away.

It wasn't difficult to fill in the rest. Isa had watched it happen over and over too many times to count. "You tried to get out."

Isaiah managed a jerky nod then winced. "Didn't get far. Leo ratted me out. Asshole." The last was muttered.

"Then what?" Locke asked.

Isaiah swallowed hard. "Carter got ugly. Said if I didn't do the job, they'd take out Micah and put Paisley to work." His gaze, ashamed and fearful, skittered to Isa. "I couldn't let that happen, so I did what I was told, but I was going to find a way out. I swear."

And if he had tried again, Isa was sure they'd have another body on their hands instead of a teen scared out of his mind and beaten to hell.

Isaiah repositioned the ice pack. "I tried to get Paisley to listen—told her we could go to Micah, and he'd help—but she just got pissed and bailed." He looked between them. "But you said she was safe, right?"

"She is," Locke said as Isa nodded.

Relief rounded Isaiah's shoulders. "Good. And Micah? How mad is he?"

Isa looked at Locke as a heavy beat of silence hung in the air. Isaiah shot unsteadily to his feet, his attention fixed on Locke, his voice cracking with panic. "What happened to Micah?"

A muscle jumped in Locke's jaw. "He's in a coma."

The ice-filled cloth fell to the floor, and Isaiah's gaze danced from Locke to Isa and back. "What?" Shock left him scrambling. "A coma? I don't understand."

Pity twisted in Isa's chest, and she kept her voice gentle. "He was looking for you."

"At the Alchemist," Locke said. "Someone drugged his drink. It messed him up enough that the doctors are keeping him in a coma while they try to find an antidote to whatever it was he took."

Isaiah started to crumple. Isa caught him and helped him back down onto the stool. The teen's pupils were blown. "Drugged?" he repeated as if it were a foreign word.

Locke nodded. "Whatever he was given, it allowed him to tear up an entire parking lot and do some serious damage."

Isaiah slowly shook his head. "That's... that's not Micah."

"We know," Isa said.

Isaiah stared at Locke as a tear slipped down his cheek. "It was him, wasn't it? Carter? He went after my brother." He covered his face with his hands and groaned. "And it's my fault. All my fault."

Isa didn't bother with platitudes. The kid was in no place to hear her. Instead, she dropped to a crouch, grabbed the crumpled cloth, then rose to toss it onto the counter. "The runs Carter was having you do. Was it drugs?"

Isaiah lifted his head from his hands, tears adding to the mess on his face but with a new hardness lurking underneath the grief. "Sometimes, yeah. Not sure what kind. I just got it from a guy and passed it along. Most times, it was packaged, so you couldn't tell what it was."

"Pills? Powder?" Locke pressed.

"Mainly pills."

"Were they his?"

Isaiah's shoulders rose and fell. "I don't know, but when he was beating the shit out of me, he was ranting about being cut out of his own deal by the leech and how he wasn't going to put up with that kind of disrespect."

Locke's expression hardened, and Isa could guess where his thoughts had gone. It didn't take a genius to put the pieces together. Carter was going to go after Angel. "Do you have any idea where Carter was headed?"

Isaiah shook his head carefully. "Things are kind of a blur. I remember him screaming at me as he pounded on my face." He swallowed hard. "I have this weird image of the room twisting around me, like walking through those carnival mirrors that mess everything up. Then things just went black."

Locke studied the young man for a long moment then came to stand in front of him. "Let me see your hands."

"What?"

"Your hands. Hold them out."

Isaiah did as told, his hands not quite steady. Locke

grabbed his right wrist and pulled out the small blade. "Hold still."

Isaiah tried to jerk back. "Hey! What—"

"Still," Locke barked.

Isaiah froze.

Carefully, Locke eased the knife's point under a bloodied nail like he was cleaning it. When he lifted the blade free, there was material on the edge. A wild light ignited in his icy eyes as he brought it close to his nose and inhaled.

Predatory satisfaction spread over his face as his gaze met hers. "Got it."

Her earlier vow rose eagerly to meet that feral intensity. "Time to hunt," she said, her voice as dark as his.

chapter 22

Locke

LOCKE'S MAGIC snapped and snarled against his imposed restraint as they drove Isaiah back to the clinic for treatment. His magic wanted to run Carter's scent to the ground, and it wasn't the only one. During the ride back to the clinic, Isa all but hummed with a dark intensity that worried Locke. Whatever was driving her was almost as feral as the instinct driving him and his magic. That wouldn't normally be a problem, but if both of them were out for blood, things could get messy, especially if he couldn't keep his footing on the thin line between personal and professional.

Speaking of which...

After pulling into the clinic's lot, he shot Zev a quick update on Carter and Isaiah via text. Locke hoped Zev would set the Cordova e-geeks loose and flush out something helpful. He and Isa got Isaiah inside and were getting ready to leave him in Mari's capable hands when a still-jittery Paisley burst into the exam room, took one look at Isaiah's bruised and bloodied face, and broke into tears. It took both Isa and Mari to talk the girl down from her hysterics and get her out of Isaiah's arms so the nurse could finish treating him. By the time Locke and Isa were free from the drama, it was late afternoon.

Isa followed him out of the clinic to the car. "Where do we start?"

He rounded the hood, stopped at the driver's-side door, and looked at her over the roof of the car. "At the apartment."

"Works for me." She yanked open the passenger door and slid inside.

When they pulled back into the apartment complex, activity at the pool was in full swing. It was clear kids were home from whatever activities held their attention during the summer months. Locke and Isa made their way up to the second floor without being stopped. At the apartment's door, Locke checked the warding he'd left behind and was not surprised to find it undisturbed. Chances were high that Carter was in the wind or on Angel's ass. Either way, Locke doubted the man would be coming back.

Inside the apartment, Locke had Isa stand near the breakfast bar and out of the way as he went to work. He freed his magic, and the world around him sharpened into painful focus, the air trapped inside the apartment becoming a myriad of competing scents, while in the wreckage, the smallest details hit his senses like small electrical strikes. He catalogued the pieces and fit them together like a multidimensional puzzle. Locke was familiar with both Isaiah and Paisley's scents, and it didn't take long to separate out the scent signatures as he moved through the apartment. Paisley's was lighter, overridden by Isaiah's, which was tinged heavily with the coppery echo of his bloody beatdown. He sank into a crouch, getting closer to the mess in the shambled closet, shifting meticulously through the scents. The third one he tagged as Carter's, not just because the man's fury rode the air like the sharp and scraping bite of pepper but because there was also an underlying note that raised Locke's hackles.

"I know this," he muttered to himself as his magic took it in, tasting the harsh chemical edge blurred by a musk of decay.

"Know what?"

He pivoted to see Isa standing in the door of the bedroom, watching him. "That scent..." He turned back to the torn-up space where Carter had cornered Isaiah and let his magic sift through the air. *There.* He dragged the odor closer and realized where he'd caught that subtle note before. The night at the Den, when Carter had stood silently in front of them, that same scent a faint hint teasing Locke's nose, and again when he'd been standing over Leo. The pieces clicked together.

"Shit."

"Shit, what?" Isa demanded from the doorway.

He rose and made his way back to her. "Is Carter an illusion mage? Do you know?"

She frowned. "A Mirage, I think."

That explained why he'd been guarding the door at the Den. Depending on their inherent strength, a Mirage could cloak things from sight—like, say, the entrance to an event that wanted to stay under the radar. The stronger ones could shield people, turning them invisible for all intents and purposes.

"How strong?" he asked.

"I don't know." She studied him. "Why?"

"Carter's dosing."

Isa's eyes widened. "With the same thing Leo took?"

"And that was given to Micah."

"That can't be good."

"It's not." His voice was all sorts of grim, but he couldn't help it. He nudged her back into the living room. "We need to get him locked down ASAP."

"That requires finding him first." She moved around the overturned sofa.

"Yeah, I'm aware." He followed her. "But the only thing we have to go on is that he's going after Angel."

She stopped near the front door and turned back to him. "Can't you track Carter?"

"Easily, but I'm betting I won't get past the parking lot downstairs. As soon as he gets in a car and takes off, I'll have limited options, none of which will allow us to move fast. Might be easier to get ahead of him before he implodes and takes everyone with him."

"Implodes?"

"Got a better description for losing your shit the way Leo and Micah did?"

She shook her head, but she looked doubtful.

"What?" he asked.

Her answer, when it came, was in an un-Isa-like, carefully modulated tone. "Even if we manage to stop Carter or Angel, it's too late. It's out there."

He knew exactly what she was implying, and since she was inexorably tangled up in this mess—and, Locke hoped, with him—he broke one of his own rules and shared confidential information with her. "Which is why Emilio is trying to get irrefutable evidence to present to the Council."

A small frown of surprise marred her forehead. "He's backing the Council into a corner?"

"He's trying."

Her attention shifted away as she processed his answer. "Huh."

Locke got close and tilted his head to catch her eye and get her to focus back on him. "So, I've got to ask—you got any ideas on where Angel would go if he's trying to slither back into the shadows?"

The gold flecks in her eyes deepened, her hazel gaze going unfocused, as she worried her lip. Long, quiet seconds ticked by before she met his eyes with wary resignation. "Maybe."

Locke pulled into an empty spot in front of a redbrick building on the downtown street. On the ride over, Isa had remained strangely stiff and silent, her *I don't want to talk about it* vibe loud and clear. He'd given her space, but now that they had arrived, he had questions. He braced an arm on the steering wheel and peered through the passenger-side window. A far cry from the modern glass office buildings and older, dust-coated adobe ones, this one-story Craftsman-style structure sat on a thick cement slab and had a peaked roof and wide wraparound porch. A discreet sign on the building's exterior bore the name Voces Unidos.

"What is this place?" he asked.

Isa stayed turned toward her door, gripping the handle. "They help local businesses get off the ground."

"And they're going to know where Angel is?" he asked incredulously.

"If anyone does, they will." Her voice was flat as tension spun around her.

"Is this a front?"

That got her attention. She turned to him, bemused. "What?"

"Is this place a front or something? Is that why they would know where to find someone like Angel?"

"No, but"—she opened her door—"my dad and Pilar run this place." She got out of the car.

"Well, shit." The quiet curse chased the slam of the passenger door.

Part of him hated putting her through this, but a bigger part understood the necessity. He waited for a break in traffic before getting out of the car then met Isa on the sidewalk. Behind her, the window blinds were drawn against the afternoon sun. Taking advantage of the momentary privacy, he took her hand and brought her into his side.

Even knowing it was a stupid question, he asked, "You sure about this?"

Her fingers tightened on his as she looked at him. "I'm sure we need to stop Angel."

He studied her face, taking in the fine lines bracketing her mouth and the grim, resolute light in her eyes. "Okay. Then let's get this done."

Together, they walked up to the porch and around the corner to the door, where a list of business hours was posted. Knowing he wouldn't be able to shield her from much, Locke still took the lead, opening the door and stepping inside. A long counter divided the space, leaving the office on one side and the reception on the other. The ends of the counter stopped short of the walls, creating walkways to reach the different spaces. An open door in the back wall led farther back.

A statuesque woman with sleek, silver-threaded dark hair rose from a desk behind the counter. The welcoming smile on her face cooled when Isa followed Locke in. "Isa."

"Pilar."

The older woman's attention shifted to him, and her voice warmed fractionally. "Good afternoon."

He inclined his head. "Afternoon."

Now that pleasantries had been exchanged, Pilar's attention returned to Isa. "Why are you here?"

"Angel's in trouble."

Locke wasn't quite sure where Isa was going with this, but he waited for his cue.

Pilar's flicker of concern was replaced by a sneer of disbelief. "And you're—what? Trying to help?"

Like a queen, Isa inclined her head and calmly said, "I am."

Pilar's eyes narrowed as heat licked along her voice. "Like you 'helped' last time?"

The air around Isa tightened, as did her body, but her voice remained level. "This is nothing like last time. One of Angel's... employees is going after him. We need to find Angel before he does."

The older woman folded her arms. "I'm not sure Angel needs your help."

Isa didn't outwardly react, but Locke swore he felt her flinch. Done with the cat-and-mouse game, he curled a finger around hers in silent support and stepped in. "He needs all the help he can get."

Dark eyes sharp with suspicion and arrogance turned to him. "Who are you?"

"Locke Turon. I work for the Cordova Family."

Alarm ignited along the stubborn lines of Pilar's face, but it was squashed quickly, replaced by quiet defiance. "What interest does the Cordova Family have with my Angel?"

Isa's fingers tightened in warning, so he went on the offensive. "Your Angel?"

Pilar's gaze flicked to Isa before returning to him, this time carrying a hint of wariness. Her self-protective instincts were intact. "Did she not tell you? Angel is my son." She swallowed and stubbornly held her ground. "You didn't answer my question."

Not wanting to escalate the situation, he angled his head and lied through his pearly whites. "The Family isn't interested in Angel. We want the employee."

Pilar turned to Isa, anger threading through her voice as she all but hissed, "*¿Ahora trabajas par las Families?*"

Isa's finger tightened painfully on his. "I —"

"I shouldn't be surprised," Pilar snapped.

He was seriously not liking this woman or her attitude. He let Isa go and moved in front of her, gaining Pilar's full attention. Her mutinous expression faltered. She might not hold any respect for the families, but she did fear them, and he could work with that.

"Isa agreed to help only after finding out that Angel was the target," he said, not tempering his icy tone.

She looked to Isa. "*¿Es verdad?*"

Isa held her gaze and dipped her chin.

Pilar folded her arms and turned back to him. "I don't know where Angel is."

Even if she did, it was clear from her tone she wouldn't be inclined to share.

"Pilar." Isa stepped around him until they were standing side by side at the tall counter, "If we don't get to him first, it could end really badly. We just need an idea of where he would go if he was being threatened."

"If he was in danger, he'd go to the police." Pilar showed only a flicker of worry.

Rock met iron as Isa started to argue. "You know that's not—"

A man walked through the door. Locke didn't need an introduction because the family resemblance to Isa was striking. Taller than Pilar, he moved with the same grace as his daughter. His dark hair was barely touched by gray, and under thick brows, the gold-streaked brown eyes were sharp. His gaze zeroed in on Isa as he crossed the room and moved into the reception area. His anguished flinch was quickly replaced by an expression of careful welcome.

"Isa, I'm surprised to see you."

Isa moved around Locke to meet her father's awkward hug. "Papá." The word held a choked roughness, the barest hint of the lost child. She cleared her throat and stepped back to Locke's side. "Angel's in trouble, and I'm hoping to find him."

There was no way to read the clutter of emotions pooling

in the man's eyes as he studied his wife and daughter. Finally, he looked at Locke and held out his hand. "Armando Serrano."

Locke took the older man's hand in his and gave it a firm shake. "Locke Turon."

"And you are with Isa?"

The question could be taken in two different ways, and there was only one answer for both. "I am."

"*Está con la Familia Cordova,*" Pilar said.

Armando frowned and looked at Isa. "The Cordovas are looking for Angel? Why?"

Locke answered before Isa could. "As I explained to your wife, we're looking for one of his employees. We've been able to track that employee's movements, but he recently got in a violent argument with Angel, and they both disappeared. Since we no longer have a viable trail for the employee and only know who the ultimate target is, we're hoping to get to Angel first."

"Violent?" Panic seeped into Pilar's voice as she moved toward one of the counter openings and came out to stand at Armando's side. "How violent?"

Armando wrapped an arm around his wife's waist and brought her close to his side.

Isa shot Locke a questioning look, silently asking how much she could share. Trusting her not to take it too far, he inclined his head. She turned back to her parents.

"A young teen got caught in the middle. When we found him, he'd been badly beaten, but he was able to confirm that the employee was determined to get his hands on Angel." She looked between her dad and Pilar. "I know I don't have the right to ask, but if you have any idea where he would go—where he would think he was safe from someone like this—we could check and make sure he's okay."

Pilar looked at Armando, and with an ease of familiarity,

the older couple held an entire silent conversation in a few tense moments. Pilar's earlier defiance melted under a mother's concern as she gave her husband a stiff nod.

Armando turned back to them. "His company has this place over by Encanto, a house they use for out-of-town visitors. He stayed there once when his condo was being repaired. He could be there."

"Do you have an address?" Locke asked.

Armando shook his head. "But I can get it. I..." He looked to Pilar, whose eyes carried a telling sheen. "We just need to go through some old texts." He gave his wife a comforting squeeze then turned to his daughter. "I'll send it to you when I find it."

"Thank you, Papá."

"Thank you," Locke added, addressing both Pilar and Armando. "We'll wait in the car while you look."

Pilar's lips were pressed together, but she dipped her chin in acknowledgment. She turned to Isa. "Will you call and let me know if he's okay?"

"Yes," Isa said without hesitation.

Locke set a hand at the base of Isa's spine. "Ready?"

A long second passed before she turned from her father to him, a stormy mix of emotions swirling deep in her hazel eyes. "Yeah."

They turned to leave, only to be stopped by Armando calling out, "Isa?"

She looked back over her shoulder.

"Do you have time soon to meet? Maybe at your place?"

There was no missing the tremor that ran through her, but she kept her voice steady. "Whenever you want, Papá. Just let me know what works."

Armando gave a short nod. "It shouldn't take long," he told Locke.

With a nod, Locke pulled Isa away from her family.

chapter 23

Isa

Isa sat in the passenger seat as they waited for her father's text and wondered if she was dreaming. "That happened, right?"

"It did."

Hope and disbelief swirled in her mind, shoving aside the more worrisome thoughts of Angel. The fact that her father had offered to come see her meant there was a very real chance she might get him back. As for Pilar, Isa wasn't sure if that damage would ever be repaired. Angel's ability to convince his mother that he was the victim had eroded the bonds between the two women to such an extent there was a time Isa feared Pilar would call a hit on her.

"Hey, you okay?" Locke asked.

"I don't know."

On the dash charger, Locke's phone vibrated with an incoming text. He picked it up, a frown forming as he read.

"What?"

He looked up, his expression grim. "Carter's apartment was buried under a shit ton of shell companies that all end with the Forge Foundation."

The name sounded familiar. It took a second to realize

he'd mentioned it when he was questioning Kelly. "You asked about them before. Who are they?"

"A group Zev's been chasing. We think they might be funding the drug's production."

He hadn't even tried to dodge her question. "And they're paying for Carter's place?"

Locke nodded. "Not only that, but it seems that Streetwise Talent has come into an influx of cash."

"Investors, you mean." She did not like the picture he was painting. "Let me guess—this foundation is one of them."

"Along with Healy's Signature Enterprises."

That would explain what they'd walked into at the Den. "And that Beto guy? Is he in it too?"

"Not yet. He and Angel had just started talking about a deal."

"So him being at the Den the other night—that was Angel currying favor?"

"Looks like it." He glanced at her. "What?"

"Why are you telling me this now?" Normally, she wouldn't be so blunt—not when she was trying to navigate the precarious minefield of a possible relationship—but after dealing with Pilar and her dad, she felt an insulating numbness that made her less cautious.

His eyebrows rose. "You'd rather I didn't?"

She grimaced. "Just waiting for the other shoe to drop."

That got her a flash of a grin. "Nothing's going to drop, *reinita*." The grin faded fast, replaced by a look of somber resignation. "This drug was the Council's Pandora's Box."

"Yeah, supercharging magic isn't going to end well for anyone."

"Especially those not used to wielding it."

Shock rocked through her as she grappled with that bombshell. "Wait! Are you saying...?"

He gave her a grim nod. "And now that it's out in the open, things are going to shift and not in a good way."

This was what he'd been keeping from her. Her mind spun at the numerous implications such a drug would have out in the wild. A shiver of foreboding ran over her skin. "Can't the families use those endless pockets to lock it down and create an antidote?"

"That short-term fix is already in the works, but the real implications run deeper."

"The Arcane Families and the Traditionalists."

The ideological rift had been growing in recent years as those with little to no access to magic decried the influence held by society's magical powerhouses. What had been grist for political discussions when she was younger had grown into divisive rhetoric infiltrating everyday life.

He nodded. "Which is why we need to find out how Carter and Angel got their hands on this shit."

She took in the lines etched around his eyes and mouth and the smudges under his eyes, and it hit her that while she'd been dealing with her own demons, he had been dealing with his. Handling the darker truths might be part of his job, but it also reflected who he was—a man willing to do what it took to keep that darkness at bay. Even if it meant shutting out those closest to him and going at it alone.

Just like me.

If he was willing to show her his truth, could she show him hers? Before she could lose her courage, she blurted, "Cora may not let Angel walk away."

Locke's gaze sharpened. "The vow you made?"

She nodded. "The only thing that will appease her is his death." Reapers understood the inherent truth of an eye for an eye to balance death's scales. Thanks to her vow, if that coin wasn't offered, it would be Isa who paid the debt. She swallowed hard. "And you need him alive."

"Not more than I need you."

Her breath stalled as his statement struck deep, slicing through the last knot of resentment and fear. His icy-blue eyes studied her face, his thoughts inscrutable. Then awareness warmed the glacial blue.

He caught her chin in his hand and brushed a thumb over her lips. "Breathe, *reinita*."

She let out a little gasp and drew in a shaky breath. "Dammit, Locke, warn a girl next time."

He tipped her chin up and pressed his lips to hers in a quick kiss. When he drew back, there was a subtle curve to his lips. "One thing at a time, yeah?"

She dipped her chin while her emotional composure scrambled for purchase. In her lap, her phone danced. She tore her gaze from Locke's, picked up the device, and checked the screen. "Papá found the address."

Locke pulled his seat belt in place. "Put it in."

She plugged the address into the GPS unit then fastened her seat belt as he started the car. "It's close."

He checked his mirrors, waiting for traffic to pass, and pulled out. "Do me a favor. Send the address to Zev and let him know we're checking it out."

She picked up Locke's phone and did as he asked. A text came zipping back. "He says he's about a half hour away, at one of the other connected properties. Do you want him to head over?" She looked at Locke. "Connected properties?"

"Other places listed under the shell corp. It's tedious as shit but has to be done if we want to run Angel to ground." He checked his mirrors as he wove through the street. "Tell Zev to hold off until I can verify whether Angel's there."

She typed out the response, set his phone back on the holder, then grabbed the passenger-door handle.

Locke shot her a look. "Ready?"

"Not even close."

He just grinned and hit the accelerator.

The address was located in an older neighborhood near the Encanto golf course, where the homes' original redbrick had been modernized in shades of white and black. Towering palm trees stood sentinel to well-worn asphalt and ribbons of sidewalks occasionally broken up by old-fashioned streetlights. While Phoenix had an appalling number of golf courses, this location held a charming mix of old and new. Even as the working day ticked down, the streets were quiet. The homes sat back behind large, neat yards, where the shadows of encroaching evening emerged around trees and behind bushes to stretch along the meticulous landscaping and welcoming walkways.

Locke rolled slowly past a gray-roofed one-story building tucked between a Tudor Revival house and a ranch-style one. A sleek two-door car was parked behind a wrought iron gate set off to the side. The rest of the paver driveway was empty except for an artful collection of large potted plants and a tall palo verde tree.

"That's probably Angel's car," Isa said.

"Doesn't look like he has visitors."

"You mentioned there were other places owned by the agency, so maybe Carter doesn't know about this place."

"Maybe." Locke didn't sound convinced.

She watched the house recede through the side mirror. "I didn't see any cameras."

"If it's used for business visitors, they wouldn't be visible."

Fair point. "So, how do we get inside?"

"We walk up and knock." He turned into a narrow alley lined with fences, garbage and recycling cans, and rear-facing garages. Tucked between two homes, the alley branched to the left, the turn partially blocked from view by a dumpster. Behind that was a small parking spot. Locke pulled into it.

"I don't think he'll just open the door."

"I don't need him to." He shut the Dodge down and tossed his sunglasses onto the dash. "I can get us in. I just don't want the neighbors involved."

She undid her seat belt. "And if we try to sneak in..."

"Someone will call the police. Better to act like we're expected."

"And when Angel decides a noise complaint isn't worth avoiding? You got a plan for that?"

He reached across her and popped his glove compartment. It dropped open, and she caught the flash of a sigil as he hit something and another compartment appeared like... well, magic. Inside sat a small black bag and thin metal case.

"Illusion spell?"

"Yep." He pulled out the bag, opened it, and poured what looked like grayish-white stones into his palm.

"What are those?"

"Warding stones." Locke ran his finger over them, turning them so she could see their etchings. He picked out three then returned the rest to the bag. Once that was back in the compartment, he reached for the case.

"And that?"

He flicked it open to reveal a set of multiple lockpicks. "Our way in." He pulled out two and tucked them and the warding stones into a back pocket.

"And if it's an electronic lock?"

He closed the hidden compartment then the glove box. "Then it'll be an even easier entry."

He popped the trunk then pushed open his door. She met him at the open trunk, where he folded back the liner, exposing a smooth metallic surface. He ran his finger over a spot, and a ward flared to life.

He traced the ward and murmured, "*Sim sala bim.*" A flare of blue was followed by a snick, and the metal shifted. He lifted the panel to reveal a padded collection of weapons.

She shook her head. "You drive around with that all the time?"

"Perk of the job." He picked up a small black compact gun. "You know how to use one of these?"

"Yeah." She took the SIG Sauer from him and racked back the slide, ensuring that the chamber was clear.

"Here." He handed over a full magazine and a leather holster. "Set it at your back."

Isa slipped the magazine in, reset the slide, then tucked the gun under her waistband at the base of her spine. She wiggled, trying to get comfortable, as she watched Locke tuck a pair of lethal-looking blades away. "Wait, where's yours?"

He lowered the metal lid and straightened the liner. "The gun's for you, just in case."

Just in case? Reality hit her hard, leaving her mouth dry and her pulse a hard, painful beat. "Maybe we should wait for Zev," she squeezed out.

Locke closed the trunk and turned to her, his expression growing gentle. "Hey." He set his hands on her hips and pulled her into him. "If you want to hang back, I can go check it out."

She flattened one palm against the steady beat of his heart. *Leave him to face Angel on his own? Oh, hell no.*

"No, I'm good," she lied and ushered her roiling anxiety into a box. The damn mental storage room was getting full.

He studied her for a long moment. "You sure?"

She scrounged up a smile. "I'm sure."

He finally let her go and stepped back. "Okay." Locke pulled one of the warding stones from his pocket and cupped it in his palm. "This old man, he played four. He played knickknack on my door."

As Locke recited the childish rhyme, a spark of blue ignited inside the warding stone, setting it aglow. He moved to the rear wheel well, bent, and set the stone inside. When he straightened, he set his palm against the Dodge's body at the counterpoint of the rear wheel.

An invisible brush of magic swept over Isa, raising goose bumps. She blinked, and her mouth dropped open as she stared down at the older-model sedan now sitting in place of the sleek dark Dodger. "What the —"

Locke brushed off his hands. "A trick Rory shared with me. Cost a pretty penny, but worth it."

She studied the illusion and shook her head. "Okay, that's cool." She went to touch it but stopped short. "Can I?"

He waved her on. She set her hand on the car's surface and drew it back along the trunk to where she knew a spoiler sat. The surface under her palm didn't change—no sign that it was anything but a flat, square trunk.

She wiped her hand along her hip. "Definitely impressive."

"Come on." Locke held out his hand, and she took it.

Together, they walked down the alley and out to the sidewalk. They passed a home whose screen door was open, with music and murmurs coming from inside. As they passed the next house, the faint yap of a dog started up. She spotted a fluff of white standing on the edge of a chair in a big window as the little Napoleon glared at them. They kept walking as a car drove past, the phone conversation in it loud enough to hear. No one paid any attention to her and Locke.

They were crossing the driveway of a Tudor Revival when a car came barreling down the road. She'd barely processed its approach when Locke stepped in front of her and turned his back to the rapidly approaching vehicle. "Come on."

He nudged her up the drive half screened by a hedge. He dug into his pocket, pulled out another warding stone, and held it. One of the heavy silver rings flared, engulfing his entire fist in a shimmering blue that quickly spread over him.

He pulled her into his body and put his lips near her ear. "Don't move."

Isa stood in his arms as a wash of magic swept over her. She kept her eyes on his chest, worried that if she dared to look beyond him, it would screw up whatever spell he was casting. She heard the engine downshift as the car got close, followed by the crunch as wheels bumped over the paver driveway. Then the engine shut down, leaving behind a vibrating quiet. A door opened and slammed closed, followed by a pause then stalking footsteps.

She felt exposed, and a chill ran down her spine. Next to her ear, she could hear Locke's steady inhalations and exhalations and found herself matching them. She almost jumped when a fist hit a door, the sound overly loud.

"Steady," Locke said, his voice barely audible.

A door opened, and a familiar voice snarled, "What are you doing here?"

Angel.

"We need to talk. Now."

There was another extended pause, then the door slammed shut.

Locke's hold relaxed, and the skin-ruffling magic eased back. "We need to move."

"Where?"

His gaze went back the way they'd come. "Back to the alley." His eyes met hers. "How good are you at fence hopping?"

She licked her dry lips. "Let's find out."

He gave her an encouraging smile and let her go. The magic receded.

She rubbed her arms. "What was that?"

"A concealment spell." He put a hand at the base of her spine as they started back.

"Why can't we use it to approach?" She stumbled over a crack in the sidewalk, her knees still shaking from the fading adrenaline rush.

Locke's arm wrapped around her waist and kept her upright. "It's a passive spell."

She matched his pace. "So if we move, it doesn't work?"

"Exactly. It's more a don't-look-here type of spell."

"Got it."

They were turning into the alley when he asked, "You good?"

"Yeah." Her knees were back to normal, and so was her heart rate.

Locke let her go, dug his phone out, hit the screen, and brought it to his ear. "Hey, Zev, going to need you." A pause. "Yeah, both of them." Another pause, then he checked his watch. "Yeah, we'll hold." He slowed to a stop near the illusion-covered Dodge, his face grim as he listened. "Got it. I'll send you a pin. Text me when you get here."

He did something else on the screen then shoved his phone back into his pocket. "Zev's about fifteen minutes out. We'll get eyes on them and make sure they don't take off before he gets here."

Easier said than done. "And if they decide to bail before the calvary rides in?"

"I'll figure something out," he said. Isa was still processing his less-than-reassuring answer when he caught her hand and pulled her around the Dodge. "Come on." They jogged down the narrow alley that stretched behind the houses. When they reached their target house, Locke stopped where the detached garage rose above the fence line. "We'll go over here."

Isa eyed the cement-block fence and reached for the top, her fingertips hitting just shy of it. Next to her, Locke dropped into a crouch and cupped his hands. She set her palms against the sun-warmed cement and placed her foot in his hands.

"On three," he said, voice low. "One, two, three." He shoved upward.

She scrambled awkwardly to pull herself up and over, ignoring the stinging bites as the rough sides of the block wall scraped first across her torso then the inside of her thigh when she threw her leg over to straddle the wall. After sitting up, she offered Locke her hand.

It wasn't necessary. Taller than her and clearly much more at ease hopping fences, Locke was already swinging his leg over the wall's edge. The muscles in his arms flexed as he rotated his body in a controlled drop into the narrow space below, then he was reaching up for her. With a lot less grace, she pulled her other leg over, rolled to her stomach, and tried her best to mimic his movements. Her arms screamed at the strain as she started to lower down. Her shirt snagged on the cement and abraded the bare skin of her stomach.

That will leave a mark.

When she felt Locke's hands on her hips, she pushed off, trusting him not to let her fall. He didn't let her down. Isa stood next to him, her heavy breathing loud in the cramped confines. She worked on calming it down as she tugged her shirt back into place and reconsidered her workout routine.

"You good?" Locke's question brushed her ear.

She nodded.

He went to the detached garage, peered around the corner, then turned back to her. "There's a half wall partially screened by bushes and trees between us and the house. Stay low and get behind it," he whispered.

"Windows?"

"Big one to the left, a double glass door on a covered patio on the other side of the wall, and another window off to the right, blinds drawn. That one's blocked by the garage. I'm betting it's a bedroom. I want you to keep an eye on those doors."

She grabbed his arm. "Wait, why? Where will you be?"

"I'm going to work my way around, see if I can't get a better angle on what's going on inside."

That didn't sound good. "Locke—"

He cut her off with a quick kiss. When he pulled back, he said, "I've got this."

She swallowed and reluctantly nodded. "All right. Let's go."

They moved out, picking their way through the shrubbery. She stayed low and followed Locke's lead. He stopped just behind a hedge, his attention on the glass doors, and held up his hand. She froze. She could see the half wall just a few feet ahead. Locke was right—it was in direct line of sight to the patio's glass doors. The way the sun hit them, she couldn't make out much through the glass. If someone inside looked up at the wrong time, she'd be screwed.

Locke held up a finger, then a second, and when the third went up, she made a hunched-over dash for the scant protection of the wall. She skidded into place, heart racing, and huddled behind the stucco. She looked over to see Locke give her a reassuring grin, then he slid back and started to edge around the yard.

As much as she wanted to watch him, she forced her trembling limbs to creep to the half wall. She peered around the corner at the covered patio and saw only a reflection of the backyard. *Tinted glass.*

Pulling back, she reconsidered her options. Locke had made it to the far side and was inching his way closer to the house. In another couple of feet, he'd lose what little protection the bushes offered. He had stilled just shy of being exposed, his attention focused on the house.

A breeze kicked up, heavy with heat. It was strangely steady and brought with it the sound of arguing.

"... tell me where she is."

"I don't know what you're talking about." There was no mistaking Angel's mocking tone.

"Don't fucking bullshit me. I got witnesses who say you were arguing with her that night, and now I can't reach her and her phone's off. I know you had something to do with it."

"Witnesses? You mean junkies like her?"

A roar of rage erupted, followed by a loud crash and a responding bellow. The strange breeze stopped, like a switch had been thrown, leaving behind a muffled quiet.

This can't be good.

She turned to look for Locke, but he was gone.

chapter 24

Locke

FROM HIS POSITION tucked behind an oleander, Locke eyed the large window, noting the reflective sheen. Treated for heat and glare, the glass kept him blind to what was happening inside while offering anyone inside a clear line of sight to the yard. He calculated his odds of getting to the house without being seen.

Slim. Very fucking slim.

Sweat beaded at the back of his neck and slid down his spine. He wiped away a rogue drop from his temple. The approaching evening wasn't offering much relief from the oppressive heat, the air heavy and still.

Too still.

His innate air magic rose at the instinctual warning, scenting through the invisible trails, and found the sharp sting of magical markers. Someone had cast a modified soundproofing spell recently. He briefly considered breaking it, but since that would alert the caster, he chose a different route. His magic swept out, avoiding the artificial boundary of the other power, and found a weak breeze riffling lazily through the upper branches of the tree guarding the back fence. Not wanting to scare it away, he threaded his magic carefully into the aerial dance, strengthening the draft into something more helpful. He directed the gust back toward the house, muting his magical signature as much as he could so it wouldn't trigger the soundproofing spell.

The reinforced breeze found its way through, slipping around the gaps in the windows. When it returned, it brought the sounds of an argument. A flex of will allowed him to share what he was hearing with Isa.

"... with her, so tell me where she is."

"I don't know what you're talking about."

He recognized Angel's voice, leaving the first to belong to Carter. He wasn't sure who "she" was, but considering the rising violence in the men's tones, Locke figured it wouldn't be long before things got physical. And when that happened, those inside would be too busy to notice what was going on outside.

Moments later, a rage-filled shout erupted, and so did he. Locke shot toward the house, staying low. His shoulder hit the stucco with bruising force as a large crash came from inside. He was just about to peek over the edge of the window when something smashed through in a shower of glass and wood. Locke covered his head with his arms and hissed as a hot slice of pain cut across one forearm before he could erect a buffer of air to deflect the cascade of sharp objects. The soundproofing spell snapped out of existence, and he caught Isa's gasp as he pivoted to see a body rolling over the pavers and hitting the wicker chairs clustered around a firepit.

The body came to a stop, but it didn't stay down as magic boiled out of the broken window frame. It skimmed just above Locke's head, so close his hair stood on end, the sensation akin to skin being raked with razor-sharp claws, but instead of spilling blood, it tore across Locke's senses in a shocking burst of pain that left his muscles frighteningly loose and his mind scrambling for purchase. He stumbled out from under the window and off to the side, somehow getting out of the river of vindictive power pouring from the house, and the invisible onslaught pulled back.

He bumped into the picnic table and caught his balance with a hand on the splintery top. He shook his head clear in time to see thick arms bulging as the man who had been thrown pushed up and lifted his close-shorn head. His eyes, bright with fury, were locked on the house.

Carter. His mouth was bloodied and twisted in animalistic rage as he got to his feet with uncanny grace. A burnt-orange glow erupted, lining his large frame as he swiped an arm over his blood-spattered chin then spat. “Let’s try something different, asshole.”

Power swept through the yard, and in a silent explosion, the world around Locke shifted sideways. The early-evening sun disappeared, replaced by tones of gray. Flashes of dull green and deep black cut through the distorted shadows like lightning. A strange mist writhed around Locke’s legs and rolled over the broken pavers. Against the dreary fog stood the once-neat house, which now appeared abandoned, its windows turned to black pits filled with jagged glass teeth. Sounds stretched and warped as if time was twisting on itself. Locke thought he heard Isa, but her cry turned into a blood-chilling shriek as something large and angry growled nearby.

His magic stalked forward, sharpening his senses to near-painful levels. For a brief disconcerting second, the normal world returned, only to be sucked back under by this nightmarish version. But it was enough for realization to sink in.

Illusionary attack.

Locke froze in place, his muscles quivering under the enforced stillness. As his mind and senses went to war, he sifted through what was real and what was being powered by Carter’s magic. Illusion mages came in three flavors: Charmer, Nightmare, and Mirage. The first two messed with your emotions, but the last one, Mirage, messed with your perception. Carter was definitely fucking with his perception.

Locke pulled out one of his blades and held it at the ready. With his empty hand, he reached out until rough wood rasped against his palm. The picnic table. He flattened his hand against it, using it as an anchor as his mind provided a snapshot of the scene.

The window Carter had flown through was to his right, and the man had landed at about two o'clock. With the house at Locke's back, that put Isa, tucked behind the garden wall, to his left at eleven o'clock, leaving only Angel unaccounted for. To join in, Angel would either have to go through the window or out the patio door.

The magic that allowed Locke to be an exceptional hunter picked through scents and sounds even as it ignored the ever-shifting landscape and implied threats. Since trusting what he saw was no longer an option, he closed his eyes. He found Isa's scent first, a faint cinnamon-laced vanilla. Then Carter's, a little beyond her, stronger with a disturbing chemical-tinged sweat and fury. But there was another scent whispering along the air, off to his left and creeping closer, a smooth, dry musk tinted with bitter ice. Angel.

The warping sounds grew clearer, and he caught Carter's angry tones, followed by the crash of something breaking. He held his position even as the ground trembled under his feet and his spine crawled in warning that someone was approaching. Locke flexed his elemental magic, thickening a layer of air and wrapping it around him like a cloak. It wouldn't stop an attack, but it would blunt it.

"Locke, your left!"

Catching Isa's warning, he swiped out, eyes flashing open. Minute changes in the air telegraphed body heat, and even though all he saw was dizzying shadows, his blade caught something lighter than muscle, likely cloth and skin. A tight grip took his forearm and pulled him forward, wrenching it backward. His fingers spasmed, his blade falling to the ground. Locke fisted his free hand and threw a sharp, vicious jab. His knuckles cracked against bone. A pained grunt sounded, and the grip on his arm loosened. He pulled back fast just as the world winked back in, the sunshine blindingly bright after the dull grays.

Locke blinked furiously, trying to clear his vision, and caught a sense of nearby movement. As the air shifted past him, he dove out of the way and stumbled into a wall, rough stucco scraping skin. He pushed off and spun around just in time to find Angel stalking toward him, thick tendrils of olive green flecked with black dancing around him in a magical storm. They struck out, hitting the dense wall of air Locke held in place, and whipped back to strike again.

Locke rushed Angel, bending low to evade the strike, and caught the man in the gut with his shoulder. As he wrapped his arms around Angel's thighs and hefted upward, a sharp pain sliced across his back. With a roar, he stumbled forward and slammed Angel into the table. The wooden top split with a loud crack.

Undaunted, Angel swung out, his fist slamming into the side of Locke's head. Even as Locke rocked and his vision blurred, he sank a vicious punch into Angel's ribs, feeling the bone give. An answering pain spiraled up from his kidneys where Angel landed a hit. Without releasing his hold, Locke punched out again, his angle awkward as Angel tried to buck free. Angel gave a grunt of pain. His fist crashed into Locke's skull, leaving his ears ringing and his vision going white.

Locke held on grimly, coiling his air magic around Angel's struggling form, and slowly cut off Angel's air supply. His vision came back in patches, providing snapshots of Angel's red face. He could feel Angel's desperation as he bucked, his magic striking out in a flurry of blows to batter at Locke's shield of air. Locke's magic held the strikes at bay, but Angel still swiped out, fingers curled into claws. Locke jerked his head back, saving his eyes but leaving his neck exposed as Angel dug bloodied furrows into his skin.

A pained feminine cry, quickly cut off, yanked Locke's attention to the yard, where Isa was struggling with the much larger Carter.

"Isa!"

His flash of panic was a momentary distraction, but that was all it took. He lost his hold on Angel, who jackknifed his legs and shot them into Locke's gut, shoving him back. Black-flecked green whipped out, found purchase in the cracks of his concern for Isa, and burrowed fast and deep. Worry spiked and deepened into crippling fear, splitting Locke's attention between threats. Bound by the unnatural terror ripping through his psyche, Locke couldn't move, his gaze fixed on where Isa continued to fight Carter as a voice whispered through his mind that she would die.

Bullshit. Isa isn't weak—never has been. She'll never go down easy. Even now, she's holding her own.

Yet he still couldn't look away. Fury burned under the unnatural icy hold, but it was too late. His hindbrain screamed in warning as pain tore through his back, sending him to his knees.

chapter 25

Isa

In the muffled quiet, Isa peered around the garden wall and caught a blur of movement near the oversized window. It was Locke. He was reaching for the edge of the window when something came flying through it. Shattering glass and pained grunts broke through the strange thick silence, and suddenly, the air was filled with noise and magic. A body rolled over the pavers, chased by a wave of magic as it crashed into the fireplace, tossing aside wicker chairs like bowling pins. It took her precious seconds to recognize who the body belonged to.

Carter. His face was twisted with rage. He rose to his feet. With his entire focus on the house, he moved a few steps forward, wiping his arm over his mouth.

Isa froze in a runner's stance, one hand on the ground, one foot behind her, ready to sprint. To where, she had no clue, but if Carter looked to his right, he would see her.

"Let's try something different, asshole," he growled as magic twisted the world into a warped version of itself.

His power swept through the air and washed over Isa, and a flash of painful cold beat at the base of her throat. Lost in the gray, with the warm stone under her hand the only solid reality, she clutched at the scythe charm against her chest and closed her eyes. Somewhere out there, Locke would be stuck in Carter's illusion, leaving him vulnerable to Angel. If she moved and tried to interfere, the chance of her getting swept up in the illusion would be high. Too high. She couldn't leave Locke alone. She needed a distraction.

Starlit darkness spun behind her closed lids as the Reaper's cloak settled on her shoulders. Whispers and needs wrapped around her, plucking at her attention, demanding to be acknowledged, but there was only one she was interested in.

"You promised me," the hungry echo of Cora's voice whispered.

Image after image swam past Isa's consciousness, each one a tale of violent retribution, with Angel in a starring role. Cora's vengeance spiraled higher. Buffered by the Reaper's analytical take, Isa spared a moment to appreciate a couple of the more inventive ideas Cora spun.

"He's here," Isa said, her voice coolly detached.

"I know." Piece by piece, the remnants of Cora's spirit reformed into a wraith and drifted close. She reached out, her fingers coming within millimeters of Isa's face. "Let me in."

"No." Isa didn't flinch at that ghostly touch—she couldn't afford to—as she wrapped the Reaper's mantle tight, holding off the unwanted connection. "Not yet."

"You promised," Cora hissed, her face twisted into a ghoulish mask.

There was a faint twinge near Isa's heart, but she held that unnatural stare. "I did, but you can't take him on your own."

An angry wail ripped through the air. Cora's image wavered as if caught in a wind funnel, one minute bone and shadows, the next an angry woman. Her attention rose beyond Isa, her face mostly monstrous as she hissed, "He's so close." When she looked back at Isa, she was once again wearing Cora's face, complete with an expression of rabid determination. "I can."

Even as pity stirred, Isa held strong. "You can't, but if you let me lead, I can give you a shot at getting your own back."

Cora cocked her head. "How?"

"Help me disable the illusion mage, and I'll play bait with Angel."

Cora's lips curved in a vicious smile. "Bait?" she said as if savoring the word. "Yes, that would work."

The arguing reached them as behind Cora, the starlit scene broke into frayed gray shadows, glimpses of a furious Carter filtering through. His features twisted with fury, his mouth moving as he wielded the rippling magic, warping the space close to him.

Cora whipped around, spotted the mage in the rift, and darted forward.

"Cora, stop!" Isa yanked on the tethers tying the spirit to her. "You can't cross without me."

The spirit froze inches away from where the two worlds met, her hands clawing at the air as if trying to tear her way through. Her head twisted around, revealing twin black holes lit by an earthly glow in a skeletal face. "Release me!"

"Not until you agree to help stop the illusion mage first then Angel."

In this space outside of time, maddened wails grew to enraged screams as invisible winds whipped around the Reaper and the spirit. Cora's storm of jagged fury and devious calculation swept over the unbending Reaper, the flood barely rippling the Reaper's cloak. Cora glided back through shadows and stopped in front of her, a shadow of cunning slipping underneath the ever-changing features.

"Illusion mage first," the spirit agreed then rushed the Reaper.

Magic flared into a bright explosion, and ice invaded every molecule of Isa's body in a breath-stealing rush that left her nerves screaming. As the chill spread, the screaming faded into an eerie nothingness. Isa felt a curious wrenching sensation as the magical vow allowed Cora control of her body. Then she was moving forward at a speed that blurred Isa's perception. One minute, she was in the starlit darkness. The next, she stood just behind Carter, tapping him on the shoulder.

The illusion mage spun around, his magic turning with him. His eyes widened as they landed on her, confused, angry, and a little unhinged. He stumbled back. "Isa? Wha—"

"I need your help." Cora shoved Isa's hands brutally hard into Carter's broad chest, a combination of magic and unnatural strength sending him flying backward. He careened into a cluster of large, plant-filled terra cotta pots. They toppled over, shattering against the pavers.

Carter caught himself on the squat chimney of the cast-iron outdoor fireplace. "What the hell are you doing?" His attention went beyond her, and with a muttered oath, he dove to the side.

Cora-Isa turned just as a whip of black-flecked olive green magic snapped past, its target Carter. Startled, Cora lost hold of Isa's body, and the off-balance Isa tried to dart out of the line of fire only to trip over her damn feet. She hit the ground hard, the impact rattling up her arms to jar her teeth. Behind her, Carter gave an angry bellow, and an answering wave of magic swept out, the world twisting as illusionary power played with reality.

Isa used her magic to fight the trailing edges of Carter's attack. She lifted her head and caught sight of Locke near the patio in a half crouch, Angel coming up on his left. "Locke, your left!"

She didn't get a chance to see if he heard her as something

heavy slammed into her hip, knocking her to her back. Pain radiated out from her hip, joining the bruising ache of the gun tucked at the base of her spine.

Carter loomed over her, raising his foot to kick her again, his face contorted into a malicious frenzy. "Bitch! Stay down!"

As Carter stomped down, she rolled and scrambled to her feet, reaching for the gun. But she was too slow. Carter lunged and caught her in a bone-bruising grip. He trapped her arms to her sides as he squeezed and lifted. Pain exploded along her torso, and the distraction was enough for Cora to reclaim physical control. Together, she and Isa slammed their head forward, smashing their forehead into Carter's nose.

A cry erupted as pain whited out their vision. They thought they heard Isa's name, but then the constricting hold rose, and they were free. They stumbled backward, trying to get air into their battered lungs, and tripped over broken pottery and dirt. They fell against the cast-iron fireplace but stayed on their feet. A good thing because Carter was shaking his head, his nose a bloodied mess, his eyes wild as he charged them again.

This time, they managed to get a grip on the gun and draw it, but Carter was too close. He slammed his fist into their arm, and their fingers spasmed, the gun tumbling from their nerveless grip. Before they could evade him, he followed up with a vicious kick. They spun out of the way, but Carter's boot clipped their thigh. They stumbled back again. A gleam of satisfaction flared in Carter's maddened gaze as he closed in.

Undaunted, they calculated their odds. Their gaze skittered around for another weapon and found one miraculously hanging on the back of the firepit's round chimney—a thick piece of wrought iron with a spiked hook. They lunged for the poker, yanked it free, and then, fueled by lethal determination and gleeful vengeance, they swung. The hooked end sank into the side of Carter's neck and held tight. Carter roared, hands going to their makeshift weapon. He jerked back as they yanked forward. The poker tore free, and Carter's shout turned to a gurgle. Blood spilled over his hands, which were hovering over his ravaged throat. He stumbled forward one step, then two. On three, his knees buckled, sending him face forward into the fireplace with a sickening thud.

They stood there, breath heaving, gore-smeared poker held to the side, as they watched Carter's limp body crumple to the pavers. Inside the Reaper's body, two spirits watched, one filled with a terrible glee, the other numb.

An unnerving giggle filled the air, then Cora said, "Your turn."

Feeling as if she was moving in a strange vacuum, Isa could only ask, "What?"

The spirit went from amused to threatening in less than a heartbeat. "I needed Carter to help me with Angel. Now bring him to me."

The inky tendrils of Isa's power were already sliding around Carter's broken body, not because she wanted to do as Cora asked but because the vow's binding demanded compliance. She called for Carter's soul—part of her horrified, another resigned—as she pulled the soul pieces together.

Carter's face was wreathed in confusion as he looked around. Cora rushed forward and threw her arms around him. "Hey, Carter! I'm so glad you're here."

The confusion on his face deepened even as his big arms came around her. "Cora? You're okay?"

The spirit pulled back. "Now I am."

Carter's attention flicked to Isa, and horrified understanding dawned. He shoved Cora back, his gaze bouncing from Isa to Cora and back. "No. What the fuck? This isn't happening. I can't be—" His mouth snapped shut as if to trap the word.

"Dead?" Isa finished for him. "Afraid so." She hitched her chin to Cora. "And you can thank her."

"You're welcome," Cora said with an infuriating casualness.

He lunged for her, but she winked out, only to reappear a few feet away. When he tried again, Isa locked his spirit in place. "Carter, stop."

His spirit stood there, trapped in the Reaper's hold. "Send me back."

She shook her head. "I can't."

Cora moved into Carter, leaving only inches between them. She cupped his face, forcing him to look at her. "I need you."

Carter stared down at her. "What happened to you?"

"Angel killed me," she said. Carter jerked against her, but Cora held tight. "That's why I need you. We have to make him pay."

She continued to croon to him, and he shook his head.

The inky tendrils of Isa's power curled slowly around the couple, binding them together. Isa started to protest, only to have Cora's voice invade her mind in a feral hiss. "You made a vow, Reaper."

I asked you for a distraction, Isa told her. The words formed in her mind, her voice silenced.

"He's distracted!" Cora snapped. "But I need his power to get Angel." She rose and covered Carter's mouth with hers in an obscene kiss.

Isa's gut lurched as realization dawned. Her vow meant she had to physically host Cora until she garnered full payment from Angel. And that vow allowed no wiggle room, so any and every power available to her was also accessible to Cora for the duration. Reapers could drain a soul and use that energy to boost their own. And now Cora was draining Carter for her own use. Isa could only stand as witness.

The part of her that was Isa slid deeper away, needing to escape the wash of self-recrimination. The Reaper part of her continued to observe with a detached curiosity. It didn't take Cora long to drain Carter to dregs that faded into nothing.

Cora, bloated with power, laughed and stepped back into the world, dragging the Reaper with her.

chapter 26

Locke

THE WORLD SPUN and settled into recognizable lines as Locke grimly forced the radiating pain aside to be dealt with later. The shattered picnic table tilted drunkenly, and as his mind started to clear, he searched out Angel's magic, but it was gone. As was the debilitating fear that had left him so exposed. Alternating waves of heat and chills washed over him as his senses came back online. He was on his hands and knees, grit scraping his palms as they pressed into the heat-warmed pavers. His tongue was coated with the bitter-copper taste of blood. He managed to spit his mouth clear, and the crimson smear marred the paver. His ears rang with a high-pitched hum. He used the table to get to his feet as he wiped at whatever was trickling into his eyes. When he dropped his hand, blood and sweat stained the back of it. He wiped it on his pants and looked around.

The once-neat yard looked like a tornado had torn through it, leaving behind broken furniture, overturned coals, and a trail of shattered pottery and glass. The air was heavy with power as flashes of olive green and onyx black clashed in silent fury. None of that compared to what stood a few feet away and left him wondering if he had hit his head earlier: three black-eyed Isas facing down one battered Angel.

What the hell is going on?

A flick of power whipped past Angel, who managed to evade it by diving to the side, and headed toward Locke. His magic flared, the air tightening around him, as he threw himself to the side and rolled over the broken picnic table. When he got to his feet, he saw that Angel had wrapped his magic around the Isa in the middle, the dull-green tendrils spearing her torso and limbs. Power swelled, the obscene strands pulling her off her feet until she hung in midair, her spine curved in a painful arc. The Isa to the left watched Angel with an avid disturbing hunger, something clutched in her hand, half hidden by her thigh, and stalked him with uncanny grace. The Isa to the right held a wrought iron poker and favored her right side, ribbons of deepest black dancing around her as she fended off Angel's magic. She missed one then another as they latched on, sinking deep. Her eyes widened, her face flinched, and her movements became jerky, the shadowed ribbons flickering like a faulty bulb.

That was his Isa. Locke reached for his second blade only to come up empty. He scanned the ground and spotted a large glass shard. Wrapping his palm in a thick layer of air, he grabbed it and, keeping it low, rushed Angel from behind.

"No!" The furious cry came from his left.

An invisible force shoved him aside, sending him crashing back into the broken table. He lost his hold on the glass shard and barely managed to avoid impaling himself on a thick splinter.

Warned by the cry, Angel half turned toward the last Isa, who lunged forward, wrapped her arm around his neck, and pulled him into her. The muffled silence fractured, and the storm of dull green winked out, as did the other two Isas. Sounds rushed back in—harsh breathing, the revving of an approaching engine, and the faint roar of an overhead jet. In the backyard, Isa and Angel stood in a strange embrace. A cruel smile curved Isa's lips as Angel's hands went to his stomach.

When his gaze rose to hers, he was frowning. "*Chiquita*?"

Isa leaned in, and Angel grunted in pain. "It's payback, asshole." She stepped back, and in her hand was a bloodied shard of thick pottery. "And it's Cora, not *chiquita*."

Angel swayed as the crimson stain grew.

"Gods dammit." Locke rushed to catch the Harvester before he hit the ground and barely caught him in time. He lowered Angel slowly, noting the sickly sheen of his light-brown complexion. He put pressure on the gut wound, ignoring Angel's pained grimace. "Hold on, Herrera." Angel tried to push him away physically and magically but was weakened on both fronts.

Locke glared up at the spirit who was clearly possessing Isa. "Is the debt paid?"

Those disturbing black eyes turned to him, the chilling smile widening. "When he takes his last breath."

Shit. We need Angel alive, at least long enough to get a damn name. "Isa, I need you."

Cora's smile disappeared as she frowned down at him. "Stop messing with my fun. She can come back when he's dead."

"No," he shot back, his voice hard as warm blood seeped from under his hands to stain the ground. "Now. He has answers we need."

"About what?" Her head cocked as if she was listening to someone. "The drug? That wasn't his deal."

Locke's mind spun with the revelation as he tried to press harder against the wound. He looked at Angel but found no help there. The man's eyes were closed, and the hand that had been battering at Locke's arms lay limp on the ground. His breaths grew shallower by the moment.

"Then whose was it?" Locke asked. When Cora didn't answer, he risked looking at her.

She was shaking her head and paying him no heed. "No, no. He's too stupid. He needed us."

Clearly, Isa was trying to help from wherever she was. Cora moved in agitated circles as she grabbed at her head. "You can't. Not until he's dead. Stop it! I know what you're doing. Stop it!" The last came out in an ear-shredding shriek.

"What the fuck?" The unexpected question came from Zev, who stalked out of the house, his attention pinned to Isa who was talking to herself. "Is she okay?"

"She's good." Locke hoped he wasn't lying, but he had to trust Isa could handle Cora. "But I'm losing Herrera."

Zev turned away from the muttering woman pacing in tight circles and joined Locke next to the bleeding man. "What do we have?"

"Gut wound. You have anything we can use? A healing charm? Something to slow the bleeding?"

"Not on me." Zev's face was a grim mask. "I might have a stasis ward in the car."

He was about to have Zev go grab it when a hand landed on his shoulder. Locke turned his head to find Isa staring down at Angel.

"Let him go."

He started to protest. "Isa—"

"He's almost gone." She looked at him, tiny pinpoints of white flashing in the black depths of her eyes as her expression wavered from resigned to coldly amused and back. "A stasis spell won't help."

Locke held those eerie eyes, torn between frustration and fury. The answers he needed were right... fucking... there, dammit.

Isa's fingers brushed over his tense jaw. "Trust me."

His gaze drifted down and snagged on the scythe charm at the base of her throat, realization striking hard and fast. His gaze jumped back to hers. "You'll be okay?"

Her touch fell away, and the small smile she gave him was more natural and real than Cora's earlier grin. "I will be."

"Make it quick."

Her lips tightened as she dipped her chin in acknowledgment.

Trusting in the woman who had made a spot for herself in his life, he turned back to Angel. Slowly, he lifted his blood-stained hands away.

Isa sank into a crouch, shadows from the encroaching evening gathering around her, deepening until she was once again draped in the familiar tattered cloak. A chill edged the warm air, bringing hints of ash and smoke, as the Reaper's skeletal mask settled over Isa's features. Tendrils stretched from the Reaper to coil around Angel. There was a spark or two of deep green that was quickly extinguished as the tendrils bound together and widened into an undulating shroud that enveloped Angel's body.

For one stretched-out moment, silence held the world still. Then Isa rose to her feet, her voice flat and cold. "The debt is paid. Leave."

Locke and Zev both stood and backed away from the shroud-covered body as a vaporous form was shoved into existence. The vapors took on the shape of a young woman with dark hair, her mouth open in a soundless scream, her fingers curled into claws. Malevolence swirled around her as she darted toward Isa.

Locke's muscles bunched as he prepared to intercept, but it wasn't needed. An invisible wind tore through the form, shredding the remnants to nothing and leaving behind a heavy press of power that dimmed the evening light.

"Hound."

Locke looked at Isa.

Her expression was empty of emotions and her voice flat as she pointed at Angel. "You should know that Cora and Carter made a deal with Angel. They provided the initial sample, and for a cut, they connected him to a supplier." The ghostly skeletal mask flickered. "I searched her memories for who the supplier was, but her recollections have been scrubbed."

"Someone used a Memory mage on her?" Zev asked.

Isa cocked her head in that disturbing alien way. "Apparently so. I was unable to get anything more than that." She turned back to Locke. "You still wish to question Angel?"

His *yes* hovered on the tip of his tongue, but considering how much of a threat the Harvester had been in life, he had to ask. "Can he hurt you?"

A flash of cold amusement was there and gone. "Harvesters feed on the living. My business is death. There's nothing for him to eat."

Not exactly reassuring, but he had to trust that Isa would respect her limits. "Then yes, I have some questions for him."

"So do I," Zev added.

"So be it," Isa murmured as the shadows clustered until the Reaper's hood settled around her, hiding her face from view.

A wind whipped the frayed edges of her cloak, and a curved staff formed in her hand, flickering in and out of view as murmurs and wails gathered, there but indistinct. The writhing shadows thickened as they moved around Angel's body, carrying an icy chill. Locke's skin crawled as ebony ribbons, dotted with lightning streaks, erupted from the body lying between him and Zev. Locke's magic sank into a crouch, ready to pounce, but held itself in check, letting Isa do her job.

Even knowing it was coming, he wasn't ready for the storm of power to switch off or the resulting unnatural stillness.

"Rise." The command held undeniable power, and it pulled at Locke's bones.

Angel's soul came together and hovered between the Hound and the Hunter. "What—who—" It caught sight of the shadow-covered body below it. Anger, arrogance, and fear washed through its face as it looked at the Reaper standing silently at its feet. "*¡No me jódes!* What did you do, *chiquita*?"

Isa said nothing.

Enraged, the wraith shot forward. "What did you do?"

Before Locke could interfere, heavy coils of magic looped around the spirit and held it in place inches from the Reaper. "You will answer the Hound's questions."

Struggling against the bonds, Angel's soul snarled in defiance. "And if I don't?"

There was a shift, then Angel screamed as the binding power whipped around him, shredding his form. "*¡Basta!*"

The power released him, and the Reaper's hood turned to Locke. "Ask your questions."

Not knowing how long Isa could hold Angel, he got to the point. "Who is the supplier Cora set you up with?"

The answer came grudgingly. "I don't know."

Locke wanted to call bullshit, but Isa didn't react, which meant it was the truth. "How is that possible? You don't strike me as the type to go into business with an unknown."

Anger and disgust twisted Angel's face. "I trusted Carter."

"He was desperate," Isa said, speaking over Angel. "He needed money fast. To replace what he stole."

The pieces started to fall into place. Desperate, Angel must have stolen from less-than-understanding sources, like those who avoided legal scrutiny. Isa had once told him Angel's legit businesses were a front.

"You were stealing from your own, weren't you?" Locke asked.

Angel jerked against the relentless chains. Magic flared, and he hissed in pain. "They are not mine. They worked for me, but if they found out the money was gone, they'd have turned. I needed a quick fix. The distribution cut would cover it until I lined up investors."

Arrogance and stupidity were not a good combination. Locke wondered how Angel had managed to hold his position as long as he had.

"Give us the name of your supplier," Zev bit out.

Angel didn't even acknowledge him. Isa had set it up so Angel had to answer Locke. So Locke repeated Zev's demand.

Angel clamped his mouth shut. Magic flared along his bindings, and the soul screamed. When the magic eased off, the remnants were hazier than before. "I don't know." Angel's voice was sullen.

"Truth," Isa intoned.

Locke and Zev exchanged a look, then Locke asked Isa, "Has he been scrubbed?"

She took a moment to answer. "No, he truly had no direct contact with the supplier. But he did tap into Carter's phone and trace a series of calls to someplace called the Forge Foundation."

chapter 27

Isa

ISA TOOK another sip of coffee from the mug cupped in her hands, appreciating the way it chased away the chill lingering in her veins. She hadn't wanted to admit to Locke how close it had been with Cora, but he didn't give her much choice during their ride over to Zev's downtown office in Dueñas Park. He kept poking at her until she admitted that after Cora gorged herself on Carter's magic and used his illusion ability to bait Angel, the wraith had garnered enough strength to keep Isa from reclaiming her body if Locke didn't agree to let Angel die.

That had gone over like a lead balloon. Isa was fairly sure the only reason it hadn't devolved into an argument was because she made a point of explaining her reasoning to the silently fuming Locke. First was that Angel's Harvester magic fed off the reactions of others, which was why Locke had ended up on his knees and susceptible to Carter's illusions. If Isa hadn't given Cora control, Angel could have leveraged her worry and fear to add to what he'd already culled from Locke. Not to mention whatever feast Carter had provided. The more Angel fed, the more vulnerable Locke and Isa became. With Cora—who was basically bits and pieces of an angry soul

—in the driver's seat, there was nothing alive to create the emotional lock for Angel. Cora's emotions were simply echoes of remembered feelings.

The Reaper, on the other hand, was all about death. That meant not only could Isa channel the soul's bitter hunger for vengeance, but she also had other ways of getting the information they needed from Angel. When dealing with Cora, Isa had tapped into the woman's memories in an effort to understand her connection to Angel and Carter. It hadn't been easy. The wraith was already fracturing under its prolonged hunt for retribution, and whichever Memory mage had ransacked her mind when she was alive had left behind seriously twisted wreckage. The mage, through luck or skill, had managed to mask the supplier's identity, but as Isa picked through the bits and pieces, she figured out that it wasn't Angel who held the answers to Locke's questions. Cora and Carter had been the middlemen, running product and messages between the shadowy supplier and Angel. It was Cora who first figured out that Angel was stealing from the Idyl Devils to shore up Streetwise Talent's financials. She shared that tidbit with Carter, who started whispering in very specific ears. Grumbles grew to threats, and backed into a corner, Angel rolled the dice and lost.

Unfortunately, others had gotten caught in the fallout—like Kelly, Leo, Paisley, and the Holmes brothers. Not to mention Isa's parents.

She winced. *Somethings never change.*

"You okay?"

She blinked and realized Locke was crouched in front of her, his hand around her knee. "Yeah, I'm fine," she said. He raised his eyebrows, and she managed a faint smile. "I'm stiff and sore, but I'm okay. Promise."

He rose and carefully took a seat next to her, stretching his arm out behind her.

She ran her gaze over him, taking in the slightly large T-shirt he'd borrowed from Zev, and thought about the nasty slice he'd taken on his side. "How about you? You good?"

She'd seen one of the cleanup crew slap a healing ward on Locke as they were taking away Carter and Angel, but she hadn't had a chance to check him over herself.

"Better now. I have to take it easy for a day or so, but otherwise, I'm good to go."

She set the coffee down and moved gently into his side, and he curled his arm around her. She rested her head on his shoulder as Zev talked to one of three screens situated on the glossy wood-grain top of his cool-as-shit desk. Zev had his earbuds activated, so all she caught was murmurs. Back at Angel's, Zev had called in the Cordova crew to scour through Angel, Cora, and Carter's known residences and businesses. Teams were still at it, but one had found a stash of the drug in question.

"Is he still talking to Emilio?" she asked.

"Yeah, they're making arrangements to get it transported to the Family scientists. Hopefully, they can figure out some kind of treatment for Micah."

"Anyone talk to Isaiah yet? Let him know what went down?"

"Nope. Emilio asked Mari to wait to share. Seems the kid's hell-bent on making amends, and Emilio's worried he'll be first in line to play guinea pig."

She lifted her head to look at him. "I doubt the doctors would go against the head of the Family if he told them to leave Isaiah out of it."

Locke shot her a dry look. "You ever dealt with a scientist who thinks they have the answer to the unanswerable?"

She shook her head.

"Let's just say you'd have a better chance at herding cats."

She gave an amused huff and resettled against him. "Well, maybe you can distract Isaiah with Paisley."

"I'll leave that to Mari." He wrapped a tendril of Isa's hair around his finger, winding and unwinding it, which was comforting.

She drifted into a sleepy haze filled with images of her and Locke snuggled together in his bed. Maybe they could lock out the world just for a little while. That happy thought was interrupted by the rumble of Zev's voice. She was blissfully content in Locke's hold, and it took a moment for Zev's words to penetrate.

When they did, she forced her eyelids open and tried to sit up, her pulse racing. "What happened with Kelly?"

"Shhh, it's okay, *reinita*," Locke said, sliding his hand along her spine. "Kelly's fine. Zev was just saying that Roxy saw a note in the DA's file that they'll be classifying Kelly's case as clear self-defense."

She rubbed at her face, relief tripping through her as exhaustion crept back in. "That's good news." She blinked. "Wait? How did Roxy get into the DA's files?"

"Trade secret." Zev sat on the arm of a nearby chair. He eyed them. "You two should head out. There's nothing more for either of you to do tonight."

"You sure?" Locke asked.

"Yeah," Zev said, rubbing the back of his neck. "I'm going to need you with me tomorrow so we can go through each of the locations. I want to see what you can pick up."

"How about early afternoon? I'm going to be busy in the morning," Locke said, dashing her hope that they could have some time to themselves.

"You are?" The question was out before Isa could censor it, her disappointment clear.

"We are," he corrected as he searched her face, his filled

with concern. "You said you wanted to see your dad and Pilar tomorrow. I was thinking maybe around nine or ten."

"You want to go with me?"

He stiffened and frowned. "Do you not want me there?"

"Yes... I mean no." She shook off her shock and tried again, this time in a firm voice. "I want you there, Locke."

Hell, if she could, she would avoid the entire scene because she had a sinking suspicion Pilar would need someone to blame. And guess who was convenient?

"Then I'm there." He pulled her close and pressed his lips to the top of her head.

She glanced at Zev, who was studying them. "How much can I tell them?" she asked.

"Whatever they need to know for closure."

She wasn't sure closure was a real thing when it came to losing someone you loved, but whatever. "So, the drug's existence? I can tell them about that?"

They'd want a reason for Angel's decisions—something they could understand—and there was no doubt that Angel enjoyed taking risks. He just never really had to deal with the consequences. Not until now.

Zev's mouth thinned with irritation, but it wasn't directed at her. "Word's out and spreading fast. Better you tell them the truth than let them get wrapped up in whatever overblown shit others will spread."

Not the answer she'd expected, but she'd take it. "Thanks."

He got to his feet. "Don't thank me. It's shit news, and I wish you weren't going to be the one giving it to them." He looked at Locke. "Take whatever time you need tomorrow. Just make sure she's good before you hit me up."

"Got it." Locke pushed to his feet then turned to help her up. "You sticking around or heading home?"

"Home." Zev went over and started powering down his computer. "Rory's waiting up for me."

"Give her a hug for me."

"Will do," Zev said as Locke guided her to the door. "Isa, thank you."

She stopped, Locke stopping with her. She gave Zev a puzzled frown. "For…?"

"For risking your life for one of mine." His dark eyes flicked to Locke then came back to her. "It won't be forgotten."

"Oh, don't worry. I wouldn't let you forget." She gave him a smirk. "Besides, he belongs to me now."

Zev's chuckles followed them out of the office and into the night.

Want to pick up the final round at Wonderland?
*Then get ready to settle up with another round of intrigue as Des and Piper join the party in **RUNE & TONIC**, wherever books are sold.*

If you don't want to miss out on exclusives and new release information, sign up for Jami's monthly newsletter at
https://www.subscribepage.com/jami-gray-books

Share the love and leave a review at your favorite book dealer!

Not ready to leave the world of the Arcane? Then go back to the starting line with the Arcane Transporter series, available at all retailers.

IGNITION POINT
JAMI GRAY
GRAVE CARGO
RISKY GOODS
LETHAL CONTENTS
JAMI GRAY
COLLISION COURSE
JAMI GRAY
BLIND SPOT
JAMI GRAY

about the author

"This story is an emotional roller coaster, from betrayal, anger, fear, love..." —InD'tale Magazine

Jami Gray is the coffee addicted, music junkie, Queen Nerd of her personal Geek Squad, Alpha Mom of the Fur Minxes, who writes to soothe the voices crammed in her head. Her series combine high-stakes urban fantasy and edgy paranormal romantic suspense into books you don't want to put down. Buckle up and get ready for a wild ride through the fascinating worlds of the Arcane, the Kyn, the PSY-IV Teams, and the Collapse.

Come visit Jami's website at **https://www.jamigray.com** and stay up to date on what kind of trouble she's getting into and when you can expect to join in.

amazon.com/author/jamigray
instagram.com/jamigrayauthor
facebook.com/JamiGrayWriter
threads.com/@jamigrayauthor
goodreads.com/JamiGray
bookbub.com/authors/jami-gray